...ks on a dairy farm. Their first poet... ..., was awarded the C. Buddingh' Prize for best poetry debut in 2015, with the newspaper *de Volkskrant* naming them literary talent of the year. In 2018, Atlas Contact published their first novel, *The Discomfort of Evening*, which won the prestigious ANV Debut Prize and was a national bestseller. It was published by Faber in 2020 and won the 2020 Booker International Prize.

Michele Hutchison was born in the UK and has lived in Amsterdam since 2004. After a period working as an editor, she became a literary translator from Dutch.

Further praise for *The Discomfort of Evening*:

'Intensely raw, shockingly graphic, and memorable . . . There is a bold beauty to the book, which for all its modernity seems to be set in a different age of automatic religious belief: the immensity and mystery of the universe coexisting alongside the claustrophobic community of farm, church and school . . . Exceptional.' *Financial Times*

'Few reading experiences are more thrilling than a first novel that feels urgent and original. In the past decade, *Open City* and *What Belongs to You* both had these qualities. *The Discomfort of Evening* . . . belongs in this company. [As] exhilarating a debut as I can remember.' *i*

'An unflinching study of a family falling apart in the madness of grief . . . Rijneveld's writing is raw and impassive, though often grotesquely vivid . . . [A] notable new talent.' *Observer*

'A strong, unique voice . . . Compelling.' *Guardian* (Book of the Day)

'Extraordinary – Rijneveld choreographs a baroque layering of horror that lands somewhere between late Hardy and Bataille . . . A book that was written for today.' *Telegraph*

'Rijneveld's poetic prose, eloquently translated by Michele Hutchison, clashes and rattles against the horrors it describes, a constant fight between terror and beauty . . . You won't forget it.' *Irish Times*

'Impressive . . . It is the strange, haunting observations . . . that give this novel of grief its particular power. A book . . . to remember.' *The Economist*

'Beautifully tender and completely compelling.' *Times Literary Supplement*

'Shudderingly vivid . . . Stunning.' *Literary Review*

'The literary name to know . . . Gripping.' *Vogue* (Top 5 Debuts of 2020)

'The most talked-about debut novel of 2020 . . . Brutal and vivid.' *Dazed & Confused*

'[An] astonishing achievement . . . The work of a poet.' *Dublin Review of Books*

'Heady imagery and sensory language . . . Haunting and beautiful.' *Monocle*

'Intense, poignant imagery . . . Extraordinary.' *AnOther*

'[A] haunting journey [of] sensory language and beautifully wild images that linger in the mind.' *Guardian* (2020 Fiction Highlights)

'This beautiful, strange novel is filled with sentences that stopped me dead.' Chris Power

'Perfectly delineates the life of a farm community in all its strange variations.' Edna O'Brien

MARIEKE LUCAS RIJNEVELD

The Discomfort
of Evening

Translated by Michele Hutchison

faber

First published in the UK in 2020
by Faber & Faber Ltd
Bloomsbury House
74–77 Great Russell Street
London WC1B 3DA
First published in Dutch by Atlas Contact, Amsterdam, in 2018
This paperback edition first published in 2020

Typeset by Faber & Faber Ltd
Printed in the UK by CPI Group (UK) Ltd, Croydon, CR0 4YY

Epigraph quotations: (top) appears on a statue of Maurice Gilliams in Antwerp
(source unknown); (bottom) from 'Spring' in *The Collected Poems of Jan Wolkers*,
published as *Verzamelde gedichten* in 2008 by De Bezige Bij

A CIP record for this book
is available from the British Library

ISBN 978-0-571-34937-1

The publisher gratefully acknowledges the support of the
Dutch Foundation for Literature

Nederlands
N letterenfonds
dutch foundation
for literature

MIX
Paper from
responsible sources
FSC® C020471
FSC
www.fsc.org

4 6 8 10 9 7 5 3

Restlessness gives wings to the imagination.

MAURICE GILLIAMS

It is written, 'I am making all things new!'
But the chords are a clothesline of grief,
Razor-sharp gusts snap the faith
Of he who would flee this cruel start.
Ice rain beats blossom to a glassy pulp,
A cur shakes his pelt bone-dry in the violence.

from THE COLLECTED POEMS
OF JAN WOLKERS (2008)

PART I

I

I was ten and stopped taking off my coat. That morning, Mum had covered us one by one in udder ointment to protect us from the cold. It came out of a yellow Bogena tin and was normally used to prevent dairy cows' teats from getting cracks, calluses and cauliflower-like lumps. The tin's lid was so greasy you could only screw it off with a tea-towel. It smelled of stewed udder, the thick slices I'd sometimes find cooking in a pan of stock on our stove, sprinkled with salt and pepper. They filled me with horror, just like the reeking ointment on my skin. Mum pressed her fat fingers into our faces like the round cheeses she patted to check whether the rind was ripening. Our pale cheeks shone in the light of the kitchen bulb, which was encrusted with fly shit. For years we'd been planning to get a lampshade, a pretty one with flowers, but whenever we saw one in the village, Mum could never make up her mind. She'd been doing this for three years now. That morning, two days before Christmas, I felt her slippery thumbs in my eye sockets and for a moment I was afraid she'd press too hard, that my eyeballs would plop into my skull like marbles, and she'd say, 'That's what happens when your eyes are always roaming and you never keep them still like a true believer, gazing up at God as though the heavens might break open at any moment.' But the heavens here only broke open for a snowstorm – nothing to keep staring at like an idiot.

In the middle of the breakfast table there was a woven bread-basket lined with a napkin decorated with Christmas angels. They were holding trumpets and twigs of mistletoe protectively in front of their willies. Even if you held the napkin up to the light of the bulb you couldn't see what they looked like – my guess was rolled-up slices of luncheon meat. Mum had arranged the bread neatly on the napkin: white, wholemeal with poppy seeds, and currant loaf. She'd used a sieve to carefully sprinkle icing sugar onto the crispy back of the loaf, like the first light snow that had fallen onto the backs of the blazed cows in the meadow before we drove them inside. The bread-bag's plastic clip was kept on top of the biscuit tin: we'd lose it otherwise and Mum didn't like the look of a knot in a plastic bag.

'Meat or cheese first before you go for the sweet stuff,' she'd always say. This was the rule and it would make us big and strong, as big as the giant Goliath and as strong as Samson in the Bible. We always had to drink a large glass of fresh milk as well; it had usually been out of the tank for a couple of hours and was lukewarm, and sometimes there was a yellowish layer of cream that stuck to the top of your mouth if you drank too slowly. The best thing was to gulp down the whole glass of milk with your eyes closed, something Mum called 'irreverent' although there's nothing in the Bible about drinking milk slowly, or about eating a cow's body. I took a slice of white bread from the basket and put it on my plate upside down

4

so that it looked just like a pale toddler's bum, even more convincing when partly spread with chocolate spread, which never failed to amuse me and my brothers, and they'd always say, 'Are you arse-licking again?'

'If you put goldfish in a dark room for too long they go really pale,' I whispered to Matthies, putting six slices of cooked sausage on my bread so that they covered it perfectly. *You've got six cows and two of them get eaten. How many are left?* I heard the teacher's voice inside my head every time I ate something. Why those stupid sums were combined with food – apples, cakes, pizzas and biscuits – I didn't know, but in any case the teacher had given up hope that I'd ever be able to do sums, that my exercise book would ever be pristine white without a single red underscore. It had taken me a year to learn to tell the time – Dad had spent hours with me at the kitchen table with the school's practice clock which he'd sometimes thrown on the floor in despair, at which point the mechanism would bounce out and the annoying thing would just keep on ringing – and even now when I looked at a clock the arms would still sometimes turn into the earthworms we dug out of the ground behind the cowshed with a fork to use as fishing bait. They wriggled every which way when you held them between forefinger and thumb and didn't calm down until you gave them a couple of taps, and then they'd lie in your hand and look just like those sweet, red strawberry shoelaces from Van Luik's sweet-shop.

'It's rude to whisper in company,' said my little sister Hanna, who was sitting next to Obbe and opposite me at the kitchen table. When she didn't like something, she'd move her lips from left to right.

'Some words are too big for your little ears; they won't fit in,' I said with my mouth full.

Obbe stirred his glass of milk boredly with his finger, held up a bit of skin and then quickly wiped it on the tablecloth. It stuck there like a whitish lump of snot. It looked horrible, and I knew there was a chance the tablecloth would be the other way around tomorrow, with the encrusted milk skin on my side. I would refuse to put my plate on the table. We all knew the paper serviettes were only there for decoration and that Mum smoothed them out and put them back in the kitchen drawer after breakfast. They weren't meant for our dirty fingers and mouths. Some part of me also felt bad at the thought of the angels being scrunched up in my fist like mosquitoes so that their wings broke, or having their white angel's hair dirtied with strawberry jam.

'I have to spend time outside because I look so pale,' Matthies whispered. He smiled and stuck his knife with utmost concentration into the white chocolate part of the Duo Penotti pot, so as not to get any of the milk chocolate bit on it. We only had Duo Penotti in the holidays. We'd been looking forward to it for days and now the Christmas holidays had begun, it was finally time. The best moment was when Mum pulled off the protective paper, cleaned the bits of glue from the edges and then showed us the brown and white patches, like the unique pattern on a newborn calf. Whoever had the best marks at school that week was allowed the pot first. I was always the last to get a turn.

I slid backwards and forwards on my chair: my toes didn't quite reach the floor yet. What I wanted was to keep everyone safe indoors and spread them out across the farm like slices of cooked sausage. In the weekly roundup yesterday, about the South Pole, our teacher had said that some penguins go fishing and never come back. Even though we didn't live at the South Pole, it was cold here, so cold that the lake had frozen over and the cows' drinking troughs were full of ice.

We each had two pale blue freezer bags next to our breakfast plates. I held one up and gave my mother a questioning look.

'To put over your socks,' she said with a smile that made dimples in her cheeks. 'It will keep them warm and stop your feet getting wet.' Meanwhile, she was preparing breakfast for Dad who was helping a cow to calve; after each slice of bread, she'd slide the knife between her thumb and index finger until the butter reached the tips of her fingers, and then she'd scrape it off with the blunt side of the knife. Dad was probably sitting on a milking stool next to a cow taking off a bit of the beestings, clouds of breath and cigarette smoke rising up above its steaming back. I realized there weren't any freezer bags next to his plate: his feet were probably too big, in particular his left one which was deformed after an accident with a combine harvester when he was about twenty. Next to Mum on the table was the silver cheese scoop she used to assess the flavour of the cheeses she made in the mornings. Before she cut one open, she'd stick the cheese scoop into the middle, through the plastic layer, twist it twice and then slowly pull it out. And

7

she'd eat a piece of cumin cheese just the way she ate the white bread during communion at church, just as thoughtfully and devoutly, slow and staring. Obbe had once joked that Jesus' body was made of cheese, too, and that was why we were only allowed two slices on our bread each day, otherwise we'd run out of Him too quickly.

Once our mother had said the morning prayer and thanked God 'for poverty and for wealth; while many eat the bread of sorrows, Thou hast fed us mild and well,' Matthies pushed his chair back, hung his black leather ice skates around his neck, and put the Christmas cards in his pocket that Mum had asked him to put through the letterboxes of a few neighbours. He was going on ahead to the lake where he was going to take part in the local skating competition with a couple of his friends. It was a twenty-mile route, and the winner got a plate of stewed udders with mustard and a gold medal with the year 2000 on it. I wished I could put a freezer bag over his head, too, so that he'd stay warm for a long time, the seal closed around his neck. He ran his hand through my hair for a moment. I quickly smoothed it back into place and wiped a few crumbs from my pyjama top. Matthies always parted his hair in the middle and put gel in his front locks. They were like two curls of butter on a dish; Mum always made those around Christmas: butter from a tub wasn't very festive, she thought. That was for normal days and the day of Jesus' birth wasn't a normal day, not even if it happened every year all over again as if He died for our sins each year, which I found strange. I often thought to myself: that poor man has been dead a long time,

8

they must have forgotten by now. But better not to mention it, otherwise there wouldn't be any more sprinkle-covered biscuits and no one would tell the Christmas story of the three kings and the star in the East.

Matthies went into the hall to check his hair, even though it would turn rock hard in the freezing cold and his two curls would go flat and stick to his forehead.

'Can I come with you?' I asked. Dad had got my wooden skates out of the attic and strapped them to my shoes with their brown leather ties. I'd been walking around the farm in my skates for a few days, my hands behind my back and the protectors over the blades so they wouldn't leave marks on the floor. My calves were hard. I'd practised enough now to be able to go out onto the ice without a folding chair to push around.

'No, you can't,' he said. And then more quietly so that only I could hear it, 'Because we're going to the other side.'

'I want to go to the other side, too,' I whispered.

'I'll take you with me when you're older.' He put on his woolly hat and smiled. I saw his braces with their zigzagging blue elastic bands.

'I'll be back before dark,' he called to Mum. He turned around once again in the doorway and waved to me, the scene I'd keep replaying in my mind later until his arm no longer raised itself and I began to doubt whether we had even said goodbye.

2

We didn't have any of the commercial channels, only Nederland 1, 2 and 3. Dad said there wasn't any nudity on them. He pronounced the word 'nudity' as though a fruit fly had just flown into his mouth – he spat as he said it. The word mainly made me think of the potatoes whose jackets my mother peeled off every evening before she dropped them into the water – that plopping sound they made. I can imagine if you think about naked people for too long shoots grow out of you, just like potatoes sprout after a while so you have to dig them out of the soft flesh with the point of a knife. We fed the forked green bits to the chickens, who were crazy about them. I lay on my stomach in front of the oak cabinet that hid the TV. One of the buckles of my skates had rolled under it when I'd kicked them off angrily in the corner of the living room. I was too young for the other side and too old to skate on the manure ditch behind the cowsheds. To be honest, you couldn't even call it skating – it was more a kind of shuffling, like the way the geese that landed there in search of something edible shuffled. The stench of manure broke free with every score in the ice and the blades of your skates turned light brown. We must have been a ridiculous sight standing there on the ditch like a pair of silly geese, our bundled-up bodies waggling from one grassy bank to the other, instead of joining in the skate on the big lake with everyone else from the village.

'We can't go and watch Matthies,' Dad had said, 'one of the calves has got the runs.'

'But you promised,' I cried. I'd even wrapped my feet in the freezer bags.

'Mitigating circumstances,' Dad said, pulling his black beret down over his eyebrows. I'd nodded a couple of times. There was nothing we could do about unforeseen circumstances and no one stood a chance against the cows anyway; they were always more important. Even when they didn't require any attention – even when their fat clumsy bodies were lying sated in the stalls – they still managed to take priority. I'd folded my arms in a sulk. All that practising in my strap-on skates had been for nothing; my calves were even harder than the porcelain Jesus in the hall that was as big as Dad. I deliberately threw the freezer bags in the bin, and pushed them deep into the coffee grounds and bread crusts so that Mum wouldn't be able to reuse them like the serviettes.

It was dusty under the cabinet. I found a hairclip, a dried-up raisin and a Lego block. Mum shut the cabinet doors whenever family members or the elders from the Reformed church came to visit. They mustn't see that we allowed ourselves to be diverted from God's path in the evenings. On Mondays, Mum always watched a quiz show called *Lingo*. We all had to be as quiet as mice so that she could guess the words from behind the ironing board; we'd hear the iron hissing at each correct answer, steam spiralling up. They were usually words that weren't in the Bible, but our mother still seemed to know them. She called them 'blush words' because some of them turned your cheeks red. Obbe once told me that when the screen was black, the television was the eye of God, and that when Mum closed the doors she wanted Him not to see us. She was probably ashamed of us because we sometimes used blush words when *Lingo* wasn't on. She tried to wash them out of our mouths with a bar of green soap, like the grease and mud stains from our good school clothes.

I felt around the floor for the buckle. From where I was lying, I could see into the kitchen. Dad's green wellies suddenly appeared in front of the fridge, bits of straw and cow shit sticking to their sides. He must have come in to fetch another bunch of carrot tops from the vegetable drawer. He'd cut the leaves off with the hoof-paring knife he kept in the breast pocket of his overalls. For days he'd been walking back and forth between the fridge and the rabbit hutches. The cream slice that was left from Hanna's seventh birthday went with him – I'd been drooling over it every time the fridge was open. I hadn't been able to resist secretly scooping off a corner of the pink icing with my fingernail and putting it in my mouth. I'd made a tunnel in the cream that had thickened in the fridge and stuck to my fingertip like a yellow hat. Dad didn't notice. 'Once he's got his mind set on something, there's no budging him,' my granny on the most religious side of the family sometimes said, and that was why I suspected he was feeding up my rabbit Dieuwertje, which I'd got from Lien next door, for the big Christmas dinner in two days' time. He never normally got involved with the rabbits – 'small stock' belonged on your plate and he only liked animals whose presence filled his entire field of vision, but my rabbit didn't even fill the half of it. He'd once said that the neck vertebrae were the most breakable part of a body – I heard them snapping in my head as though my mother was breaking a handful of raw vermicelli above the pan – and a rope with a noose in it had recently appeared in the attic, hanging from the rafters. 'It's for a swing,' Dad said, but there was still no swing. I didn't understand why the rope was hanging in the attic and not in the shed with the screwdrivers and his collection of bolts. Maybe, I thought, Dad wanted us to watch; maybe it would happen if we sinned. I briefly pictured my rabbit hanging broken-necked from the rope in the attic, behind Matthies's bed, so that our father could skin it more easily. It would probably come off the same way as the skin from the big cooked sausage that Mum peeled with her potato knife in the mornings: only they'd put Dieuwertje in a layer of butter in the big casserole dish on the gas stove, and the whole house would smell of broiled rabbit. All of us Mulders would be able to smell from afar that Christmas dinner was ready to be served; we'd know not to spoil our appetite. I'd noticed that while I used to have to be sparing with the feed, I was now allowed to give my rabbit a whole scoopful, as well as the carrot tops. Despite the fact that he was a buck, I'd named him after the curly-haired female presenter on children's TV because I found her so pretty. I wanted to put her at the top of my Christmas list, but I waited a while as I hadn't seen her in any of the toy catalogues yet.

There was more going on than plain generosity towards my rabbit, I was sure of it. This was why I'd suggested other animals when I'd joined Dad bringing in the cows for their winter treatment before breakfast. I was holding a stick to drive them. The best thing to do was to whack their flanks so they'd walk on.

'Other children in my class are having duck, pheasant or turkey, and you fill them with potatoes, leek, onions and beets, stuffed up their bums until they're overflowing.'

I glanced at my dad and he nodded. There were various kinds of nods in our village. That in itself was a way of differentiating yourself. I knew them all by now. This was the nod that dad used for the cattle dealers when they offered him a price that was too low but that he had to accept, because there was something wrong with the poor creature and he'd be saddled with it for good otherwise.

'Plenty of pheasants here, especially among the willows,' I said, glancing at the overgrown area to the left of the farm. I saw them there sometimes in the trees or sitting on the ground. When they saw me, they'd let themselves drop to the ground like a stone and would stay there playing dead until I'd gone. That's when their heads would pop up again.

Dad had nodded again, whacked his stick against the ground and hissed, 'Sssssssjeu, come on,' at the cows to drive them on. I'd looked in the freezer after that chat but there was no duck, pheasant or turkey to be found among the packets of mixed mincemeat and vegetables for soup.

Dad's boots disappeared from sight again, and only a few

strands of straw remained behind on the kitchen floor. I put the buckle in my pocket and went upstairs in my stockinged feet to my bedroom, which overlooked the farmyard. I sat on my haunches on the edge of the bed, and thought about my father's hand on my head when we'd brought in the cows and walked back to the meadow to check the mole-traps. If they were empty, Dad would keep his hands stiffly in his trouser pockets: there was nothing that deserved a reward, not like when we'd caught something and had to prise the twisted, bloodied bodies from the claws with a rusty screwdriver, which I did bent over so that Dad couldn't see the tears running down my cheeks at the sight of a small creature that had walked unsuspectingly into a trap. I pictured the way Dad would use that hand to wring my rabbit's neck, like the child-proof top of a canister of nitrogen: there was only one right way to do it. I imagined Mum laying out my lifeless pet on the silver dish she used for Russian salad on Sundays after church. She'd display him on a bed of lamb's lettuce and garnish him with gherkins, tomato chunks, grated carrot and a sprig of thyme. I looked at my hands, at their irregular lines. They were still too small to be used for anything other than holding stuff. They still fitted in my parents' hands but Mum's and Dad's didn't fit in mine. That was the difference between them and me – they could put theirs around a rabbit's neck, or around a cheese that had just been flipped in its brine. Their hands were always searching for something and if you were no longer able to hold an animal or a person tenderly, it was better to let go and turn your attention to other useful things instead.

I pressed my forehead harder and harder against the edge of my bed; I felt the pressure of cold wood on my skin and closed my eyes. Sometimes I found it strange that you had to pray in the dark, although maybe it was like my glow-in-the-dark duvet: the stars and the planets only emitted light and protected you from the night when it was dark enough. God must work the same way. I let my intertwined hands rest on my knees. Angrily I thought about Matthies who'd be drinking hot chocolate from one of the stalls on the ice. I thought of him skating with red cheeks, and about the thaw that would start tomorrow: the curly-haired presenter had warned of roofs that might be too slippery for Saint Nicholas to get down the chimney, and mist which might lead him to get lost and perhaps Matthies too, even though it was his own fault. For a moment, I saw my skates before me, greased and back in their box, ready to be returned to the attic. I thought about being too small for so much, but that no one told you when you were big enough, how many centimetres on the door-post that was, and I asked God if He please couldn't take my brother Matthies instead of my rabbit. 'Amen.'

'But he's not dead,' Mum said to the vet. She got up from the edge of the bath and extricated her hand from a pale blue flannel. She'd been just about to clean Hanna's bottom, otherwise there was a chance she'd get worms. They made little holes in you like in cabbage leaves. I was old enough to make sure I didn't get worms, and I wrapped my arms around my knees to look less naked now the vet had suddenly come into the bathroom without knocking.

In a hurried voice, he said, 'Just by the far side, the ice was much too weak because of the navigation channels. He'd been in front for a long time, everyone had lost sight of him.' I knew instantly this wasn't about my rabbit that was sitting in its hutch as usual, gnawing at carrot tops. And the vet sounded serious. He often came into the house to talk about the cows. Not many people came here who didn't come to talk about the cows, but this time something wasn't right. He hadn't even mentioned the cattle once, not even when he actually meant us – the children – when he asked how the livestock was doing. When he hung his head, I stretched my upper body to be able to see through the little window above the bath. It was already starting to get dark: a group of deacons wearing black were approaching, closer and closer until they'd wrap their arms around us, arriving each day to bring the night in person. I told myself that Matthies had lost track of time: it wouldn't be unusual for him and that's why our father had given him a watch with a luminous dial, which he was probably accidentally wearing upside down – or was he still delivering the Christmas cards?

I let myself sink back into the bath-water and rested my chin on my damp arms, peering through my eyelashes at my mother. We'd recently had a brush-like draught-excluder added to the letterbox in the front door so that we'd stop feeling the wind inside the house. I sometimes peeked through it to the outdoors and now I was looking through my eyelashes, I got the idea that Mum and the vet hadn't realized I was listening in: that in my thoughts I could erase the lines around my mother's eyes and mouth because they didn't belong there, and press dimples into her cheeks with my thumbs. My mother wasn't the nodding sort; she had too much to say for that, but now she only nodded and for the first time I thought: please say something, Mum, even if it's about tidying up, about the calves that have got the runs again, the weather forecast for the coming days, the bedroom doors that keep jamming, our ungrateful attitude, or the dried-up toothpaste at the corners of our mouths. She said nothing and looked at the flannel she was holding. The vet pulled the step-stool out from under the sink and sat down on it. It creaked under his weight.

'Evertsen pulled him out of the lake.' He paused for a moment, looked from Obbe to me and then added, 'Your brother is dead.' I looked away from him, at the towels hanging from the hook next to the sink that were stiff from the cold. I wanted the vet to get up and say it was all a mistake, that cows are not that much different from sons: even if they go into the big wide world they always return to their stalls before sunset to be fed.

'He's out skating and he'll be back soon,' Mum said.

She squeezed the flannel into a ball above the bath-water; the drips made rings. Mum bumped against my raised knees. To give myself something to do, I floated a Lego boat on the waves my sister Hanna made. She hadn't understood what had just been said and I realized that I could also pretend my ears were blocked, that they'd been tied in a permanent knot. The bath-water began to get tepid and before I knew it, I'd peed. I looked at pee that was ochre yellow and billowing into cloud-like swirls before mixing with the water. Hanna didn't notice, otherwise she'd have jumped up immediately with a shriek and called me a dirty girl. She was holding a Barbie above the surface of the water. 'She'll drown otherwise,' she said. The doll was wearing a stripy swimsuit. I'd once put my finger under it to feel the plastic tits, and no one had noticed. They felt harder than the cyst on my dad's chin. I looked at Hanna's naked body which was the same as mine. Only Obbe's was different. He was standing next to the bath, still dressed; he'd just been telling us about a computer game in which he had to shoot people who burst apart like big tomatoes. He was going to use the bath-water after us. I knew he had a little tap he could pee from down below and under it was a wattle like a turkey's. Sometimes I worried that he had something hanging there that nobody talked about. Maybe he was dangerously ill. Mum called it a winkle, but maybe it was actually called cancer and she didn't want to frighten us because my granny on the less religious side had died of cancer. Just before she'd died, she'd made eggnog. Dad said the cream had curdled when they found her, that everything curdled when somebody died, unexpectedly or not, and for weeks I hadn't been able to sleep because I kept seeing Granny's face in her coffin, her half-opened mouth, eye sockets and pores beginning to ooze eggnog as thin as yolk.

Mum pulled me and Hanna out of the bath by our upper arms, her fingers leaving white marks on our skin. Usually she'd wrap towels around us and check whether we were fully dry at the end so that we didn't start to rust, or worse, grow mould like the cracks between the bathroom tiles, but now she left us, teeth chattering, on the bath-mat, soap-suds still in my armpits.

'Dry yourself properly,' I whispered to my shivering sister as I passed her a rock-hard towel, 'otherwise we'll have to descale you later.' I bent down to check my toes which is where the mould would start first, and this way no one could see that my cheeks were bright red, like two Fireball gobstoppers. *If a boy and a rabbit take part in a race, how many miles per hour does one of them have to go faster to win?* I heard the teacher inside my head say, as he stabbed his pointer into my stomach, forcing me to reply. After my toes, I quickly checked my fingertips – Dad sometimes joked that our skin would come loose if we stayed in the bath for too long and that he'd nail it to the wooden wall of the shed, next to the pelts of the skinned rabbits. When I stood up again and wrapped the towel around myself, Dad suddenly appeared beside the vet. He was shaking and there were snowflakes on the shoulders of his overalls; his face looked deathly pale. Again and again he blew into his cupped hands. At first I thought about the avalanche our teacher had told us about, even though you surely never get them in the Dutch countryside. I only realized it couldn't be an avalanche when Dad began to cry, and Obbe moved his head from left to right like a windscreen wiper to get rid of his tears.

At Mum's request, our neighbour Lien took down the Christmas tree that very evening. I was sitting on the sofa with Obbe, hiding behind the happy faces of Bert and Ernie on my pyjama top, though my own fears towered over them. I kept the fingers of both hands crossed, like you do in the school playground when you've said something you don't mean, or want to undo your promises, or your prayers. We looked on sadly as the tree was carried from the room, leaving behind a trail of glitter and pine needles. It was only then that I felt a stab in my chest, more than at the vet's news. Matthies was sure to return but the Christmas tree wouldn't. A few days earlier, we'd been allowed to decorate the tree with tiny fat Santas, shiny balls, angels and chains of beads, and wreath-shaped chocolates, all to the tune of 'Jimmy' by Boudewijn de Groot. We knew the lyrics off by heart and would sing along, looking forward to the lines containing words we weren't allowed to use. Now we watched through the living room window as Lien used a wheelbarrow to dump the tree at the side of the road, wrapped in an orange tarpaulin. Only the silver star was left sticking out; they'd forgotten to take it off. I didn't mention it, as what was the point of a star if we didn't have a tree any more? Lien rearranged the orange tarpaulin a couple of times as though it might alter our view, our situation. Not long ago, Matthies had pushed me around in the same wheelbarrow. I'd had to use both hands to hold on to the sides that were covered in a thin layer of dried manure. I noticed at the time that his back had become more crooked through the hard work, as though he was working his way down to the earth. My brother had suddenly broken into a sprint, causing me to be thrown up higher and higher at every bump. It should have been the other way round, I thought now. I should have pushed Matthies around the farmyard while making engine sounds, even though he'd have been much too heavy to dump at the side of the road afterwards and cover in the orange tarpaulin like the dead calves, so that he could be collected and we could forget him. The next day he'd be born again and there'd be nothing that made this evening any different from all the other evenings.

'The angels are naked,' I whispered to Obbe.

They lay on the dresser in front of us next to the chocolate stars that had melted in their jackets. These angels didn't have trumpets or mistletoe in front of their winkles. Dad couldn't have noticed that they weren't wearing any clothes otherwise he'd certainly have put them back in their silver paper. I'd once broken the wings off an angel to see whether they'd grow back.

God could surely make that happen. I wanted some kind of sign that He existed and that He was there for us during the daytime too. This seemed sensible to me because then he could keep an eye on things, and look after Hanna, and keep the cows free of milk fever and udder infections. When nothing happened and the broken-off white patch remained visible, I buried the angel in the vegetable patch between a couple of leftover red onions.

'Angels are always naked,' Obbe whispered back. He still hadn't had a bath and he had a towel around his neck; he held on to both ends as though he was ready for a fight. The bathwater with my pee in it must have been stone cold by now.

'Don't they catch cold?'

'They're cold-blooded, just like snakes and water fleas, and then you don't need clothes.'

I nodded but quickly laid my hand over the porcelain willy of one of the angels as a precaution when Lien from next door came in. I heard her in the hall wiping her feet for longer than normal. From now on, every visitor to the house would wipe their feet for longer than necessary. I learned that at first, death requires people to pay attention to small details – the way Mum checks her nails for dried-up bits of rennet from making cheese – to delay the pain. For a moment I hoped Lien had Matthies with her, that he'd been hiding in the hollow tree at the top of the meadow and that he'd had enough of it now and had come out again; the temperature had dropped below freezing outside. Ice would be closing over the holes caused by the wind: my brother wouldn't be able to find a way out from under it and would have to look around the whole lake on his own in the pitch dark. Even the construction lamp at the skating club had gone out by now. When Lien had finished wiping her feet, she talked to Mum, so quietly I couldn't hear. I only saw her lips moving and my mother's pursed shut, like mating slugs. I let my hand slide off the angel's willy when no one was paying attention and watched Mum go to the kitchen, pushing another hair-grip into her bun. She put in more and more, as though she was trying to fix her head so that it wouldn't suddenly flip open and reveal everything that was happening inside it. She came back with the Christmas biscuits. We'd bought them at the market together. I'd been looking forward to their brittle interiors, to the crunch of the sprinkles, but Mum gave them to Lien, as well as the rice pudding from the fridge and the rolled meat that Dad had got from the butcher's, and even the eighty-metre-long roll of red and white string to tie up the meat. We could have wrapped the string around our bodies so that they didn't fall apart in slices. Later I sometimes thought that this was when the emptiness began. It wasn't because of Matthies's death but those two days of Christmas that were given away in pans and empty Russian salad tubs.

4

The coffin with my brother in it was in the front room. It was made of oak and had a viewing window above his face, and metal handles. He'd been there for three days. On the first day, Hanna had rapped on the glass with her knuckles and said, in a small voice, 'Now, I've had enough of this – stop messing around, Matthies.' She remained motionless for a moment as though she was afraid he might be whispering and she wouldn't hear him if there wasn't total silence. When there was no reply, she went back to playing with her dolls behind the sofa, her thin body trembling like a dragonfly. I'd wanted to take her between my finger and thumb and blow on her to keep her warm, but I couldn't tell her that Matthies had gone to sleep forever, that from now on we'd only have viewing windows in our hearts with our brother laid out behind them. Apart from our granny on the less religious side, we didn't know anyone who was asleep for all eternity, though in the end we all got up again. 'We live according to God's will,' Granny on the more religious side often said about this. When she got up in the morning her stiff knees troubled her, as well as bad breath, 'as though I'd swallowed a dead sparrow'. Neither that bird nor my brother would ever wake up again.

The coffin was on the dresser on a white crocheted cloth

that was usually taken out for birthdays when there would be cheese sticks, nuts, glasses and punch laid out on it, and just like at the parties, people stood in a ring around it now, their noses pressed into hankies or other people's necks. Although they said nice things about my brother, death still felt ugly and as indigestible as the lost tiger nut we found days after a birthday party behind a chair or under the TV cabinet. In the coffin, Matthies's face looked like it was made of beeswax, so smooth and tight. The nurses had stuck tissue paper under his eyelids to keep them shut, while I'd have preferred them to be open so that we could look at each other one more time, so that I could be sure I didn't forget the colour of his eyes, so that he wouldn't forget me.

When the second group of people had left, I tried to spread open his eyes, which made me think of the paper nativity scene I'd made at school, with coloured tissue paper as stained glass and Mary and Joseph figures. At the Christmas breakfast, a tea light had been lit behind them so the tissue paper would light up and Jesus could be born in an illuminated stable. But my brother's eyes were dull and grey and there wasn't a stained glass pattern. I quickly let the eyelids drop again and closed the viewing window. They'd tried to replicate his gelled locks but they just hung on his forehead like brown wilted pea pods. Mum and Granny had dressed Matthies in a pair of jeans and his favourite sweater, the blue and green one with HEROES in big letters across the chest. Most of the heroes I'd read about in books could fall from tall buildings or find themselves in an inferno and end up with just a few scratches.

I didn't understand why Matthies couldn't do this too and why he'd only be immortal in our thoughts from now on. He'd once rescued a heron from the combine harvester just in time, otherwise the bird would have been shredded, added to a bale of straw and fed to the cows.

From behind the door where I was hiding, as she was dressing his body, I'd heard Granny tell my brother, 'You always have to swim to the dark patch. You knew that, didn't you?' I couldn't imagine how you managed to swim to the dark patch myself. It was about differences in colour. When there was snow on the ice you had to look for the light, but when there wasn't any snow, the ice would be lighter than the hole and you had to swim to the dark. Matthies had told me this himself when he'd come into my bedroom before skating and shown me in his socks how to slide your feet toward and away from each other in turn. 'Like riding two fish,' he said. I had watched from my bed and made a clicking sound with my tongue against the roof of my mouth, the way the skates sounded on television as they went across ice. We loved that sound. Now my tongue lay curled in my mouth like an increasingly dangerous navigation channel in a lake. I didn't dare make clicking sounds any more.

Granny came into the front room with a bottle of liquid soap – maybe that's why they'd put papers under his eyelids, so that the soap wouldn't get in and sting. Once they'd tidied him up, they'd probably take them away again, like the tea light in my nativity scene which was blown out so that Mary and Joseph could get on with their lives. Granny pulled me to her chest for a moment. She smelled of beestings pancakes with ham and syrup: there was still a big pile of them on the counter left over from lunch, greasy with butter, their edges crispy. Dad had asked who had made a face of bramble jam, raisins and apple on his pancake, looking at each of us one by one. His eyes stopped at Granny who smiled at him just as cheerfully as his pancake.

'The poor lad is laid out nicely.'

More and more brown patches were appearing on her face, like the apples she'd cut up and used as mouths on the pancakes. You get overripe from old age in the end.

'Can't we put a rolled-up pancake in there with him? It's Matthies's favourite food.'

'That would only smell. Do you want to attract worms?'

I removed my head from her breast and looked at the angels that were on the second step of the stairs in a box, ready to be taken back to the attic. I'd been allowed to put them back in the silver paper, one by one, facing downwards. I still hadn't cried. I'd tried but hadn't been able to each time, not even if I tried to picture Matthies falling through the ice in great detail: his hand feeling the ice for the hole, looking for the light or the dark, his clothes and skates heavy under the water. I held my breath and didn't even manage it for half a minute.

'No,' I said, 'I hate those stupid worms.'

Granny smiled at me. I wanted her to stop smiling, I wanted Dad to take his fork to her face and mash up everything like he'd done with his pancake. I didn't hear her muffled sobs until she was alone in the front room.

In the nights that followed, I kept sneaking downstairs to check whether my brother was really dead. First I'd lie in my bed wiggling around or 'making a candle', as I called it, by throwing my legs up in the air and supporting my hips with my hands. In the mornings his death seemed obvious but as soon as it grew dark, I'd begin to have my doubts. What if we hadn't looked hard enough and he woke up under the ground? Each time, I'd hope that God had changed his mind and hadn't listened to me when I'd prayed for him to protect Dieuwertje, just like the time – I must have been about seven – when I'd asked for a new bike: a red one with at least seven gears, and a soft saddle with double suspension so that I didn't get a pain in my crotch when I had to cycle home from school into the wind. I never got the bike. If I went downstairs now, I hoped, it wouldn't be Matthies lying beneath the sheet but my rabbit. Of course I'd be sad, but it would be different from the beating veins in my forehead when I tried to hold my breath in bed to understand death, or when I made the candle for so long my blood ran to my head like candlewax. Finally, I let my legs drop back onto my mattress and carefully opened my bedroom door. I tiptoed onto the landing and down the stairs. Dad had beaten me to it: through the banisters I saw him sitting on a chair next to the coffin, his head on the glass of the viewing window. I looked down at his messy blond hair that always smelled of cows, even when he'd just had a bath. I looked at his bent body. He was shaking; as he wiped his nose on his pyjama top, I thought how the fabric would become hard with snot, just like my coat sleeves. I looked at him and began to feel little stabs inside my chest. I imagined I was watching Nederland 1, 2 or 3 and could zap away at any moment if it got too much. Dad sat there for so long my feet got cold. When he pushed his chair in and returned to bed – my parents had a waterbed that Dad would sink back into now – I descended the rest of the stairs and sat down on his chair. It was still warm. I pressed my mouth to the window, like the ice in my dreams, and blew. I tasted the salt of my father's tears. Matthies's face was as pale as fennel; his lips were purple from the cooling mechanism that kept him frozen. I wanted to turn it off so that he could thaw in my arms and I could carry him upstairs so that we could sleep on it, like Dad sometimes ordered us to when we'd misbehaved and been sent to bed without any dinner. I'd ask him whether this was really the right way to leave us.

The first night he was in the coffin in the front room, Dad saw me sitting with my hands around the banisters and my head pushed through them. He'd sniffed and said, 'They've put cotton wads in his bottom to stop his crap coming out. He must still be warm inside. That makes me feel better.' I held my breath and counted: thirty-three seconds of suffocation. It wouldn't be long before I could hold my breath for so long that I'd be able to fish Matthies out of his sleep, and just like the frogspawn we got out of the ditch behind the cowshed with a fishing net and kept in a bucket until they were tadpoles and tails and legs slowly began to grow out of them, Matthies would also slowly transform from lifeless to alive and kicking.

*

On the morning of the third day, Dad asked from the bottom of the stairs whether I wanted to go with him to Farmer Janssen's to pick up some mangels and drop them off at the new bit of land. I would have preferred to stay with my brother so that I could be certain he didn't thaw in my absence, melting out of our life like a snowflake, but I didn't want to disappoint him so I put on my red coat over my overalls, the zip done up to my chin. The tractor was so old I was shaken back and forth at every bump; I had to cling on to the edge of the open window. Anxiously I glanced over at my father: the lines of sleep were still on his face, the waterbed made rivers in his skin, an impression of the lake. Mum's bobbing body had stopped him from sleeping, as had his own bobbing body, or the idea of bodies heaving as they fell into water. Tomorrow they'd buy a normal mattress. My stomach rumbled.

'I need to poo.'

'Why didn't you go at home?'

'I didn't need to then.'

'That's impossible, you feel it coming on.'

'But it's the truth. I think I've got the runs.'

Dad parked the tractor on the land, turned off the engine, and reached over to push open my door for me.

'Squat down over by that tree, the ash there.'

I quickly climbed out of the cab, pulled off my coat and let my overalls and pants drop to my knees. I imagined the diarrhoea splattering onto the grass like the caramel sauce my granny poured onto the rice pudding, and squeezed my buttocks together. Dad leaned against the tractor's tyre, lit up a cigarette and looked at me.

'If you take any longer, moles will start tunnelling up your bum hole.'

I began to sweat, picturing the cotton wads my dad had mentioned, the way the moles would burrow into my brother when he was buried, and the way they'd dig up everything in me afterwards. My poo belonged to me, but once it was between the blades of grass, it belonged to the world.

'Just push,' Dad said. He came over and handed me a used tissue. His eyes were hard. I wasn't used to this expression on him, even though I knew he hated waiting because then he had to stand still for too long, which made him dwell on things, and then he smoked more. No one in the village liked to dwell: the crops might wither, and we only knew about the harvest that came from the land, not about things that grew inside ourselves. I breathed in Dad's smoke so that his cares would become mine. After that, I said a quick prayer to God that he wouldn't give me cancer from the cigarette smoke if I helped with the toad migration when I was old enough. 'The righteous care for the needs of their livestock,' I'd once read in the Bible, so I was safe as far as illness was concerned.

'The urge went away,' I said. I pulled my pants back up and put my overalls back on, closed my coat and zipped it up to my chin. I could hold in my poo. I wouldn't have to lose anything I wanted to keep from now on.

Dad stamped out his butt on a molehill. 'Drink lots of water, that helps with the calves too. Otherwise it will come out the other end one day.' He laid his hand on my head, and I tried to walk as upright as I could beneath it. Now there were two things I'd have to watch out for at both ends.

We walked back to the tractor. The new bit of land was older than me and yet it continued to be called that. It was like the way there used to be a doctor living at the bottom of the dike where there was now a playground with a bumpy slide, which we still called the Old Doctor's when arranging play dates.

'Do you think worms and maggots are going to eat Matthies?' I asked my father as we walked back. I didn't dare look at him. Dad had once read out from Isaiah, 'All your pomp has been brought down to the grave, along with the noise of your harps; maggots are spread out beneath you and worms cover you,' and now I was worried this would happen to my brother too. Dad tugged open the tractor's door without answering me. I feverishly pictured my brother's body full of holes like strawberry matting.

When we arrived at the mangels, some of them were rotten. The mushy white pulp that looked like pus stuck to my fingers when I picked them up. Dad tossed them nonchalantly over his shoulder into the trailer. They made a dull thud. Whenever he looked at me I felt my cheeks burning. We had to agree upon times when my parents couldn't look at me, I thought, the same as with the TV. Perhaps that was why Matthies didn't come home that day – because the doors to the TV cabinet were closed and no one was keeping an eye on us.

I didn't dare ask my father any more questions about

Matthies and threw the last mangel into the trailer, taking my place next to him in the cabin afterwards. There was a sticker on the rusty rim above the rearview mirror that said MILK THE COW, NOT THE FARMER.

Back at the farm, Dad and Obbe dragged the dark blue waterbed outside. Dad pulled off the nozzle and the safety cap and let the water drain out into the farmyard. It wasn't long before a thin layer of ice had formed. I didn't dare stand on it, afraid that I would fall through. The dark mattress slowly shrank like a vacuum-sealed packet of coffee. Then my father rolled up the waterbed and laid it at the side of the road, next to the wheelbarrow containing the Christmas tree that would be picked up on Monday by the waste disposal company. Obbe nudged me and said, 'There he is.' I stared at the place he was pointing to and saw the black hearse approaching over the dike; it came closer and closer like a large crow, then it turned left and drove onto the farm, across the layer of ice from the waterbed, which had indeed cracked. Reverend Renkema got out with two of my uncles. Dad had chosen them and Farmer Evertsen and Farmer Janssen to lift the oak coffin into the hearse and later carry it into the church as Hymn 416 was sung, accompanied by the band in which Matthies had played the trombone for years, and the only thing that was right about that afternoon was that heroes are always borne aloft.

PART II

From close up the warts on the toads look just like capers. I hate the taste of capers, those little green buds. And if you pop one between your thumb and index finger, some sourish stuff comes out, just like from a toad's poison gland. I poke at a toad's fleshy rump with a stick. There's a black stripe running down its back. It doesn't move. I push harder and watch the rough skin fold around the stick; for a moment its smooth belly touches the tarmac that has been warmed by the first rays of spring sun, where they love to squat.

'I only want to help you,' I whisper.

I put down the lantern they gave us at the Reformed church next to me on the road. It is white with sticking-out folds in the middle. 'God's word is a lamp to your feet and a light to your path,' Reverend Renkema had said as he handed them out to the children. It's not yet eight o'clock and my candle has already shrunk to half its size. I hope God's word isn't going to start fading too.

In the light of my lantern I see that the toad's front feet aren't webbed. Maybe a heron bit them off or he was born like that. Maybe it's like Dad's gammy leg that he drags around after him across the farmyard like one of those tube sandbags from the silage heap.

'There's squash and a Milky Way for everyone,' I hear a church volunteer say behind me. The thought of having to eat a Milky Way in a place where there are no toilets makes my stomach heave. You never know whether someone's sneezed onto the squash or spat in it or whether they've checked the sell-by dates of the Milky Ways. The chocolate layer around the malt nougat might have turned white, the same thing that happens to your face when food makes you sick. After that death will follow swiftly, I'm sure of that. I try to forget about the Milky Ways.

'If you don't hurry up, you won't just have a stripe along your back but tyre tracks,' I whisper to the toad. My knees are starting to hurt from the squatting. Still no movement from the toad. One of the other toads tries to catch a lift on his back, trying to hang on with its front legs under its armpits, but it keeps sliding off. They're probably scared of water like me. I stand up again, pick up my lantern and quickly shove the two toads into my coat pocket when no one's looking, then I search the group for the two people wearing fluorescent vests.

Mum had insisted we put them on. 'Otherwise you'll be as flat as the run-over toads yourselves. Nobody wants that. These will turn you into lanterns.'

Obbe had smelled the fabric. 'No way I'm going to put that on. We'll look like total idiots in these dirty, stinking sweat-bags. No one else will be wearing safety vests.'

Mum sighed. 'I always get it wrong, don't I?' And she turned the corners of her mouth downwards. They'd been constantly turned downwards recently, as though there were fruit-shaped weights hanging on them, like on the tablecloth that goes with the garden set.

'You're doing fine, Mum. Of course we'll wear them,' I said, gesturing to Obbe. The vests are only used when the kids in the last year of primary take their cycling proficiency test, which Mum oversees. She sits on a fishing chair at the only crossroads in the village, and puts on her concerned face, lips pursed – a poppy that just won't open. It's her job to check that everyone sticks out their arm to indicate and gets through the traffic safely. The first time I felt ashamed of my mum was on that crossroads.

A fluorescent vest comes towards me. Hanna is carrying a black bucket of toads in her right hand, and her vest is half open, its panels flapping in the wind. The sight of it makes me feel anxious. 'You have to close your vest.' Hanna raises her eyebrows, staples in the canvas of her face. She manages to keep looking at me like this – with slight irritation – for a long time. Now the sun is becoming hotter during the day, she's getting more freckles around her nose. An image flashes into my mind: a flattened Hanna with the freckles splattered around her over the tarmac, the way some run-over toads end up in pieces. And then we'd have to scrape her off the road with a spade.

'But I'm so hot,' Hanna says.

At that moment, Obbe joins us. His blond hair is long and hangs in greasy strings in front of his face. He repeatedly smooths it behind his ear before it slowly tumbles back again.

'Look. This one looks like Reverend Renkema. See that fat head and those bulging eyes? And Renkema doesn't have a neck either.' A brown toad is sitting on the palm of his hand. We laugh but not too loudly: you mustn't mock the pastor, just like you mustn't mock God; they're best friends and you have to watch out with best friends. I don't have a best friend yet but there are lots of girls at the new school who might become one. Obbe started secondary ages ago, and Hanna is two years below me at primary school. She's got as many friends as God had disciples.

Suddenly Obbe holds his lantern above the toad's head. I see its skin glow pale yellow. It squeezes its eyes shut. Obbe begins to grin.

'They like heat,' he says, 'that's why they bury their ugly heads in the mud in the winter.' He moves the lantern closer and closer. When you fry capers they go black and crispy. I want to knock Obbe's hand away, but then the lady with the squash and the Milky Ways comes over to us. He quickly puts the toad in his bucket. The squash lady is wearing a T-shirt that says LOOK OUT! TOADS CROSSING. She must have seen Hanna's shocked expression because she asks us if everything's all right, if all the crushed bodies aren't upsetting us. I lovingly wrap my arm around my little sister who has put on a sulky pout. I'm aware there's a risk she could suddenly burst into tears, like this morning when Obbe flattened a grasshopper against the stable wall with his clog. I think it was mainly the sound that scared her, but she stuck to her guns: to her it was that little life, the wings folded in front of the

40

grasshopper's head like mini fly-screens. She saw life; Obbe and I saw death.

The squash lady smiles crookedly, and fetches a Milky Way for each of us from her coat pocket. I accept it out of politeness and, when she's not looking, take it out of its wrapper and drop it into the bucket of toads: toads never get tummy ache or stomach cramps.

'The three kings are OK,' I say.

Since the day Matthies didn't come home, I've been calling us the three kings because one day we'll find our brother, even though we'll have to travel a long way and go bearing gifts.

I wave my lantern at a bird to drive it away. The candle wobbles dangerously, and a drop of candle-grease falls on my welly. The startled bird flies up into a tree.

Wherever you cycle through the village or the fields, you see the dried-up reptilian bodies like little tablecloths. With all of the children and volunteers who have come to help, we carry our full buckets and lanterns to the other side of the verge which runs down to the lake. The water looks so stupidly innocent today and in the distance I can see the outlines of the factories, the tall buildings with dozens of lights and the bridge between the village and the city, like Moses' path when he stretched out his hand over the sea like the Bible says: 'Then the Lord drove the sea back by a strong east wind all night and made the sea dry land, and the waters were divided. And the children of Israel went into the midst of the sea on dry ground, the waters being a wall to them on their right hand and on their left.'

Hanna stands next to me and peers across to the other side.

'Just look at all those lights,' she says. 'Maybe they have a lantern parade every single night.'

'No, it's because they're afraid of the dark,' I say.

'*You're* afraid of the dark.'

I shake my head but Hanna is busying emptying her bucket. Dozens of frogs and toads spread across the surface of the water. The gentle splashing sounds make me feel dizzy. I suddenly notice that the fabric of my coat is sticking to my armpits. To waft away the heat I flap my arms like a bird that wants to take off.

'Do you ever want to go to the other side?' Hanna asks.

'There's nothing to see there; they don't even have any cows.' I block her view by standing in front of her, and drawing the left side of her safety vest to the side with the Velcro and pressing it hard so that it sticks.

My sister steps to one side. She's put her hair in a ponytail that gives her an encouraging pat on the back with every movement. I really want to pull the elastic out. I don't want her to think that anything's possible, that she can put on her ice skates one day and disappear.

'Don't you want to know what it's like there?'

'Of course not, you blockhead. You know that . . .' I don't finish my sentence, but chuck the empty bucket into the grass next to me.

I walk away from her and count my footsteps. By the time I reach four, Hanna is walking next to me again. Four's my favourite number. A cow has four stomachs, there are four seasons, a chair has four legs. The heavy feeling I just had in my chest pops, like the air bubbles in the lake that float to the surface and go their separate ways.

'It must be boring there without any cows,' she says quickly.

In the candlelight you can't see that her nose is crooked on her face. She has a cast in her right eye; it's as though she's continually adjusting her gaze to focus on you, like a camera's shutter speed. I wish I could put in a new roll of film to be sure she'll see well enough to stay safe. I hold out my hand to Hanna and she takes it. Her fingers feel sticky.

'Obbe's talking to a girl,' she says.

I look back. His lanky body suddenly seems to know how to move better; he makes a few exaggerated gestures with his hands and laughs with sound again, the first time in ages. Then he squats down at the lakeside. Now he's probably telling a nice story about toads, about our good intentions, but not about the water, barely warmed by the sun, where the toads are now swimming and at the bottom of which our brother lay a year and a half ago. He walks back along the dike with the girl. After a few yards we can no longer see them; they've dissolved into the darkness. All we find is his half-burned lantern on the tarmac. The little green candle lies next to it, stamped flat like a goose dropping. I scrape it up with my spade. We can't just leave it here alone like that after a whole evening's faithful service. When we get back to the farm, I hang it on a branch of the knotted willow tree. The trees stand in a row with their heads bent towards my bedroom, like a group of church elders listening in on us. I suddenly feel the toads moving in my coat pocket. I lay my hand over them protectively. I turn ninety degrees and say to Hanna, 'Don't say anything to Mum and Dad about the other side, they'll get even more upset.'

'I won't say anything. It was a stupid idea.'

'Very stupid.'

We can see Mum and Dad through the window, sitting on the sofa. From behind, they look just like the candle stubs in our lanterns. We use some spit to put them out.

2

Mum is getting the amount of food on her plate wrong more and more often. As soon as she's sat down after dishing it up, she says, 'It really did look like more than that from above.' Sometimes I'm worried it's our fault, that we're nibbling away at her from the inside, like what happens to a black lace-weaver spider. The teacher told us about them during a biology lesson – once she's given birth, the mother gives herself to her young. The tiny hungry spiders devour the mother: every last bit of her, until not even a leg is left. They don't mourn her for a second. Mum always leaves a bit of her chicken cordon bleu on the edge of her plate, 'leaving the best till last', saving herself until the end of the meal just in case we, her young, have not yet filled our bellies.

I gradually start looking down at our family from above, too, so it's less noticeable how little we amount to without Matthies. The empty place at the table now only has a seat and a chair-back that my brother can no longer casually set his weight against, causing my dad to roar, 'Four legs!' No one's allowed to sit on that chair either. I guess that's in case he comes back one day. 'If Jesus returns, it will be a day just like any other. Life will go on as usual. Just like when Noah built his ark, people will be busy working and eating, drinking and getting married. Matthies will be as entirely expected as He is, when he returns,' Dad had said at the funeral. When he comes back, I'll push his chair in so much it touches the edge of the table, so that he won't spill his food or slip away without a sound. Since his death, we've been eating in fifteen minutes. When the big hand and the small hand are standing upright, Dad gets up. He puts on his black beret and goes to do the cows, even if they've just been done.

'What are we eating?' Hanna asks.

'New potatoes and beans,' I say after I've lifted one of the pan lids. I see my pale face reflected in the saucepan. I cautiously smile at myself, just briefly, otherwise Mum glares at you until the corners of your mouth go down again. There's nothing here to smile about. The only place we sometimes forget about that is behind the covering shed, out of the sight of our parents.

'No meat?'

'Burnt,' I whisper.

'Again.'

Mum slaps my hand, I drop the lid and it falls, leaving a damp circle behind on the tablecloth.

'Don't be so greedy,' Mum says, closing her eyes. Everyone copies immediately, even though Obbe, just like me, keeps one open to keep an eye on things. There's never any warning that we're about to pray or that Dad's going to say grace, so you just have to sense it.

'But may our souls not cleave to this transient life but do everything that God bids us and end up finally by Him.

46

Amen,' my father says in a solemn voice before opening his eyes. Mum fills the plates one by one. She has forgotten to turn on the extractor fan – the whole house stinks of charred fillet steak and the windows have steamed up. Now no one can look in from the street and see that she's still in her pink dressing gown. In the village people stare in through each other's windows a lot, to check what kind of hours they work and how the family keep each other warm. Dad is sitting at the table with his head in his hands. He's held it high all day long but at the table it falls down; it has become too heavy. From time to time he lifts it again to put his fork in his mouth before letting it droop again. The little stabs inside my belly get worse, as though holes are being pricked in the lining. No one says anything, just knives and forks scraping on plates. I pull the cords of my coat even tighter. I wish I could squat on my chair. My stomach, which is swelling, would hurt less then and I'd have a better view. Dad finds that position irreverent and taps his fork on my knee until I'm sitting on my bottom again. Sometimes there are red stripes on my knees, like a tally of the days without Matthies.

Suddenly Obbe leans towards me and says, 'Do you know what an accident in an underpass looks like?' I've just pricked four holes in a string bean with my fork – the juice is seeping out and now it's a recorder. Before I can reply, Obbe has opened his mouth. I see watery mashed potato dotted with bits of beans and some apple puree. It looks like vomit. Obbe laughs and swallows the casualties. There's a pale blue line on his forehead. He butts his head against the edge of the bed

47

in his sleep. He's still too young to worry about it. Dad says children can't have worries because they only come when you have to plough and grub your own fields, even though I keep discovering more and more worries of my own and they keep me awake at night. They seem to be growing.

Now that Mum has got thinner and her dresses baggier, I'm afraid she'll die soon and that Dad will go with her. I follow them about all day so that they can't suddenly die and disappear. I always keep them in the corner of my eye, like the tears for Matthies. And I never switch off the light globe on my bedside table until I've heard Dad's snores, and the bedsprings creaking twice. Mum always rolls from right to left to right before she finds the right fit. Then I lie in the light of the North Sea, waiting for it to go quiet. But when they go to visit friends in the village in the evenings and Mum shrugs when I ask what time they'll be back, I lie for hours staring at the ceiling. Then I imagine how I'll cope as an orphan and what I'll tell the teacher about the cause of their deaths. There is a list of the top ten causes of death. I once Googled them at break time. Lung cancer was number one. I've secretly put together my own list: drowning, traffic accidents and slipping in the cowshed are at the top.

After I've figured out what I'm going to tell the teacher and stop wallowing in self-pity, I press my head into my pillow. I'm too old to believe in the tooth fairy but too young not to still long for her. Obbe sometimes jokingly calls her 'the tooth bitch' because she just stopped paying him one day and his back teeth, roots and all, were under his pillow. They left

48

a bloody mark behind because he never rinsed them. If she comes to visit me one day, I'll flatten her. Then she'll have to stay and I'll wish for new parents. I've still got my wisdom teeth to use as bait. Very occasionally I go downstairs when they're not back yet. I sit in the dark in my pyjamas on the sofa, my knees together, hands folded, and I promise to God that I'll take another bout of diarrhoea if He brings them home safely. I expect the phone to ring at any moment and to hear they lost control of the wheel, or the handlebars of a bike. But the phone never rings, and usually I get cold after a while and go back upstairs where I continue my wait under the covers. They're not brought back to life until I hear the bedroom door and the shuffle of Mum's slippers. And then I can fall asleep with peace of mind.

Before we have to go to bed, Hanna and I play a bit. Hanna sits on the carpet behind the sofa. I look at my socks pulled up high, the tops folded twice. I rub them flat. My sister is sitting next to the Thunderbirds island. It used to belong to Matthies, and we often played with it together. We'd fire rockets into the sky and fight with the enemy – we could choose who that was ourselves back then. Obbe is lying on his chest across the sofa, headphones over his ears. He looks down on us. There's a mayonnaise stain in the shape of France on his grey T-shirt.

'I'll let anyone who breaks the trees on the drive listen to the new *Hitzone* for ten minutes on my Discman.'

Obbe lets his headphones sink from his ears until they're around his neck. Almost everyone in my class has got a

Discman, except for the squares. I don't want to be a square and that's why I'm saving up for a Discman: a Philips one with an anti-shock system so that it doesn't keep cutting out on my way to school over the bumps in the fields. And a protective jacket the same colour as my coat. I don't have to save up much more. Dad gives us two euros every Saturday for helping on the farm. He hands it over solemnly: 'Put this in your bottom drawer for later.' The thought of the Discman allows me to forget everything around me, even the fact that Dad is hoping we'll move out.

The island's trees were once olive green, but they've faded over the years and the paint has chipped off. As though someone's urging me on, I've broken off a whole row of plastic trees before I know it. I hear them snap between my fingers. Anything you can break with just one hand isn't worth breaking. Hanna starts to yell at once.

'It was just a joke, you idiot,' Obbe says quickly.

He turns around as Mum comes out of the kitchen and puts his headphones back over his ears. Mum has tied the belt of her dressing gown tight. Her eyes dart from Hanna to me to Obbe. Then she sees the snapped-off trees in my hand. Without a word she pulls me up by my arm, digging her nails into my coat – which I don't even want to take off indoors any more – which press through the fabric. I try not to react and most of all not to look at Mum so that she doesn't get it into her head to take my coat off me, without mercy, the way she peels potatoes. She lets go of me at the bottom of the stairs.

'Go and fetch your piggy bank,' she says as she blows a lock of blonde hair away from her face. My heartbeat quickens with every step. For a moment I think of the proverb from the Book of Jeremiah that Granny sometimes quotes when she's reading the paper, licking her thumb and first finger so that the world's problems don't stick together: 'The heart is deceitful above all things, yes, and desperately wicked: who can know it?'

Nobody knows my heart. It's hidden deep beneath my coat, my skin, my ribs. My heart was important for nine months inside my mother's belly, but once I left the belly, everyone stopped caring whether it beat enough times per hour. No one worries when it stops or begins to beat fast, telling me there must be something wrong.

Downstairs I have to put my piggy bank on the kitchen table. It's a china cow with a slot in its back. There's a plastic stopper in its bum hole so you can take money out. There's duct tape over it so that I have to get through two barriers before I spend my money on rubbish.

'Because of your sins He keeps Himself hidden and He no longer wants to hear you,' Mum says. She is holdig a claw hammer – she must have been waiting for me with it. I try not to think about the Discman I want so much. My parents' loss is much worse – you can't save up for a new son.

'But there's a hole . . .' I try.

Mum presses the side of the hammer you use to get nails out of wood – they look like two metal rabbit's ears, reminding me briefly of what I sacrificed to keep Dieuwertje alive – gently against my swollen belly. I quickly take the hammer. Its handle

51

feels warm. I lift it up and let it fall onto the piggy bank with a big smack. It breaks into three pieces. My mum carefully fishes out the red and blue notes and a couple of coins. She gets the dustpan and brush and sweeps up the pieces of the cow. I grip the handle's hammer so tightly my knuckles turn white.

3

My head full of black-and-white images, I lie on top of my dinosaur duvet cover. I keep my arms stiff alongside my body, my feet slightly parted, like a soldier at ease, my coat as armour. At school today we did the Second World War and we watched a film about it on School TV. I get a lump in my throat again instantly. I see the images of Jews, lying on top of each other like braising steaks, the bald-headed Germans in old cars. They looked like the plucked bums of our laying hens, pinkish with black stubble, and once you get an outbreak of feather pecking amongst them, they won't let anyone escape.

I raise myself half up on my mattress and scratch a fluorescent star from the sloping roof. Dad has already taken away a few, which he does whenever I come home with a bad grade and it's his turn to tuck me up at night. Dad always used to make up a story about little Johnny who was up to no good. He was always doing something that wasn't allowed. Now Johnny's a good boy so he doesn't get punished – either that or Dad keeps forgetting to tell me about him.

'Where's Johnny?' I asked.

'He's tired and crushed.'

Then I knew right away that Dad's head is tired and crushed inside because that's where Johnny lives.

'Is he ever coming back?'

'Don't count on it,' Dad replied in a dejected voice.

When he takes off a star he leaves behind the white Blu-Tack: each bit stands for a question I got wrong. I stick the pulled-off star on my coat at heart height. When the teacher was telling us about it, I wondered what it would be like to kiss a tash-face like Hitler. Dad only has a moustache when he drinks beer. He gets a line of foam along his top lip. Hitler's was at least two fingers thick.

Under the desk, I'd put my hand on my belly to calm down the tickling insects. I got them more and more often in my belly and crotch. I could also make them start by thinking that I was lying on top of Johnny. Sometimes I thought that was why he was crushed, but as long as Dad's head was still round and on top of his body, I didn't take that seriously. I rarely asked questions – they just didn't occur to me. But this time I'd raised my hand.

'Do you think that Hitler sometimes cried when he was alone?'

The teacher, who is also my form tutor, looked at me for a long time before answering. She had eyes that always shone, as though there were battery-run tea lights behind them that lasted a long time. Maybe she was waiting for me to cry so that she could see whether I was a good or a bad person. After all, I still hadn't cried about my brother, not even soundlessly, as my tears got stuck in the corner of my eye. I guessed it was because of my coat. It was warm in the classroom, which meant my tears would surely evaporate before they reached my cheeks.

'Villains don't cry,' the teacher said then. 'Only heroes cry.'

I'd looked down. Were Obbe and I villains? Mum only cried with her back to us, and so quietly you couldn't hear it. Everything her body did was silent, even her farts.

The teacher told us that Hitler's favourite pastime was daydreaming and that he was afraid of illness. He suffered from stomach cramps, eczema and wind, although that last one was because he ate a lot of bean soup. Hitler had lost three brothers and a sister, none of whom made it to the age of six. I'm like him, I thought, and nobody must know it. We even share the same birthday – 20 April. On good days, Dad tells us from his smoking chair that it was the coldest April day in years and that I came into the world light blue that Saturday, and they almost had to chisel me out of the womb like a statue out of ice. In my baby album, there's a coil stuck next to my first scan: a copper tube with a bow on it and little white hooks like tiny shark's teeth that could bite every sperm dead, and a thread at the bottom that looks like a mucus trail. I'd managed to avoid the coil and had swum through it. When I asked why Mum had shark's teeth in her, Dad had said, 'Be ye fruitful and multiply, bring forth abundantly in the earth, and multiply, but make sure you've got enough bedrooms first. This was a stop-gap solution, God knew that, only you were already as stubborn as a mule.' After I was born, my mum didn't get another coil. 'Children are the Lord's legacy.' You can't say no to legacies.

I secretly Googled my birthday later. We can only get on the internet when the phone cable is out and the internet cable is plugged in, so it crackles and beeps as it connects – and we're not allowed on for long in case our parents get an important phone call, even though they never get important phone calls and they're usually only about a cow that's got out again on the new bit of land. They think everything on the internet is wicked, but as Dad sometimes says, 'We're in the world, not *of* the world.' We're only allowed to use it for school sometimes, even though I have my doubts about Dad's line (which is from John) when people say they can see from our Reformed faces which village we come from. I saw that there were powerful gusts of wind on that day, but Dad had said that it was so calm outside that even the knotted willows kept their branches reverentially still. On that day in April, Hitler had been dead for forty-six years already. And the only difference between him and me is that I'm afraid of vomiting and diarrhoea, not Jewish people – even though I've never seen a Jew in real life, but maybe they are still hiding in people's attics or cellars, hidden by Dutch farmers like in the war, or perhaps that's why we're not allowed down in the basement. There must be a reason Mum takes two full supermarket bags down there on Friday evenings. There are tins of hot dogs in them, even though we never eat hot dogs.

I take the crumpled letter from my coat pocket that the teacher made us write to Anne Frank. I thought that was a crazy thing to do. Anne Frank was dead, and I knew the letterbox in the village only had two slots – one for 'other postcodes' and one for more local numbers, 8000 to 8617. Heaven wasn't included. That would be mad too, because dead people are always missed more than living ones so there would be too much post going there.

'It's about empathizing with her situation,' the teacher said. She felt I was good at putting myself in another's shoes but not so great at kicking off my own and having fun. Sometimes I'd get stuck in the other person for too long because that was easier than staying inside myself. I shunted my chair a bit closer to Belle. We'd been sitting next to each other since the first week of secondary school. I'd liked her at once because she had big ears that stuck out through her straw-blonde hair and her mouth was a bit crooked on her face, like a clay doll that had dried before it was completely finished. The sick cows were always sweeter too; you could stroke them gently without them suddenly kicking back at you.

Belle leaned towards me for a moment and whispered, 'Don't you ever get tired of your uniform?' I followed her eyes – they were made up with eyeliner, and the lines under and over looked like curves on a number line that made jumps too big to work out an answer – in the direction of my coat. The cords of my hood lay on my chest, hard from dried-up spit. In the wind they sometimes wound around my neck like umbilical cords.

I shook my head.

'They talk about you in the playground.'

'So what?'

In the meantime, I opened the drawer under my desk slightly. I was the only person who still had a drawer; the desk was actually from the primary school that was next to the secondary school. The sight of the foil-wrapped packages

57

made me feel calm: a mass grave of milk biscuits. My stomach rumbled. Some of the biscuits had already gone soft, as though someone had put them in their mouth and then spat them back out into the silver foil. After it had been through your intestines, food turned into poo. All of the toilets here had a ledge inside – my turd would be served up to me on a white plate, and I didn't want that. I had to keep it inside me.

'They say you can't grow tits and that's why you always wear your coat. And that you never wash it. We can smell cow.'

Belle used her fountain pen to make a full stop after the title on her page. I wanted to be that blue dot for a moment. And then for there to be nothing else after me. No lists, thoughts or longings. Just nothing at all.

Belle looked at me expectantly. 'You're just like Anne Frank. You're in hiding.' I pushed my pencil into the grinder of my pencil sharpener that I'd got out of my bag, and turned it until there was a very sharp point. I let it break twice.

I roll over on the mattress that used to belong to Matthies so that I'm lying on my belly. For the last couple of weeks I've been sleeping in his bedroom in the attic. Hanna's got my old room now. Sometimes I think that Johnny has stayed in my old room, that he finds it too scary in the attic because since then, Dad hasn't told me anything about him, and only his absence has made an impression. In the middle of the mattress there's the hollow of my brother's body. It's the shape left by death and whichever way I turn it or flip it over, the hollow stays a hollow that I try not to end up in.

I look for my teddy bear but can't see it anywhere. Not at the foot of the bed, not under the duvet, not under the bed. Immediately I hear my mum's voice inside my head: 'Disgusting.' That's what she'd said and it was in the look on her face when she suddenly came into my room, the stress on 'gust'. It was an ugly word and if you said it, it was a bit like needing to vomit. She'd first said the word and then spelled it out: d-i-s-g-u-s-t-i-n-g, her nose stuck up in the air. I suddenly realize where my bear must be. I slip through the opening in the covers and look out of my bedroom window into the garden where I see my bear hanging on the washing line. There are two red wooden pegs in each ear. He is being rocked roughly back and forth by the wind, making exactly the same movement I made when I was lying on top of him, causing Mum to clap her hands three times like she was chasing a crow from the cherry tree. She'd seen the way I was pushing my crotch into its fluffy bottom. Since I've been sleeping here in the attic I've been doing that. I close my eyes and first run through the day as I move, repeating everything everyone said to me and the way they said it, and only then do I think about the Philips Discman I really wanted, about two snails having sex on top of each other, the way Obbe separated them that time with a screwdriver, about Dieuwertje Blok from the TV, about Matthies on the ice, about a life without my coat but with myself. Just until I need to pee.

'An idol is what you flee to before you go to God,' she said to me a bit later, when I came down for a beaker of warm milk with aniseed. As a punishment she's put my bear in the wash and hung him on the line. I creep down the stairs in my socks, slip through the hall to the back garden, and step into the tepid evening air. Behind me in the farmyard, the construction light is still on. My parents are giving the calves their milk before they go to bed, a sum I'm not allowed to forget: one scoop of protein powder to two litres of water. That's how the calves get extra protein; after drinking it, their noses smell of vanilla. I can hear the milk tank buzzing, the clatter of the drinking troughs. I quickly pull on my mum's clogs which are next to the door, sprint across the grass to the washing line, take the pegs from my bear's ears and clutch him tight to my chest, rocking him gently back and forth a few times as though he's Matthies, as though I've fished him out of the dark lake in the dead of the night. He feels heavy and wet. It will be at least a night before he's dry, a week before the smell of washing powder has worn off. His right eye is watering. When I walk back across the lawn, Mum and Dad's voices become louder. By the sound of it they are arguing. I can't handle arguments, just like Obbe can't handle anyone talking back to him, and presses his hands to his ears and begins to hum. Since I don't want to stand out in the darkness, I lay one hand over the fluorescent star on my coat, hold my bear in the other, and hide behind the rabbit hutches. The warm ammonia smell of the rabbits seeps through the splits in the wood. Obbe had got a couple of fat maggots from the muck-heap to use for fishing. When he went to thread the hook through those little bodies, I quickly looked the other way. From here I can hear what the row's about, and I see

Mum standing next to the manure pit with a pitchfork.

'If you hadn't have wanted to get rid of the child . . .'

'Oh, so now it's my fault?' Dad says.

'That's why God took away our oldest son.'

'We weren't married yet . . .'

'It's the tenth plague, I'm sure of it.'

I hold my breath. My coat feels damp from the wet bear against my chest, and its head droops forwards. I wonder for a moment whether Hitler would have told his mum what he was planning and that he was going to make a mess of it. I haven't told anyone that I prayed for Dieuwertje to survive. Could the tenth plague be my fault?

'We have to get along with what we've got,' Dad says.

I see his outline in the light of the construction lamp. His shoulders are higher than normal. Just like the coat rack he's hung higher now that we're taller, his shoulders are raised a couple of centimetres. Mum laughs. It's not her normal laugh: it's the laugh she does when she actually *doesn't* find something funny. It's confusing, but grown-ups are often confusing because their heads work like a Tetris game and they have to arrange all their worries in the right place. When there are too many of them, they pile up and everything gets stuck. Game over.

'I'd rather jump off the silo tank.'

The stabs in my belly get worse. It's as though my stomach is Granny's pincushion, which she pricks her pins in so as not to lose them.

'You haven't told anyone about the baby. Who knows

what the family thinks. Only God knows and he'll forgive a thousand times over,' Dad says.

'As long as you're keeping count,' Mum says, turning her back. She is almost as thin as the manure fork leaning against the wall of the barn. Now it dawns on me why she's stopped eating. During the toad migration, Obbe told me that after they've hibernated, toads don't eat again until they've mated, no sooner. My parents no longer touch each other, not even briefly. This must mean they don't mate either.

Back in my bedroom I look at the toads in the bucket under my desk. They're not on top of each other yet and the lettuce leaves are untouched at the bottom of the bucket.

'Tomorrow you're going to mate,' I say. Sometimes you have to be clear about things, set down rules, otherwise everyone will walk all over you.

Then I stand in front of the mirror next to my wardrobe and brush my hair sideways across my head. Hitler combed his hair like this to hide the scar of a bullet that had grazed his face. Once my hair is combed, I go and lie on my bed. In the light of my globe, I can see the rope hanging above my head from a beam. There still isn't a swing on it, or a rabbit. I see a loop at the end. Just big enough for a hare's neck. I try to reassure myself by thinking that my mum's neck is at least three times thicker and she's scared of heights.

4

'Are you angry?'

'No,' Mum says.

'Sad?'

'No.'

'Happy?'

'Just normal,' Mum says, 'I'm just normal.'

No, I think to myself, my mum's anything but normal. Even the omelette she's making right now is anything but normal. There are bits of eggshell in it and it's stuck to the bottom of the frying pan, and both the white and the yolk have dried out. She's stopped using butter and she's forgotten the salt and pepper again. Her eyes have been deeper in their sockets lately too, like my old flat football is sinking further and further into the manure pit next to the cowshed. I throw the eggshells on the counter into the bin and see the shards of my smashed cow amongst the rubbish. I fish out its head, which, apart from the horns, is still intact, and quickly put it in my coat pocket. Then I get the yellow dish-cloth from the sink to wipe up the slimy trails left by the broken eggs. A shiver runs through me: I don't like dried-up dish-cloths; they feel less dirty when they're wet than when they're dry and are still full of bacteria. I rinse it under the tap and stand next to my mother again, ever closer in the hope that she'll accidentally touch me when she moves the frying pan to the plates set out ready on the counter. Just for a moment. Skin against skin, hunger against hunger. Dad had made her stand on the scales before breakfast, otherwise he'd refuse to accompany her to church. It was an empty threat. I could hardly imagine a service without my dad being there, the way I sometimes ask myself what would become of God without my father. To underline his words, he'd put on his Sunday shoes immediately after breakfast rather than putting them in a row to be polished: we were only to appear before the Lord with polished toecaps, Mum sometimes said. Especially today, because it's the day of prayer for the crops, an important day for all the farmers in the village. Twice a year, before and after the harvest, the members of the Reformed community come together to pray and give thanks for the fields and the crops, that everything might blossom and grow – even while Mum is just getting thinner and thinner.

'Less than one and a half calves,' Dad said when Mum finally got on the scales. He bent over the numbers on the scales. Obbe and I stood in the door opening and glanced at each other. We all knew what happened to calves that were born too light, which were too skinny to go to the slaughter-house and too expensive to feed up. That's why most of them were given an injection. The longer Dad left her standing there, the more the numbers tried to crawl back, like snails, Mum getting quieter and seeming to shrink, as though the entire year's harvest was going to seed before our very eyes and there was nothing we could do about it. I wished I could have put on a packet of pancake flour and castor-sugar so that Dad would stop this. He'd once told us that a single calf could feed fifteen hundred people, so it would be a long time before we'd nibbled away at all of Mum, until there were only bones left. All of us staring at her all the time was causing her not to eat: my rabbit Dieuwertje didn't start gnawing at the carrots poking through his manger until he got the idea I was no longer around. When Dad put the scales back under the sink later, I quickly took out the batteries.

Mum doesn't touch me once while portioning out the omelette, not even by accident. I take a step back and then another. Sadness ends up in your spine. Mum's back is getting more and more bent. This time there are two plates missing, one for Mum and one for Matthies. She has stopped eating with us, even though she keeps up appearances by making herself a sandwich, and she still sits at the head of the table opposite Dad, watching us with the eyes of Argus, bringing our forks to our mouths. For a moment I picture a dead baby and the Big Bad Wolf Granny used to tell us about when we stayed at her house and she tucked us in beneath an itchy horse blanket. One day they cut open the Big Bad Wolf's belly to rescue the seven goats and put stones in instead and sewed his belly up again. They must have put a stone back in my Mum's belly, I realize, which is why she's so hard and cold sometimes.

I take a bite of my bread. During dinner, Dad tells us about the cows that won't lie in the free stalls but sleep on the slats, which isn't good for their udders. He holds up a piece of omelette.

'No salt on this,' he says, pulling a face and taking a sip of his coffee at the same time. No salt on the egg but still a sip of coffee with it.

'And the bottom's burnt,' Obbe says.

'There are bits in it,' Hanna says.

All three look at Mum, who gets up from the table abruptly and dumps her cumin cheese sandwich in the bin and puts her plate in the sink. She wants us to think she wasn't planning on eating the sandwich, that we're the reason she's got so thin. She doesn't look at anyone, as though we're the crusts she always carefully cuts off and lays next to her plate, like points to deduct from our scores later. Her back to us, she says, 'See, you always take his side.'

'It's just a poor egg,' Dad says. His voice is lower, the sign he's waiting for a disagreement; sometimes even when there isn't one, he changes the other person's mind. He sniffs as he continues to inspect the piece of omelette. The tension makes me poke my little finger up my nose and hook a piece of snot. I glance at the yellowish ball and then put it in my mouth. The salty taste of snot makes me feel calm. When I move my hand back up to my nose, my father gives my wrist a tug. 'Just because it's the day of prayer it doesn't mean you should start the harvest.' I quickly move my arm back down, push my tongue back into my throat as far as it can go and snort. It works. Snot fills my mouth so that I can swallow again. Mum turns around. She looks tired.

'I'm a bad mother,' she says.

She fixes her gaze on the light bulb above the kitchen

66

table. It's time for it to be covered by a lampshade. With or without floral motif. Whenever we mention it, she says it's no longer worth the bother, that she's old and it's only more work for us when we have to divide up the lampshade and all the furniture after their death, just like all the other things she no longer wants to spend money on with an eye on the Day of Judgement. I quickly stand next to her with my plate in my hand. When we play football at school it's about getting the positions right. Someone has to be captain, be an attacker or defender. I put too big a piece of egg in my mouth.

'It's a perfect egg,' I say, 'not too salty, not too watery.'

'Yes,' Hanna says, 'and there's calcium in the shell.'

'Listen to that, Mother,' Dad says, 'you're not that bad.'

He smiles for a moment and lets his knife glide across his tongue, which is dark red with a blue stripe on the underside – a moor frog at breeding time. He gets a muesli roll from the bread-basket and studies it from every side. Every Wednesday we fetch bread from the baker's in the village before school. All the bread is past its sell-by date and actually supposed to go to the chickens, but we mainly eat it ourselves. Dad says, 'If the chickens don't get ill from it, neither will you.' I still get worried sometimes that mould will grow inside me, that one day my skin will turn blue and white, like the spiced buns Dad slices the mould off with a big knife before serving to us, and that in due course, I'll only be good as chicken feed.

The bread usually tastes nice though, and the trip to the baker's is the best one of the week. Dad proudly shows off his haul: glazed currant buns, egg cakes, sourdough bread, spiced biscuits, doughnuts. Mum always takes out the croissants, even though she finds them too greasy. She looks for the best ones, and it gives her peace of mind if we want to eat them. The rest go to the chickens. I think we feel happy for a brief moment then, even if Dad says that's not for us, that we weren't made to be happy, just like our pale skins can't be in the sun for more than ten minutes so we always long for the shade, for darkness. This time we had a feed-bag of extra bread. Must be for the Jews in the basement. Maybe Mum makes good omelettes for them and cuddles them, making her forget to hold us, really tightly the way I sometimes hold Lien next door's cat – I feel the ribs through its fur against my belly, its little heart beating against mine.

We always sit in the front pew of the Reformed church on the dike – in the morning, evening and sometimes in the afternoon too for the children's service – so that everyone can see us coming in and know that despite our loss we still visit the House of the Lord, that despite everything we still believe in Him – even though I'm beginning to have more and more doubts about whether I find God nice enough to want to go and talk to Him. I've discovered that there are two ways of losing your belief: some people lose God when they find themselves; some people lose God when they lose themselves. I think I'll belong to that second group. My Sunday clothes are tight around my limbs, as though they were measured for the old version of myself. Granny compares going to church three times with tying your shoelaces: first you make a flat knot, then a noose and tie them, and last a double knot to be sure they're securely tied, and in the same way we won't remember the message properly until after the third time. And on Tuesday evenings, Obbe, a few old classmates from primary school and I have to go to catechism at Reverend Renkema's house in preparation for confirmation. His wife gives us orange squash and a slice of Frisian gingerbread. I like to go, but more for the gingerbread than for God's word.

During the service I secretly hope that one of the oldies in the last pew – who sit there so they'll get home first – will faint or feel unwell. This happens regularly, and you'll hear the loud bang of an oldie folding in on themself like a prayer book, and if someone has to be carried out of the church, a wave of distress rushes through the congregation, distress that unites us more than all the words in the Bible. The same wave that often rushes through me. But I'm not the only one. Our heads half turned, we watch the fallen until they've disappeared around the corner, before starting on the next psalm. Granny is old too but she's never been carried out of the church. During the sermon, I fantasize sometimes that she's collapsed and that I'm the one who will carry her outside like a hero, everyone turning their heads for me. But Granny is still as fit as a young heifer. She says that God is just like the sun: He always stays with you, however hard you cycle away from Him. He always travels with you. I know she's right. I've sometimes tried to lose the sun by being quicker, by playing hide and seek, but it stays visible behind my back or in the corner of my eye.

I look at Obbe who is sitting next to me on the bench. He's closed his hymn-book: its thin pages remind me too much of my mother's skin, as though with each psalm we turn her over and forget about her. He is picking at a blister on the palm of his hand. Now summer's coming, the stalls have to be mucked out so that they'll be spotless for the winter. We never really live in the seasons as we're always busy with the next one.

In time, the blister's soft membrane will become rock hard and you roll it off between your thumb and forefinger. We are constantly renewing ourselves – apart from Mum and Dad. Just like the Old Testament they keep repeating their words, behaviour, patterns and rituals, even if we, their followers, are moving further and further away from them. The pastor asks us to close our eyes and to pray for the fields and the crops. I pray for my parents: for Mum to get the silo out of her stubborn head and not to notice the rope hanging from the beam when she's dusting my bedroom. I think about her every time I make a loop in my exercise book or tie a knot in a bread-bag, because the clip never gets put on top of the bread-bin now. I suspect Dad's been putting them in the pocket of his overalls. And sometimes, when I'm lying on my belly on my mattress, moving on top of my bear, I fantasize that we have a little machine in the kitchen like the one they have on Stoepje's market stall that seals the bread-bag with a red plastic ribbon. Then it won't matter any more if we lose the clips and Mum will no longer be sad.

I peek through my eyelashes at my dad. His cheeks are wet. Maybe we're not praying for the crops but for the harvest of all the children in the village, for them to grow big and strong. And Dad's realized that he hasn't paid attention to his own fields and he's even allowed them to become flooded. Apart from food and clothes we also need attention. They seem to keep forgetting that. I close my eyes again and pray for the toads underneath my desk, hoping for the mating season that might encourage Mum and Dad too, and for the Jews in the basement, even though I don't think it's fair they're allowed cornflakes and hot dogs. I don't open my eyes until I feel a roll of peppermints pressing into my side.

'Only people with a lot of sins pray for a long time,' Obbe whispers.

5

The side of Obbe's forehead is blue like bread mould. Every few minutes he feels for his crown and smooths the hair around it flat with three fingers. Mum says we all have difficult skulls. I think it's because we all miss the pressure on our foreheads since Dad stopped laying his hand on our heads and just keeps his hands stiffly in the pockets of his overalls. The crown is the starting point from which we have grown, where all the separate bits of skull have come together. Perhaps that's why Obbe keeps touching his, to make sure he exists.

Mum and Dad don't see our tics. They don't realize that the fewer rules there are, the more we start inventing for ourselves. Obbe thought we should get together and talk about it, so after the service we've all gathered in his room. I'm sitting on the bed with Hanna who is leaning on me listlessly. I tickle her neck gently. She smells of Dad's restlessness, the smell of his cigarette smoke in her cardigan. There are little cracks in the headboard of Obbe's bed where he bangs every night or thrashes from one side of his pillow to the other, making a monotonous sound. Sometimes I try to guess the tune through the wall. Sometimes it's singing but more often just humming. He doesn't do psalms, which I'm glad about because they make me miserable. When I hear him banging, I go to his room and tell him to be quiet otherwise Mum will lie awake worrying how we're going to sleep in a tent in a campsite, if we ever get to go on holiday. It helps for a while but after a few minutes the banging starts up again. Sometimes I'm worried the wood won't split but his head, that we'll have to sand him and varnish him again. Hanna bangs too, which is why she's been sleeping in my bed more often, so I can hold her head until she falls asleep.

Downstairs we hear Mum vacuuming the front room. I hate that sound. Mum vacuums three times a day, even when there are no crumbs, even when we pick up all the crumbs from the carpet in our hands and carry them to the door and throw them into the gravel.

'Do you think they still kiss?' Hanna asks.

'Maybe they French kiss,' Obbe says.

Hanna and I giggle. Kissing with tongues always makes me think of those slimy, purplish-red cooking pears that Mum makes with cinnamon, blackcurrant juice, cloves and sugar, all tied up with each other.

'Or they lie on top of each other in the nuddy.'

Obbe gets his hamster out of the cage next to his bed. It's recently been renamed Tiesey. It's a little desert hamster. Its wheel is yellow from caked piss and there are sunflower seed cases everywhere. First you have to move your finger in the sawdust before you get him out of his nest, otherwise he'll be startled and bite. I want to be approached with the same caution, because every morning I'm dragged from Matthies's hollow by my dad who pulls the duvet off me and says, 'Cow

73

time. They're mooing with hunger.' It's easier to get into a hollow than to come out of one.

The hamster walks along my brother's arm. Its cheek pouches are round and full with food. It reminds me of Mum: but no, hers are the opposite – sunken. She can't be saving food in them to nibble away at later in the evening – although I did catch her licking out a yoghurt carton yesterday after dinner. She'd torn it open along the fold. She spread a bit of blackberry jam over the sides. I heard her finger keep disappearing into her mouth, the gentle plop, a string of saliva. Once a week the hamster gets a beetle or an earwig that we get from the cows' straw. But it's not enough to live off. Mum has to start eating again.

'Tiesey? That's short for Matthies,' I say.

Obbe gives me a big shove in my side; I fall off his bed and land on my funny bone. I try not to cry, even though it hurts and a light electric shock runs through my body. It wouldn't be fair not to cry about Matthies but then cry about myself. It still takes me some effort to hold back the tears. Maybe I'm becoming as fragile as Mum's dinner service and over time I'll have to be wrapped up in newspaper when I go to school. *Be brave*, I whisper to myself. *You have to be brave.*

All of a sudden Obbe acts kind, he makes his voice gentle. He touches his crown briefly. With fake cheeriness he says he didn't mean it like that – I don't know how he did mean it then, but it's not wise to go into it. Hanna looks nervously at the door. Dad sometimes gets so angry when he hears us arguing that he chases you around the farm, even though it looks more like hopping because he can't run on his gammy leg. If he does get hold of you, he gives you a kick up the backside or a slap against the back of your head. The best thing to do is run to the kitchen table. After going round and round a few times, he gives up, getting more oxygen to his brain, absorbing it like the butterflies do through the holes in the cottage cheese box where Obbe keeps them captive in his desk drawer. When a silence falls you can hear their wings beating against the plastic lid. They're for an important school experiment about the lifespan of a certain type of butterfly, he told us. Dad keeps his leg hidden. He never wears shorts, not even when it's boiling hot – I sometimes imagine that his legs are just like a twin-stick ice lolly, and that one day they'll break loose from each other and we'll throw away the bad leg, or let it melt in the sun behind the covering shed.

'If you don't cry, I'll show you something amazing,' Obbe says.

I breathe in and out deeply and pull my coat sleeves right down to my knuckles. They are beginning to fray at the seam. I hope they don't slowly get shorter until I'm totally exposed. It's not good to pick open the cocoons in the back garden before the butterflies have hatched. Crippled butterflies might come out and I'm sure they wouldn't be allowed to take part in Obbe's experiment.

I nod as a sign that I'm not going to cry. Being brave starts with holding back the tears.

My brother lets Tiesey go inside the collar of his pyjamas, pulling up the waist of his boxer shorts when the hamster reaches his belly. I can see his willy lying there with black curls around it like Dad's tobacco. Hanna begins to giggle again.

'Your willy's doing something strange, it's standing up.'

Obbe grins proudly. The hamster runs down along his willy. What if it bites or wants to burrow?

'If I pull at it, white stuff comes out.'

Now that sounds painful to me. I've already forgotten about my funny bone. I get a brief urge to touch his willy, to stroke it like Tiesey's fur. Just to see what it feels like, what material it's made of and whether you can move it, maybe to tug at it gently. If you do that to a cow's tail, they look back for a moment, except if you keep on doing it and then they kick back at you.

Obbe lets go of the waist of his blue and white striped boxers. We see the bulge moving around, like a wave in the ocean.

'Tiesey might suffocate,' Hanna says.

'My dick doesn't suffocate, does it?' Obbe says.

'That's true.'

'Isn't he going to stink of pee?'

My brother shakes his head. It's a shame I can no longer see his willy. I can feel the tickly insects tickling inside my belly, though that should be impossible because since the incident with the bear, Mum has been giving me a big spoonful of some syrupy stuff that tastes of liquorice every evening. It says on the label on the bottle: *To treat worms*. I hadn't told her I had been thinking about Johnny and Dieuwertje Blok, though mainly about Dieuwertje. Then she'd probably have a row with Dad because Mum doesn't like made-up things, because stories in your imagination often leave out suffering and Mum thinks it should be part of things. She can never take a day off from thinking that because she'd feel guilty; she believes that everyone should bear their sins like lines for punishment in an exercise book.

Obbe wiggles his leg and Tiesey rolls out onto the duvet. His black eyes look like match ends, there's a black stripe along his back, and his right ear is folded double. It doesn't matter how often you stroke it flat, the ear just curls back. Hanna's just settling in against me when he picks up the glass of cloudy water from his bedside table. There's a pile of milk caps next to the glass. They're covered in sand. They used to call him the Flipper King at primary school. He beat everyone, even the cheats.

'I was about to show you something, right?'

'Wasn't that it already?' My mouth suddenly feels dry, and it's hard to swallow. I keep picturing the white stuff that Obbe was talking about. Is it like the filling in the piping bag we use to make stuffed eggs on birthdays? Mum keeps it in the basement otherwise the whole house stinks of it. It must be difficult for the Jews not to secretly eat it, not to flick out the yellowish goo with green bits of basil with their fingers like I've secretly done sometimes. I left the egg whites, as there was no point to them without the filling. When Matthies was still here, they said, 'It's that time of year again, the egg-eaters have been busy,' and I'd smile and get the second piping bag out of the fridge which they'd kept back just in case. Now they no longer celebrate their birthdays and Mum has stopped making stuffed eggs.

'No,' he says, 'I'm only doing it now.'

He drops Tiesey into the glass of water, covers it with his hand and begins to move it slowly back and forth. I can't help laughing, it looks funny. Everything you can turn into a maths sum has a reassuring solution – I bet he'll need to breathe again after one minute. The hamster moves faster and faster from one side of the glass to the other, its eyes beginning to pop out, its legs kicking about wildly. It's only a few seconds before he starts to float like a grey air bubble in a spirit level. No one speaks. All we can hear are the butterflies flapping their wings. Then Hanna begins to cry with great sobs. There are footsteps on the stairs almost immediately. Startled, Obbe quickly puts the glass behind his Lego castle where the enemy is holding a ceasefire.

'What's going on?' Dad pushes open the door and looks around in irritation. My cheeks are red. Hanna is lying in a ball on the grey bedcovers.

'Jas pushed Hanna off the bed,' Obbe says. He looks me in the face. Nothing noticeable in his eyes. No air bubble being kept level. They're as dry as a bone. When Dad's looking the other way, Obbe briefly opens his mouth and pushes his finger in and out as though he needs to throw up. I quickly slide off the bed.

'Right,' Dad says, 'off to your bedroom, you, and pray.'

His shoe hits my bum; the poo stuck up it might have shot back up into my intestines now. When Mum learns the truth about Tiesey she'll get depressed again and won't speak for days. I glance at Hanna and Obbe one last time, then the Lego castle. My brother is suddenly busy with his butterfly collection. He probably just beat them out of the air with his bare hands.

6

My sister is the only person who understands why I've stopped taking off my coat. And the only one who tries to think of a solution. Our evenings are filled with this. Sometimes I get afraid that one of her solutions is going to work, that I'll take away something from my sister, because as long as we still have desires we're safe from death, draped around the farm's shoulders like the suffocating smell after a day of muck-spreading. At the same time my red coat is fading, just like my image of Matthies. There isn't a photo of him anywhere in the house, just his milk teeth, some of which have dried-up blood on them, in a little wooden pot on the windowsill. I try to picture him every evening like an important history test, to learn his features off by heart – just like I learned the slogan 'liberté, égalité, fraternité' which I repeat constantly, especially at grown-up parties to show off what I've learned – afraid of the moment other boys might get into my head and let my brother slip out from between them. My coat pockets are heavy with all the things I'm collecting. Hanna bends over me and offers me a handful of salty popcorn: a sacrifice to make up for not having stuck up for me just now. If only I had pushed her from the bed Tiesey might still be alive. I don't feel like talking to her. The only person I'd like to see now is Mum or Dad, and for them to say that I didn't do anything wrong. But Dad doesn't come. He never says sorry. He can't get the word across his chapped lips – only God's word rolls out smoothly. You don't know that things are good again until he asks you to pass the sandwich filling at the table. Then you can be happy you can pass him the apple syrup again, even though sometimes I'd like to take my knife and smear the syrup over his face so that our gazes stick to him, so that he sees the three kings can't find the Orient.

Suddenly I wonder whether Dad doesn't only scratch the sticky stars from my ceiling but also from the sky. That might be the reason everything looks blacker and Obbe meaner: we've lost our way and there's no one to ask for directions. Even the Big Bear from my favourite picture book, who takes down the moon every night for the Little Bear who is afraid of the dark, is hibernating. Only the night light in my socket offers some comfort. I'm actually too old for it, but in the night everyone is ageless. Fear has more disguises than my mother has floral dresses, and that's saying something as she's got a wardrobe full – though now she often wears the same one, the one with the cacti, as though it'll keep everyone away from her, even though she now wears her dressing gown over the top of it.

I lie with my face to the wall, which has a black-and-white poster of Boudewijn de Groot on it, the one with the lonely cyclist on a narrow mountain track with a child on the front of his bike. Sometimes, before I go to sleep I fantasize that I'm the child and Mum is riding the bike, even though Mum doesn't like cycling, as she's much too afraid of getting her dress caught in the spokes, and we'll never get so lonely that we end up on the same path. When I turn over, Hanna lays the popcorn between us. It sticks to my bottom sheet right away. We take a piece in turn. A verse from Proverbs pops into my head: 'To do justice and judgement is more acceptable to the Lord than sacrifice.' I can't resist this sacrifice as we rarely have popcorn, and I know that Hanna means well because she gets this guilty look on her face, her eyes raised, like the pastor when he's listing the sins of the community and looks up at the ceiling that's just been whitewashed.

From time to time, my hand arrives too late and I'll touch Hanna's fingers and feel her bitten-off nails. They're set deep in red-ringed flesh, chunks of white fat in a sausage. I only have a problem with black dirt stuck under mine. Hanna says my nails are going black because I think about death too much. I immediately picture Tiesey's bulging eyes, the emptiness that settled inside my head when he stopped treading water, and then the blow, the all-destructive silence of an ending, of an empty wheel.

As Hanna eats the last of the popcorn and talks about the new Barbie she wants, I realize that I've had my hands folded under my duvet for a while. Maybe God's been waiting for half an hour already for what I'm going to say. I unfold my hands: falling silent is also a way of saying something in the village. We don't have answering machines, but we do let long silences fall, silences in which sometimes you can hear the cows lowing in the background or the whistle of a kettle.

'Car accident or burning?' I ask.

Hanna's face relaxes now she knows I'm not angry with her and we're simply repeating our daily ritual. Her lips look red and fat from the salt. You get more from sacrifices than you give away. Is that why Obbe killed Tiesey? To get Matthies back? I don't want to think about my sacrifice that has four legs and more than a hundred million olfactory cells.

'How are they supposed to burn?'

'I don't know. Sometimes they forget to blow out the tea lights, the ones next to the window on the yard side,' I say.

Hanna nods slowly. She's wondering about the plausibility. I know I go too far, but the further I go in thinking up the different ways in which Mum and Dad might end their days, the less chance of surprises.

'Murdered or cancer?'

'Cancer,' I say.

'Jumped off the silo or drowned?'

'Why would you jump off the silo? That's just stupid,' Hanna asks.

'People do that when they feel very sad, they jump off things.'

'I think it's an idiotic idea.'

It hasn't occurred to me before that Mum and Dad couldn't only be overcome by death but they could beat death to it. That you could plan the Day of Judgement just like a birthday party. It must be because of what I heard my mother say the other day, and the rope on the beam. I think about the different coloured scarves she wraps around her before she goes to church but worry they'll only make her crazier. She ties them so tightly that you can see the stripes on her skin after church. Maybe she wears them to reach the high notes of a psalm, as sometimes they're so high you have to clench your buttocks. But I say to my sister, 'It's a very stupid idea. I'll bet on a heart attack or a car accident, Mum drives so recklessly.'

I quickly put the last bit of popcorn in my mouth. It had rolled under my belly. I suck out the salt until it becomes tasteless and pappy on my tongue. It reminds me of the time that Obbe made me put a dead bumblebee in my mouth. It had been lying on the windowsill next to Mum's piece of chewing gum – before she goes to bed, she takes it out of her mouth, rolls it into a ball and leaves it to go hard overnight before chewing on it again the next day. I did it for a pile of milk caps; Obbe swore I wouldn't dare. I felt the bumblebee's little hairs against the roof of my mouth, its wings like sliced almonds on my tongue. Obbe counted to sixty. I pretended that it was a honey sweet, but a whole minute long I'd had death in my mouth.

'Has Dad got a heart, do you think?'

The image of the bumblebee makes way for Dad's chest. I saw it today. It was so hot he walked around the fields with the cows without his white vest on. He's got all of three hairs on his chest. Blond. I can't imagine a heart behind his ribs, more like a slurry pit.

'Most likely,' I say. 'He's always generous with the collection at church.'

Hanna nods and sucks in her cheeks. Her eyes are still

84

red from the crying. We don't talk about Tiesey. We don't talk about all the things we will never forget. The slurry pit only gets emptied once a year. This isn't the moment to pour out our hearts, even though I don't know when is. Granny sometimes says that praying makes your heart less heavy, but mine still only weighs three hundred grams. About the same as a packet of mincemeat.

'Do you know the story of Rapunzel?' Hanna asks.

'Of course I do.'

'She's our solution,' Hanna says. She turns onto her side so she can look me in the face. In the light of my globe, her nose looks like a capsized sailing boat. She has the kind of beauty you rarely see, like the drawings she does with crayons: they're lopsided and crooked and that's what gives them their beauty, their naturalness.

'One day she was rescued from her tower. We need a rescuer. Someone to take us away from this ridiculous village, from Dad and Mum, from Obbe, from ourselves.'

I nod, it's a good plan. Only my hair comes down to just under my ears and it will be years before it's long enough for someone to climb up with. Aside from that, the highest point here on the farm is the hayloft, and you can just get up there with a ladder.

'And to get you out of your coat,' Hanna continues. She runs her sticky fingers through my hair. I can smell the salty odour of popcorn. She moves them across my head, drumming, the way the tickling insects often push against my skin. I never touch Hanna, only when she asks me to. It doesn't occur to me to. You've got two kinds of people, those who hold on and those who let go. I belong to the second category. I can only hold on to a person or a memory with the things I collect. I can safely stow them away in my coat pocket.

There's a popcorn husk caught on one of Hanna's incisors. I don't mention it.

'But can't we go together?' I ask.

'The other side is just like the off-licence in the village. You can't get in if you're under sixteen.'

Hanna gives me a determined look. There's no point arguing with her now.

'And it has to be a man. Rescuers are always men.'

'What about God, then? He's a rescuer, isn't he?'

'God only saves those who have sunk. You don't dare swim. Apart from that,' Hanna goes on, 'God's too friendly with Dad. He's sure to tell and then we'll never get away.'

Hanna is right. Even though I don't know whether I want a rescuer – first, you have to learn how to hold on yourself, but I don't want to disappoint my sister. I hear Dad screaming to us: 'He who leaves his brethren becomes a wanderer, adrift from his original existence.' Is this our original existence, or is there another life waiting for us somewhere on Earth that will fit around us like my coat?

'You've got twenty-four hours to make a choice,' Hanna says.

'Why twenty-four hours?'

'We don't have much time, our lives depend on it.' She says this in the same tone she uses when we're playing table tennis in the barn, when the ball keeps ending up in the wrong place. Then she says, 'And now the real one.' As if we'd just been waving our bats around to chase away the dung flies.

'What then?' I ask.

'Then, then it will start,' Hanna whispers.

I hold my breath.

'Kissing. Rapunzel had her long hair, we've got our bodies. You always have to use your charms if you want to be rescued.' Hanna smiles. If I had a chisel I'd give her nose a tap to straighten it.

You should remove everything that attracts unwanted attention, my father once said when I hadn't been able to resist getting my Pokémon cards out of my bag. He threw them onto the fire, saying, 'No man can serve two masters: for either he will hate the one, and love the other; or else he will hold to the one, and despise the other.'

He forgot that we already serve two – Dad and God. A third could make things complicated, but that's something to worry about later.

'Yuck.' I pull a disgusted face.

'Don't you want to be rescued and go to the other side of the bridge?'

'What shall we call our plan?' I say quickly.

Hanna ponders for a moment.

'Just The Plan?'

I pull the cords of my coat tighter and feel the collar close around my neck. Would the noose on the beam feel the same around your neck? I hear a quiet plopping sound under my desk. Hanna doesn't know I'm keeping two toads captive, that I've already got a bit of the other side in my room. It doesn't seem very sensible to tell her now – I don't want her to free them in the lake, to let them swim and see them dive down to the place where Matthies disappeared. Touching them I've finally got something I can hold, even though they feel funny. Luckily Hanna hasn't heard: her head is full of The Plan.

We hear footsteps beneath us. Dad pokes his head up the stepladder. 'Are the two of you reflecting on your sins?' Hanna laughs and I go red. That's the biggest difference between us: she's light and I go dark, ever darker.

'Go to your own bed, Hanna. School tomorrow.' Dad goes back down the ladder. I look down at his parting, and his head looks like a slotted head screw. Sometimes I'd like to bore him into the ground so that he could only do two things: watch and listen, listen a lot.

7

I jolt awake in the middle of the night. My duvet feels clammy with sweat, and the planets and moons on it seem to give off less light. Or maybe they give off the same amount of light but it's no longer enough for me, as the effect is gradually fading. I push away the damp duvet and sit on the edge of my bed. Immediately my body begins to shiver beneath the thin fabric of my pyjamas, and the draught that comes under the door grabs me by the ankles. I pull the duvet over my shoulders and think about the nightmare I had, in which my parents were lying under the ice like two frozen eels, which Farmer Evertsen sometimes gives us, wrapped up in the *Reformist Daily*. Dad always used to say, 'Wrapped up in God's words they taste even better.'

Evertsen was there too. He was wearing his Sunday suit with the narrow lapels and a shiny black tie. When he saw me, he began to sprinkle salt on the ice and he said, 'They'll be preserved for longer like that.' I lay flat on the ice, like a snow angel fallen from heaven, and looked at my parents – they looked like the dinosaur figures in a pot I got for my birthday once that were stuck in a kind of jelly. Obbe and I had dug them out of the jelly with an apple corer. Once they were out there wasn't much point to them: their inaccessibility made them interesting, like my frozen parents. I tapped the ice, laid my ear to it, and heard the singing sound of skates. I wanted to call out to them but nothing escaped my throat.

When I got up again I suddenly noticed Reverend Renkema standing at the edge of the water in the special robe he only wears at Easter, when all the children from the community walk down the aisle with wooden crosses. An Easter bunny made of freshly baked bread with two currants for eyes hangs on each cross. Before we leave the church, Obbe has often scoffed half of his. I never dare start mine for fear that I'll come home to an empty rabbit hutch, that if I break off its ears, the same will happen to Dieuwertje. I let the bunny go mouldy in my desk drawer. That's less awful. Going mouldy is at least a long process of disintegration. But in my nightmare, Renkema stood there in the tufts of reeds, waiting like a cormorant to peck at something. Before I woke up, he said in a solemn voice, 'As the heavens are higher than the earth, so are my ways higher than your ways and my thoughts than your thoughts. God's plans are your plans.' After that everything went black: the grains of salt beneath me began to dissolve, and I seemed to glide slowly under the ice until I saw a hole in it: the light in the socket in my bedroom, next to the bookcase.

'God's plans are your plans.' Could the pastor be referring to Obbe and Hanna's missions? I turn on the globe on my bedside table, and feel around the floor with my feet until I find my slippers, and smooth the creases from my coat. I don't know what my plan is, except I want Mum and Dad to mate and become happy again one day, so that Mum starts eating and they don't die. Once I've fulfilled that mission, I can go to the other side with peace of mind. I take the milk pail out from under my desk and glance at the toads that look up at me with drowsy eyes. They seem thinner, their warts whiter, like the pictures of bang snaps that Obbe circles in the fireworks brochure for New Year's Eve – he spends weeks poring over the rockets and fountains to put together the best package. Hanna and I just pick the ground spinners, as we find them the prettiest and the least scary.

I tilt the bucket slightly so that I can see whether they've eaten anything, but the lettuce leaves at the bottom are brown and soggy. Toads can't see motionless things, I know that, and that's why they can starve. I move a lettuce leaf up and down in front of their faces. 'This will taste nice. Eat it up. Eat it up,' I sing quietly. It doesn't help, and the stupid creatures refuse to eat.

'Then it's time to mate now,' I say decisively, picking up the smallest of the two. I gently rub its underbelly over the back of the other toad. I once saw this on a nature programme on School TV. The toads sat on top of each other for days, but there's no time for that now. My parents don't have days left: they lie in our hands like touchpapers waiting for someone to light them so they can give us warmth. While I rub the toads together, I whisper to them, 'Otherwise you'll die. Do you want to die or what? Well?' I feel the webbed feet pressing against my palm. I clutch the toads tighter and tighter and press them together more and more insistently. After a few minutes it gets boring and I put them back in the bucket. I take a couple of leaves of spinach I stole from dinner out of a paper napkin, and a chunk of toasted bread which has gone soft in the meantime. The toads still look like they're dead. I wait for them to eat but nothing happens. I sigh and stand up. Perhaps they need time, change always takes time. The cows don't just eat a new food mix: you have to add it handful by handful to their old food, until they no longer notice that the pellets are different.

I push the bucket back under my desk with my food, and see a pin lying on the top of it next to my pen pot. It's fallen from my pinboard, from Lien next door's postcard. She sends me a postcard every once in a while because I complained about never getting any post when Dad did – pretty blue letters. I think that some of them are about the Jews. Someone must miss them now they've been in hiding with us for so long? I'd wanted to tell my teacher about them but was worried someone might overhear. A couple of boys in my class are a bit Nazi-ish, especially David, who smuggled his mouse to school once in his pencil case. He kept it hidden among his leaky pens all day and finally let it out during biology, shouting, 'A mouse! A mouse!' The teacher caught it in a trap with some breadcrumbs, where it died because of the shock and all the class's cheers.

Lien next door doesn't write much on the cards she sends. It's often about the weather or their cows, but the pictures on the front are lovely – white beaches, small and big kangaroos, one of Villa Villekulla where Pippi Longstocking lives, and a brave jerboa that has finally dared to swim. I suddenly get an idea. The teacher once stuck a pin in the world map on the wall at the back of the classroom. Belle wanted to go to Canada because her uncle lives there. It's good, the teacher said, to dream about places you'd like to visit one day. I pull up my coat and shirt until my navel is bare. Hanna's the only one with a sticking-out belly button – a pale bobble like a newborn mouse that is still blind and curled up, the way we sometimes find them under the tarpaulin in the mound of silage grass.

'One day I'd like to go to myself,' I say quietly, pushing the pin into the soft flesh of my navel. I bite my lip so as not to make a sound, and a trickle of blood runs down to the elastic of my pants and soaks into the fabric. I daren't take out the pin, afraid blood will gush out everywhere, and everyone in the house will know that I don't want to go to God but to myself.

8

'You have to keep your buttocks as wide apart as possible.'

I'm lying on my side on the brown leather settee like a breech calf, looking back at my father. He's wearing his blue skipper's jersey, which means he's relaxed and the cows have been nice to him today. I'm anything but relaxed. I haven't been able to poo for days, which has made my belly hard and swollen under my coat, like the Bundt cake my mother sometimes lets rise under a striped tea-towel. The three kings were given Bundt cake on their way back from Bethlehem, and their turbans were used as a mould, which is why it is ring-shaped. I mustn't let go of my poo before we find the star, though even sitting hurts. I can't imagine travelling for hours.

'What are you going to do, Dad?' I ask.

He says nothing, just unzips his skipper's collar a little further. I see a chunk of bare chest. Using his thumbnail, he breaks off a chunk of the bar of green soap he's holding. In panic, I run through the last few days in my head. Have I said a blush word without *Lingo* being on? Have I been mean to Hanna? Before I can think about it any further, Dad has shoved the chunk of soap deep into my bum hole with his index finger. I just manage to smother a scream in the cushion under my face. I sink my teeth into the fabric. I can see the pattern on the cover through my tears. Triangles. For the first time since Matthies's death, I cry. The lake inside my head empties. Dad pulls out his finger as fast as he's pushed it in. Again he breaks a chunk of soap off the bar. I try to stop crying by imagining that we are playing 'land grab', a game I sometimes play in the village with a couple of classmates. You throw a stick into the opponent's area, and Dad's finger is the stick, it's no more than that. And still I clench my buttocks and look nervously over my shoulder at my mother who is sitting at the kitchen table, sorting out the ear tags of the cows that have died – blue with blue, yellow with yellow. I don't want her to see me like this but there's nothing to hide myself with, though my blushes of shame cover me as heavily as a horse blanket. She doesn't look up from her work, even though we always have to be economical with the soap and the fact it's disappearing inside me, chunk by chunk, must affect her. An ear tag lands on the floor. She bends down, her hair falling in front of her face.

'Open wider,' Dad roars.

Still sobbing, I pull my buttocks further apart with my hands, as though it's the mouth of a newly born calf that has to be held open when it refuses the bottle. The third time Dad sticks his finger inside, I no longer react. I just stare at the sitting room window which has been covered with old newspapers, which is crazy because they like to talk about the weather and now there's not much to see of it. 'To stop Peeping Toms,' Dad said when I asked about it, and actually I could say that about him now, with my buttocks like two open curtains. But according to my father, soap in your bum hole is a tried and tested method that has been used for centuries on children – in a couple of hours I'll be able to shit again. The last time Dad picked up the bar of green soap, Mum looked up briefly and said, 'Number 150's missing.' She's wearing her reading glasses, and everything far away from her is suddenly close up. I try to make myself as small as Hanna's Playmobil doll, which Obbe once sat on the edge of the settee with another doll right behind it, pushed up to its bum. I didn't understand what he found so funny about it and why he swiped them off the sofa when the elders came to visit. Making myself smaller doesn't help as I only feel bigger, more conspicuous.

Then Dad tugs at the hem of my pants as a sign that the procedure is finished, that I can get back up again. He wipes his finger on his skipper's jersey, and then uses the same hand to take a slice of gingerbread from the dresser before taking a large bite. I get a pat on my lower leg. 'It's only soap.' I quickly pull my trousers back up and raise myself on my knees to close the stud. Then I drop back down onto my side like a cow collapsing on the slats, wiping the tears from my cheeks with the palms of my hands.

'Number 150,' my mother says again. Now she takes off her glasses.

'Shipping disease,' Dad says.

'Poor creature,' Mum says.

Number 150 falls into the tray with all the other dead cows. For a moment I want to see that number which tumbles, tarnished and lonely, and will soon disappear into the filing cabinet never to be seen again. The cabinet gets locked, and the key hangs on a hook on the side of the cupboard: it's about the gesture, closing something off so that a stall comes free in their heads. I can still feel my father's finger inside. Not long afterwards, the bar of green soap is back in the metal tray on the sink in the toilet. No one will worry about the broken-off chunk that is now roaming about my body somewhere.

When I look at the bar of soap as I'm peeing, I hear Obbe's words about how the unrolled wall of the small intestine has the surface area of a tennis court. When Obbe wants to tease me, he no longer just makes vomiting noises but now acts like he's about to toss up a tennis ball. I feel sick at the idea that a tennis competition could be held inside me and that I'm made up of more space than I actually take up. From time to time, I picture a little man smoothing out the gravel of the tennis court with a dragnet so that a new game can take place inside me and I can poo again. Hopefully the little man won't get green soap in his eyes.

On the table next to the new ear tags, my pale blue swimming costume lies lifelessly across my rucksack, a packet of ready salted crisps and a carton of strawberry yoghurt drink next to it. Sometimes there are crisps on the floor in the swimming pool, and the wet bits stick to your feet like soaked-off blisters and you have to flick them off with the corner of your towel. Later you see them hitching a ride under other people's feet.

'The giraffe is the only animal that can't swim,' I say.

I try to forget the piece of green soap roving about my body,

97

like I tried to forget my father's finger.

'Are you a giraffe?' Mum asks.

'Now I am.'

'You only have one part of the diploma left to do.'

'But it's the most difficult part.'

I'm the only person my age who hasn't passed their swimming proficiency test, the only one who freezes when I have to go 'swimming through a hole': it's important you can do this, as the winters are harsh here in the village. And even though Dad burned my strap-on wooden skates after that day in December, and it's now mid-May more than a year later, a time will come when I will have to brave the ice again. The holes in the ice are now mainly inside our heads.

'If God hadn't wanted people to be able to swim, He wouldn't have made us this way,' Mum says, putting my swimming costume and the packet of crisps into my rucksack. There's a box of plasters at the bottom. I mustn't forget to put one over my belly button, otherwise the green pin will be visible through my cozzie. Everyone will know then that I never go on holiday, otherwise I'd long for foreign countries, for beaches so white they look like they've been covered in sun cream.

'Maybe I'll drown,' I say cautiously, searching my mum's face in the hope she'll be startled, that more lines will appear in her skin than when she's crying for herself, that she'll stand up and hold me, rock me back and forth like a cumin cheese in a brine bath. My mum doesn't look up.

'Don't be so daft. You're not going to die.' She says it as

though she'd begrudge it me, as though I'm not clever enough to die young. Of course she doesn't know that we, the three kings, are trying to meet death. We caught a glimpse of him with Tiesey, but it was too brief, too fleeting. Besides, if you aren't prepared for it, you don't know what you should watch out for. Good preparation makes the man – God knew during creation that we'd need a day to rest from everything we'd created during the week.

'And we can't go on holiday until you've got your diploma.'

I sigh and feel the pin stick into my navel. The skin around it has turned light purple. Last week they'd put a white tarpaulin across the pool with holes in it, and the divers hung on to the side. The swimming teacher had told us that panic and hypothermia were our greatest enemies. The divers had ice-piercers around their necks to make it look more real. That day at Christmas, Matthies had forgotten his steel-tipped pin for breaking the ice. It was on the little table beneath the mirror in the hall. No one knows that I saw it there, that I considered running after him, but that my anger at not being allowed to go along held me back.

In the swimming pool, Belle pokes me in my side. She's wearing a pink swimming costume; there's a fake Pokémon tattoo on her right arm, the kind you get with two packets of chewing gum and that slowly disappears from your skin, bit by bit. She passed her diploma years ago, and now she's allowed to swim on her own in the pool and jump from the high diving board and go on the big slide.

'Eva's got tits.'

I glance furtively at Eva who is standing in the queue for the big slide. At the start of the school year she whispered to me that I must have got 'spunky' and 'funky' mixed up. Of course she was referring to my coat. Eva's two years older than us, and they say she knows a lot about the things boys like about girls and how to behave. As the end of the swimming lesson, she's always got the most frog sweets in her bag though we all started with the same number. One tip about boys costs two frogs. She's the only one who showers apart. I think it's because of her verrucas, which she says don't exist but I can see them on the sides of her foot, like the mucous glands on my toads, both full of poison.

'Will we ever grow some?' Belle asks.

I shake my head. 'We'll stay tit-less forever. You only grow them if a boy looks at you for longer than ten minutes.'

Belle looks around at the boys who are getting ready to dive through the hole. We're not being looked at, only observed, which is something quite different.

'Then we'll have to make sure they see us.'

I nod and point at the swimming teacher. His hand is feeling for the whistle around his neck. My words seem to get stuck, just like the children who choke up the slide – only the odd one shooting into the water now and again – until it's a train. My body begins to shiver, and the drawing pin rubs against my swimming costume.

'Panic is not an enemy but a warning,' the teacher said. 'That leaves just one enemy,' I say. And just before I get up onto the starting block, I see Matthies before me. I hear the clatter of his skates, the gurgling of the air bubbles under the ice. The divers said that your heartbeat increases underwater, but I haven't even dived in yet and my heart is beating against my chest like my fists against the ice in my nightmares. Belle wraps her arm around me: we are taught how to rescue people from under the ice, but above water we don't know how to keep someone on dry land, so it's not strange that Belle's arm is heavy and awkward. Her swimming costume is stuck to her body, and I can see the narrow line between her skinny legs. I think about the verrucas on Eva's feet, the way they'll burst open and fill the pool with green poison that will change the divers one by one into frog sweets, croaking.

'Her brother,' Belle tells the swimming teacher.

He sighs. Everyone in the village knows about our loss, but the longer Matthies is away from home, the more people get used to there being just the five of us. Those who are new to the village don't even know any better. My brother is slowly fading out of various minds, while he moves more and more into ours.

I free myself from Belle and escape into the changing rooms, where I put my coat on over my costume and lie down on the bench. It smells of chlorine. I'm convinced the water's going to start bubbling with soap-suds from the chunk of green soap in me. Everyone will point at me and then I'll have to tell them what's wrong inside. I carefully begin to make swimming movements lying on my belly. Eyes closed, I do the butterfly stroke and let myself sink into the ice hole. Soon I realize that my arms have stopped and I'm only moving my hips up and down. The divers are right: an increased heartbeat and accelerated breathing. It's not hypothermia but imagination that is the enemy.

The bench creaks beneath my belly like black ice. I don't want to be rescued now, I want to sink. Deeper and deeper until breathing starts to become difficult. In the meantime I chew the frog sweets into tiny bits, taste the gelatine, the reassurance of sweetness. Hanna's right: we have to get away from this village, away from the cows, away from death, away from life in its original form.

9

Mum plunges a cumin cheese into the brine bath. It needs to soak for two to five days. There are two large sacks of vacuum salt on the floor next to her. Every once in a while, she throws a large scoopful into the water so that the cheese keeps its flavour. Sometimes I wonder if it would help if we dunked Mum and Dad in the brine bath, if we re-baptized them 'in the name of the Father, the Son and the Holy Spirit' so that they'd firm up and keep well for longer. I've only just noticed that the skin around Mum's eyes looks yellowish and dull, like the light bulb above the dining table with her floral apron as a lampshade, flicking from light to dark. We mustn't use an angry tone with her, we mustn't be surly and we definitely mustn't cry. Sometimes I think it would be more peaceful if they were ducked forever, but I don't want Obbe to take care of us. There'd be even less of us left then and we're already so few.

From the window of the brining shed, I see my brother and sister walking to the furthest cowshed. They're going to bury Tiesey with the dead chickens and the two stray cats, and it's my job to distract Mum. Dad won't notice, as he's just gone off on his bike. He said he was never coming back. It's because of me. Yesterday I pulled the freezer plug out of the socket to plug in the toastie maker, but forgot to plug it back in again. When Mum and Dad rescued the beans they had just frozen, they lay wet and floppy on the kitchen table. The little green bodies looked dismal, like an exterminated plague of bush crickets. All our work had been for nothing – four evenings in a row we'd had to shell them with a tray on our laps for the rubbish and two milk pails next to us on the floor, so that all Mum had to do was wash and blanch them before packing them in freezer bags. When the thawed harvest lay on the table, Dad cut the plastic bags open with a bread knife, tipped the limp beans into a wheelbarrow and rolled them to the muck-heap – I'm worried we'll have to roll Mum and Dad in a wheelbarrow to the muck-heap and that it will all be my fault. After that he said we'd have to figure things out for ourselves – but we already knew he had to go to the trade union and when he got back he'd have forgotten he'd threatened to leave for good. Lots of people want to run away, but the ones who really do rarely announce it beforehand: they just go.

After Dad had left, we'd put Tiesey in a Russian salad container. Hanna wrote in felt pen on the lid: *Let us never forget*. Obbe looked on with a steely expression. He didn't betray anything but touched his crown more and more, and I knew he'd lain in bed tossing and turning and banging his head all night, so hard that Dad taped bubble wrap to the wood. I kept hearing the bubbles pop. Sometimes I wonder whether that's why Obbe's so mixed up; maybe he's muddled up his brains.

'Could you help with the curds a minute?' Mum asks.

I walk away from the window, with my hair still damp from the swimming pool. No one asks how anything went; they just announce – when they think of them – the things we have to do, and forget to find out what happens next. They don't want to know if and how I got out of the hole. I'm still alive, and that's the only thing they pay attention to. That we get up every day, however slowly, is enough proof for them that we're doing all right. The three kings continue to heave themselves onto our camels, even though the saddles disappeared long ago and we're just sitting on a bare hide, and all the bumps chafe our skin.

I use my fingers to press the damp white chunks into the cheese mould and slide it across to the wooden cheese press, pushing down on it to get the whey out of the curds. Mum closes the lid of the rennet. I bring the press down on the curds again. White pieces stick to my fingers, and I wipe them off on the seam of my coat.

'How's it going in the basement?'

I don't look at my mother but fix my gaze on the flowery meadow on her apron. It's possible that Mum will move into the basement one day; that she'll find the family, the Jewish people that live there, nicer than us. What will happen to the three kings then, I don't know: Dad is still incapable of even heating up milk for coffee, and if he lets even that boil over, how could he ever keep his children at the right temperature?

'What do you mean?' Mum asks. She turns around and goes to turn the cheeses lying on the wall shelving. Of course I should have known she wasn't going to give away her operating base just like that. Just as you have to be careful with the cows when combining different races. Maybe she's preparing to go away, to leave us. Maybe that's why she's stopped wearing her glasses, so that we stay at a distance.

'Nothing,' I say, 'nothing is your fault, not even that stone in your tummy.'

'Don't talk nonsense,' Mum says, 'and don't pick your nose. Do you want to get worms again?' Mum grabs my arm hard; for the second time her nails prick through the fabric of my coat. She hasn't cut her nails for a long time, I notice. They've got white tips, partly yellow from the whey. 'What have we got to thank for this?' I don't reply. There are some questions Mum doesn't want a reply to. She doesn't say this, so you have to sense it. If you reply it only makes her sadder. She lets go of me more carefully than she grabbed me. I think of the plague she was talking to Dad about that night I got my bear down off the washing line. The plagues broke out in Egypt because the people wanted to go to the other side. Here they break out because we're not allowed to go to the other side although we long for it. It could even be that if Hanna and I leave, the stone in my mother's tummy would get less heavy. Maybe I could ask the vet to operate on her. He once cut a couple of abscesses from a cow after the neighbour trod on her udder. He threw them onto the muck-heap and less than an hour later, the crows had already eaten the bloody lumps.

Behind us the shed door opens. Mum has just started testing a new cheese. She looks back and puts the cheese scoop down beside her on the counter.

'Why isn't there any coffee?' Dad asks.

'Because you weren't here,' Mum says.

'But I am here, and it's already long past four.'

'You'll have to make it yourself then, if you need some.'

'What I need is a bit more respect!'

He strides back through the door, slamming it behind him. Anger has hinges that need oiling. For a moment Mum pretends to continue with her work, but then she begins to sigh and goes to make coffee all the same. Everything here is a maths sum: respect equals four sugar lumps and a shot of condensed milk. I quickly stuff the cheese scoop into my pocket with all my memories.

'Boudewijn de Groot,' I whisper a couple of hours later to the darkness and the place I'm expecting Hanna's ear to be. I didn't have to think for very long. If there's anyone whose voice has been running through my head for days, it's his. I even have a photo of Boudewijn in my purse, along with the photo of my first love: a boy called Sjoerd. There are cracks in his photo, and I remember how I felt when I found out that he swapped his love for me for two Pokémon cards and a milk biscuit behind the bike shed. From that moment on, I always emptied my dinosaur beaker of syrup and buttermilk into the bushes there as a memorial, especially because my classmates said it stank – they got real drinking yoghurt in a box. The ground and the plants behind the bike shed turned white. No, Boudewijn de Groot seemed the right choice to me because anyone who sings so beautifully about love must be able to save love. And Mum and Dad like him. Surely they won't mind if he takes us away. Mum always used to sing along to 'Het land van Maas en Waal' so loudly that I thought she was longing for another place. Now she only listens to *The Musical Fruit Basket* – the requests programme for psalms, hymns and spiritual songs.

Hanna and I are lying on our backs in my bed with our arms hooked, like a pretzel. The duvet covers us to the waist, but it's too hot to lie under it completely. I'm picking my nose and put my little finger in my mouth.

'Gross,' Hanna says. She pulls her arm out of mine and frees herself from me. She wasn't able to see it but she knows I often fill my silences with picking my nose. It helps me think, as though looking for ways out in my thoughts also has to be expressed physically. Hanna says it will give me wide nostrils, that the elastic will get stretched, just like on my undies. You can buy new underwear but you can't buy a new nose. I lay my hand on my belly beneath my coat. A scab is forming around the drawing pin. With my other hand I feel Hanna's face, taking her earlobe between my thumb and forefinger for a moment. It's the softest part of a human body. Hanna snuggles up to me again. Sometimes I like it but more often I don't. When someone stands or lies too close I get the feeling I have to admit something, that I have to justify my presence: I'm here because Mum and Dad believed in me and from that thought I could be born – even though they've been having more doubts recently and they're paying less attention to us. There are creases in my clothes. I'm crumpled like the screwed-up shopping list in the bin, waiting for someone to smooth me out and read me again.

'Mr Herbert is my choice,' Hanna says.

We're sharing my pillow. I move ever further away from her and picture my head falling off the edge, causing a tipping point in my thoughts, hoping that I'll be able to convince Hanna I don't need a saviour, that I do want to go to the other side, far away from here, that maybe we need something other than a man, that we can't simply swap God – he's the strongest Pokémon card we have. Even though I don't have any other solutions for getting out of here.

'Why Boudewijn?' Hanna asks.

'Why Mr Herbert?'

'Because I love him.'

'And I love Boudewijn de Groot,' I say. Maybe it's because he looks a bit like Dad, even though Dad's blond and he's got a smaller nose and can't sing as well. He never wears colourful shirts either, just his overalls, his blue skipper's jumper and a black suit with shiny lapels on Sundays. Dad can only play the recorder too. Every Saturday and Sunday morning, he accompanies us to the psalm of the week so that on Mondays we'll make a good impression at school. Every few couplets he presses his index finger to the air hole and blows, as if he knows that I always stray from the line I should be following. Sometimes I feel like I'm not singing for my father but for the whole village, with a voice as soft as butter and clear as a song thrush's; a thrush that's fallen into the butter churn – that's how they'd revere me, Mulder's girl. The shrill, flat sound of the recorder hurts my eardrums.

'You have to know where he lives. That's a condition,' Hanna says. She leans over me and switches on the globe. My eyes have to get used to the light, as though the things in the room quickly have to put on a straight face, smooth down their clothes and become silent, so they match the idea I have of them. It's a bit like the way Mum always jumps if we go into her bedroom when she's only half-dressed, as if she's afraid she'll no longer satisfy the image we have of her, and decks herself out like a Christmas tree every morning.

'On the other side of the bridge.'

Hanna's eyes narrow. I'm not even sure Boudewijn de Groot lives on the other side, but I realize how exciting it sounds: the other side. Mr Herbert lives in the house one further than the sweet-shop, exactly the way we think about things: first what you want is sweets and later it's love. We understand that order of events.

'That's it,' Hanna says, 'we have to go there. There are tons of saviours and Mum and Dad won't dare to go there.'

I pinch the drawing pin under my coat, a lifebuoy in the middle of the North Sea.

'Do you want to kiss Boudewijn?' my sister suddenly asks.

I shake my head frantically. Kissing is for old people, and they do it when they've run out of words. Hanna is now lying so close to me that I can smell her breath. Toothpaste. She moistens her lips with her tongue. An overdue milk tooth is still trying to become a grown-up tooth.

'I've got an idea,' she says, 'I'll be right back.'

She slides out from between the sheets and comes back carrying Dad's Sunday suit.

'What do you want with that?' I ask.

Hanna doesn't reply. There's a perfume bag on the hanger – lavender. I watch her put on the suit over her nightdress. I grin but Hanna doesn't smile. Using a black marker from my pen pot she draws a moustache above her top lip. Now she looks a bit like Hitler. I wish I could cover her entirely in pen so that I can always remember her and mark her as mine. She's too big for my coat pockets.

'Come on. You have to lie on your back otherwise it won't work.'

I do what she says, as I'm used to her taking charge and me obeying her. She's dressed her bony legs in Dad's much too baggy trousers and has planted them next to my hips, her hair swept out of her face. In the light of the globe she looks creepy with a black moustache that looks more like a bow-tie.

'I'm from the city and I'm a man,' she says in a deep voice. I instantly know what I have to do, as though it's dead normal for her to be sitting on me in the middle of the night wearing Dad's suit. The jacket with the shiny lapels makes her shoulders bigger and her head as small as a porcelain doll's.

'I'm from the village and I'm a woman,' I say in a higher pitched voice than my own.

'And you were looking for a man?' Hanna growls.

'That's right. I'm looking for a man to save me from this terrible village. Someone who is very strong. And handsome. And kind.'

'Well madam, then you've come to the right place. Shall we kiss?'

Before I can answer, she presses her lips to mine and immediately pushes her tongue inside. It's lukewarm, like a leftover steak that Mum's warmed up in the microwave and served again. She moves it around rapidly a few times, her saliva mixing with mine and dripping down my cheek. As quickly as she's pushed it in, she pulls it out again.

'Can you feel it too?' Hanna asks, breathlessly.

'What do you mean, sir?'

'In your belly and between your legs?'

'No,' I say, 'just your moustache. It tickles a bit.'

We laugh as though we can't stop and for a moment it feels like that. Then Hanna collapses next to me.

'You taste of metal,' she says.

'You of wet milk biscuits,' I say.

We both know how bad that is.

10

My sister and I wake up with black stripes on our faces and Dad's Sunday suit all creased. I sit up in bed at once. If Dad catches us, he'll get the Authorized Version out of the drawer in the dining room table and read to us from Romans: 'If you declare with your mouth, "Jesus is Lord," and believe in your heart that God raised Him from the dead, you will be saved.' With that same mouth we kissed each other last night. Hanna pushed her tongue inside me as she was looking for words she didn't possess herself. You can refuse the guilt of sin entry to your heart but never to your home. That's why when he comes to drum us out of bed, Dad will quickly find out that we've invited this sin in, the way we once let in a stray cat. We put it in the walnut basket behind the wood stove and fed it milk and crusts until it grew stronger. Neither Hanna nor I is going to be saved now.

Hanna smooths the creases out of Dad's suit and takes half a roll of peppermints from the breast pocket. She puts one in her mouth. I ask myself why she's doing this because the peppermints are meant for getting through the sermon, to keep us quiet so we don't start swinging our legs, which makes the pew creak so everyone in the row knows that Mulder's kids aren't listening to the words of Reverend Renkema. We have no reason to sit still now – we have to get moving. After the service when we complain about how long it was, he says, 'Anyone displaying impatience can listen for twice as long for punishment,' before saying, 'Lien next door, now she rambles on. She could talk the hind legs off a donkey, or the ears off your head.' For a moment I picture my father and Lien standing facing each other on the farm track, with his ears falling off like autumn leaves. We'd have to stick them back on with Pritt stick. I'd rather put them in a little velvet box and whisper the sweetest and the most terrible words into them every night, before putting the lid back on and shaking the box so I'm sure the words have slid into the ear canal. I've got so many words but it's as if fewer and fewer come out of me, while the biblical vocabulary in my head is pretty much bursting at the seams. I can't stop smiling at the idea of Dad's glued-on ears. And as long as Dad is making jokes about Lien next door and keeps repeating them, just like this week's weather forecast, we've got nothing to fear.

Yet Dad eats the most peppermints during the silent contemplation and, just recently, as soon as we get home he's been asking what the sermon was about to check whether we were paying attention. Secretly I think he asks for himself because he's been distracted and is using us to get a summary. Last Sunday I said the sermon had been about the prodigal son, which wasn't true but Dad didn't correct me. The return of the prodigal son is my favourite story. Sometimes I picture Matthies arriving on foot with snow-white skin, and Dad taking the best calf from the cowshed and slaughtering it.

Despite the fact that Mum doesn't like parties because of all the 'jigging about and bam-bam-bam' as she calls dancing and music, we'd organize a big party on the farm with lanterns, streamers, Coke and deep-ridged crisps 'because he was lost and is found again'.

'Do you think we did something wrong?' I ask Hanna. She tries to suppress a yawn behind her hand. We've only had three hours' sleep.

'What do you mean?'

'Well, you know. Maybe we're the reason why things are like they are with Mum and Dad. Maybe it's our fault that Matthies and Tiesey are dead.'

Hanna thinks for a moment. When she thinks she moves her nose up and down. There is marker pen on her cheeks too now. She says, 'Everything there's a reason for comes good in the end.'

My sister often says wise things, but I don't think she understands much of what she says herself.

'Will it be all right, do you think?'

I feel my eyes moisten. I quickly turn them onto Dad's suit, the padded shoulders that give him more authority on Sundays. We could easily puncture them with a knife. I pick the yellow trails of sleep out of my eyes with my little finger and wipe them on my duvet.

'Of course. And Obbe didn't mean it that way, it was an accident.'

I nod. Yes, it was an accident. Here in the village it's always that way: people fall in love by accident, buy the wrong meat by accident, forget their prayer book by accident, don't speak by accident. Hanna has got up and is hanging Dad's jacket back on the hanger. The perfume bag of lavender has burst open, and there are little purple flowers all over my duvet. I lie on my back in the lavender. Please let the day wait so that I don't have to go to school, long enough for the grass in the fields to be dry enough to make hay, long enough for the dampness in me to slowly subside.

11

On the news they've recommended drinking a large glass of water every hour, and even show a picture of what a big glass looks like – though it doesn't look like the glasses we own. Here in the village no two houses have the same glasses, and you can use glasses to make yourself different from the others. We use the ones that used to have mustard in them. In turn we drink water from a Coke bottle that Dad fills the glasses with. The bottle wasn't rinsed properly, giving the water a Coke taste, lukewarm from the sun. My nose itches from the dust that was whipped up by the haymaking. When I pick my nose the snot comes out black. I wipe it on my trousers, and don't dare eat it, afraid I'll get ill and return to dust. The hay-bales lie around me like bars of green soap in the field. I don't want to think about my dad's finger in me, and take a bite of the doughnut he's just given us. I can barely manage another soggy doughnut: they're coming out of our ears as the baker's hardly had anything else recently. I take a bite all the same, even if only to feel connected to Obbe and Dad: three people sitting on a hay-bale eating doughnuts need some kind of connection. Its soggy skin sticks to my teeth and the roof of my mouth. I swallow without really tasting it.

'God's knocked over his pot of ink,' Obbe says as he stares at the darkening sky above our sweaty heads. I grin and even Dad smiles for the first time in ages. He gets up and wipes his hands on his trouser legs as a sign we should get back to work. Soon he'll start getting nervous that it will rain on the bales and they'll go mouldy. I get up too and pluck a handful of dried grass to protect my palms from the string around the bale. I take another quick peek at the smile on Dad's face. Look, I think, we only have to make sure that the ropes don't leave impressions behind, then everything will come good with us, and we don't have to be afraid of the Day of Judgement descending on our parents at any moment like a jackdaw on its prey, or that we sin more than we pray. As I pick up a new bale, my coat sticks to my sweaty skin. Even now it's boiling hot I don't take it off. I throw the bales onto the hay-cart so that Dad can arrange them in neat rows of six.

'We have to hurry up before the sky breaks open,' Dad says, staring at the ever-darkening sky above us.

As I look up at him I say, 'Matthies could lift two bales of hay in one go; he stuck his pitchfork into them as though they were chunks of nettle cheese.' Dad's smile immediately sinks into the skin of his face until nothing is left. There are people whose smiles are always visible even when they're sad. The smile lines can no longer be erased. It's the other way round with Mum and Dad. Even when they smile they look sad, as though someone's put a set square next to the corners of their mouths and drawn two lines pointing down.

'We don't think about the dead, we remember them.'

'We can remember out loud, can't we?' I ask.

Dad gives me a penetrating look, jumps from the hay-cart and sticks his pitchfork in the ground. 'What did you say?'

I see the muscles in his upper arms tense.

'Nothing,' I say.

'Nothing what?'

'Nothing, Dad.'

'That's what I thought. How dare you talk back to me after ruining the entire supply of beans when you unplugged the freezer.'

I stare up at the sky because I don't know what to do with myself. For the first time I notice that I've tensed my muscles too, and that I'd like to push Dad's head into the ink like a fountain pen before writing an ugly sentence with it – or one that's about Matthies and how much I miss him. My thoughts startle me immediately. 'Honour thy father and thy mother: that thy days may be long upon the land which the Lord thy God giveth thee.' And straight away I think: and hopefully the days on the other side, not just here in this stupid boring village. Obbe grabs the Coke bottle from the ground and greedily drinks the last bit without asking me if I want any more. Then he gets up to continue with the hay.

The last round goes slower. It's my job to steer the tractor and Obbe's to throw the bales onto the cart so that Dad can stack them. Dad keeps shouting that I have to speed up or slow down. Now and then he suddenly tears open the tractor door and pushes me roughly from the seat, before tugging hard at the wheel to stop us from driving into a ditch, sweat dripping from his forehead. As soon as he's back on top of the stack, taking bales from Obbe, I think: if I accelerate hard, just once, he'll fall off the cart. Just once.

After the haymaking, Obbe and I lean against the back wall of the cowshed. He has a piece of straw sticking out through the gap between his front teeth. In the background you can hear the buzzing of the cow brushes that spin across their backs to stop them itching. It's long before feeding time so we're free for a while. Obbe chews on his straw and promises to tell me the password for *The Sims* on the computer if I help him with his mission. With the password you can get stinking rich and make the avatars French kiss each other. A shiver runs through my body. Sometimes when Dad comes to wish me goodnight, he sticks his tongue in my ear. It's not as bad as the finger with green soap, but still. I don't know why he does it. Maybe it's just like the lid of the vanilla custard that he licks clean every evening with his tongue, as it's a waste otherwise, he says – and the same with my ears as I often forget to clean them with cotton buds.

'Not something to do with death, is it?' I say to Obbe.

I don't know if I'm strong enough to meet death now. We're only allowed to appear before God in our Sunday best, but I don't know what the rules are for death. I can still feel Dad's anger weighing down on my shoulders. At school I don't take sides when there are fights. I watch from a distance and support the weakest person inside my head. When it comes to death, I can hardly stick up for myself, as I've never learned how to. Even though I sometimes try to look at myself from a distance, it doesn't work, I'm stuck inside. And the incident with the hamster is still fresh in my memory. I know how I'm going to feel afterwards, but this doesn't outweigh my curiosity to see death and understand it.

'There's always the risk of running into him.'

Obbe spits the straw out from between his teeth, and a white splatter lands on the pebbles.

'Do you get why we're not allowed to talk about Matthies?'

'Do you want the password or not?'

'Can Belle join in too? She's coming over in a bit.'

I don't tell him she's mainly coming for the neighbour's boys' willies, because I'd been boasting about them and said they looked a bit like the pale croissants we sometimes had at hers for lunch, made from dough her mother got out of a tin and rolled up before putting them in the oven and baking them brown.

'Sure,' Obbe says, 'as long as she doesn't start blubbering.'

A little later Obbe gets three cans of Coke out of the basement, hides them under his jumper and gestures to me and Belle. I know what's going to happen and feel calm. So calm that I forget to clamp my zip between my teeth. Maybe it's also to do with the fact that Lien next door and her husband Kees have complained. They think the way I cycle along the dike with my sleeves pulled over my fingers and my zip between my teeth is dangerous. Mum and Dad had waved away their concerns like a low bid for a calf at auction.

'It's temporary,' Mum said.

'Yes, she'll grow out of it,' Dad said.

But I won't grow out of it – I'm actually growing into it and getting stuck, and no one will notice.

When we open the door to the rabbit shed, Belle is talking about the biology test and Tom, who sits two rows behind us, has black hair down to his shoulders, and always wears the same checked shirt. We suspect he doesn't have a mother, as why else does no one wash his clothes or make him wear something else? According to Belle, Tom's stared at her for at least ten minutes, which means that at any moment tits could start growing under her T-shirt. I'm not happy for her but I smile all the same. People need small problems in order to feel bigger. I'm not desperate to get tits. I don't know if that's strange or not. I'm not longing for boys either but for myself, but you must never reveal that, just like how you keep the password to your Nokia secret so that no one can break into you unexpectedly.

It's warm and dark in the rabbit shed. The sun has shone down on the plasterboards of the roof all day long. Dieuwertje lies stretched out in his hutch. Mum took yesterday's soggy leaves out of his hutch and replaced them with fresh ones: she forgot sweets for the sweets tin, but not the leaves. Obbe slides the manger from the wood and puts it on the floor. He takes a pair of scissors from his pocket: there's a bit of tomato sauce sticking to the edges from when Mum cuts open the tops of the Heinz packets. Obbe makes a cutting gesture, and sunlight falls through the chinks in the shed wall momentarily and reflects off the metal of the blades. Death is giving a warning signal.

'First I'll cut off the whiskers, as those are the sensors, and then Dieuwertje won't know what he's doing.' One by one he cuts off the whiskers and lays them in my outstretched palm.

'Isn't that bad for Dieuwertje?' asks Belle.

'It's about the same as if we burn our tongue and then taste less. It's pretty harmless.'

Dieuwertje darts into all the corners of his hutch but fails to dodge Obbe's hand. Now that all the whiskers are gone, he says, 'Do you want to see them mating?'

Belle and I look at each other. It's not part of our plan to cut off the whiskers and see whether they grow back, but the worms have returned to my belly. Since Obbe showed me and Hanna his willy, Mum's worm drink has been going through me even faster: I deliberately complain about having an itchy bottom. Sometimes I dream that worms as big as rattlesnakes are coming out of my anus: they have lions' jaws and I've fallen into the hollow in my mattress like Daniel in the lion pit and have to promise that I trust in God, but I keep seeing those filthy hungry faces with their snakes' bodies. It's not until I'm crying for mercy that I awake from the nightmare.

Obbe nods at the dwarf rabbit in the hutch opposite Dieuwertje's. I think of Dad's words: never let a large rabbit cover a small one. It's wrong: Dad's two heads taller than Mum and she survived when she gave birth to us. This must be possible too then, and that's why I press the little rabbit into Belle's arms. She hugs it for a moment, then puts it in Dieuwertje's hutch. We watch in silence as Dieuwertje carefully sniffs at the dwarf rabbit, hops around it, begins to stamp its back feet on the ground and then first jumps onto the front before jumping onto the back. We can't see his willy. All we can see are his heated movements and the look of fear in the little rabbit's eyes, the same look I saw on the hamster.

'Desire without knowledge is not good – how much more will hasty feet miss this way!' Dad sometimes says when we get too covetous about things we want, and at that moment Dieuwertje lets himself fall sideways off the little animal. I briefly wonder whether Dad lets himself fall the same way each time he's done it. Perhaps that's why his leg is deformed and always hurts. Maybe the story of the combine harvester was invented because it's more believable and free from shame. Just when we want to take a breath of relief, we see that the dwarf rabbit is dead. There's nothing spectacular to look at. It closed its eyes and departed. No convulsions or cries of pain; not a glimpse of death.

'What a stupid game,' Belle says.

I see that she's going to cry. She's too soft for this kind of thing. She's like the whey cheese is made of, while we're already further in the process with a plastic layer around us.

Obbe looks at me. There are pale downy hairs growing on his chin. We say nothing but both know that we'll have to repeat this until we understand Matthies's death, even though we don't know how. The stabs inside my belly become more painful, as though someone's poking a pair of scissors into my skin. The soap still hasn't helped yet. I put the whiskers in my coat pocket with the shards of the cow and the cheese scoop, pull the tab from the can of Coke and put the cold metal to my mouth. Over the edge of it I see Belle looking at me expectantly. I have to fulfil my promise now. Jesus had followers too because He always gave them something that made Him seem credible. I have to give something to Belle so that she doesn't turn from a friend into an enemy. Before I take her to the peephole in the yew hedge, I tug at Obbe's sleeve and whisper, 'What's the password then?'

'Klapaucius,' he says, grabbing the little rabbit from Dieuwertje's hutch and putting it under his jumper where it must still be cold from the Coke cans. I don't ask what he's going to do with it. Everything that requires secrecy here is accepted in silence.

Belle is sitting on a fishing chair on the other side of the yew hedge. I curl my little finger in front of the peephole.

'That's not a willy,' Belle cries, 'that's your little finger.'

'It's not the right weather for willies. You're out of luck,' I say.

'When's a good day then?'

'I don't know, you never do. Good days are rare here in the countryside.'

'It's all just a pack of lies, isn't it?'

A lock of Belle's hair is stuck to her cheek – it had dangled into the can of Coke. She burps behind her hand. At that moment we hear laughter behind the hedge, and see the boys next door jumping into the inflatable paddling pool and float-ing on their brown backs, like raisins being soaked in brandy.

I tug at Belle's arm.

'Come on, let's ask if we can play at theirs.'

'But how are we going to get to see the willies?'

'They always have to pee at some point,' I say, with a conviction that makes my chest swell. The idea that I've got something someone else is longing for makes me bigger. Side by side we go next door. My belly is full of bubbles. Will the worms inside me survive the Coke?

My fascination with willies must have come from when I played with the naked little angels when I was ten. When I took them out of the Christmas tree, I felt the cold porcelain between their sturdy legs like a bit of seashell in the chicken grit, and laid my hand on top like a twig of mistletoe, at the time protectively and this time out of an endless longing that has mainly nestled in my underbelly and is growing in there.

'I'm a paedophile,' I whisper to Hanna. I feel my breath travel across the hairs on my arms and try to lie back against the edge of the bath so that I don't feel it. I don't know what makes me more nervous: feeling my breath on my skin, or the idea that one day I'll stop breathing and that I don't know which day that will be. However I rearrange myself, I still keep feeling my breath. The hairs on my arms stand up; I dip them into the water. *You're a paedophile, you're a sinner.* Obbe taught me that word after he saw it on TV at a friend's house. They're not on Nederland 1, 2 or 3 because no one wants to see their faces on TV. Obbe said that they touched little boys' willies, though from the outside they look like normal people with normal lives who are older than us. There are five years between me and the boys next door, a whole hand's worth. It must be the case that I'm one of them, and that someday I'll be hunted down and driven into a corner like the cows into the racks when we want to move them to a new bit of field.

After eating, Mum had passed around a damp flannel for us to take turns cleaning our ketchup mouths and sticky fingers. I didn't want to take it. Mum wouldn't forgive me if I wiped my sinful fingers on the same flannel she pressed her lips to – she hadn't eaten any macaroni with ketchup at all but still scrubbed her mouth clean. Maybe it was a veiled attempt to give us an advance goodnight kiss on our mouths – she was coming to give us one less and less often. I went upstairs myself now and pulled the duvet up to my neck, the way I'd seen in a film at Belle's house, and then someone always came and tucked the duvet under the main character's chin, which never happened to me, and sometimes I woke up shivering from the cold, pulled up the duvet myself and whispered, 'Sleep tight, dear main character.'

Before the flannel got to me, I pushed my chair back and said I felt the urge. The word 'urge' made everyone around the table look up hopefully: maybe I'd finally have to poo at last. But on the toilet, I waited until I heard all the chairs being shunted back, until my bottom grew cold and I'd read the birthdays on the calendar above the sink three times. With a pencil from my coat pocket I drew very faint crosses after each name, so faint you could only see it from close up, with the biggest cross after my birthday in April, and I wrote A.H. after it for Adolf Hitler.

The boy next door's willy had felt soft, like Granny's meatloaf I had to roll sometimes on Sundays on the counter, sprinkled with herbs. Only meatloaf is greasy and rough. I wanted to keep holding on to the willy but the stream grew thinner and stopped. The boy moved his hips back and forth, making his tinkle jig around, and splashes ended up on the grey tiles. After that he pulled up his boxers and jeans. Belle watched from a distance. She was allowed to do up his jeans. You always have to begin from the bottom with an important job – from there you can grow to the top. Belle won't be able to forget the dead rabbit in a hurry, but this calmed her: I'd kept my word. I'd grabbed her finger and pushed it against the boy's willy, saying unnecessarily, 'This is a real one.'

'I'm a paedophile,' I repeat. Hanna squeezes a bit of shampoo from a bottle and rubs it in her hair. Coconut. She says nothing but I know she's thinking. She can do that, think before she speaks; with me it's the other way around. When I try it, my head suddenly empties out and my words are like the cows that lie down in the wrong place in the shed to sleep, where I can't get to them.

Then Hanna begins to giggle.

'I'm serious!' I say.

'You can't be.'

'Why not?'

'Paedophiles are different. You're not different. You're like me.'

I let myself sink back into the bath-water, pinch my nose shut and feel my head touch the bottom. Underwater I can see the hazy contours of Hanna's naked body. How long will my sister keep believing that I'm no different from her, that we form a unit, while there are enough nights when we lie separate from each other in bed and sometimes she can no longer keep up with my train of thoughts.

'And you're a girl,' Hanna says as soon as I resurface. There's a crown of bubbles around her head.

'Are all paedophiles boys then?'

'Yes, and much older, at least three hands, and with grey hair.'

'Thank God.' I may be different but I'm not a paedophile. I picture the boys in my class. Not one of them has grey hair. According to the teacher, only Dave has an old soul. We've all got an old soul. Mine is already twelve years old. That's older than the neighbour's oldest cow and he says she's ready for the scrap-heap – she hardly produces any milk.

'You can say that again – thank God,' Hanna says loudly and we giggle, get out of the bath and dry each other, before pulling our heads into our pyjama tops like snails in search of protection.

13

The warty skin hangs loose around the skeletons. Every few seconds they puff out their cheeks, as though they are gathering air so they can say something but keep changing their minds. For a moment I want to cut open the warts to see what's inside them, but instead I rest my arms on my desk and lay my chin on my hands. They've hardly eaten anything since the toad migration. Maybe they've joined the resistance like Mum, although I wouldn't know what they were rebelling against. In the Second World War, resistance was always against others – now it's only directed at ourselves, like with my coat, which is a rebellion against all the illnesses listed in the radio requests on *The Musical Fruit Basket*. I'm more and more scared of all the things you can catch. And sometimes, I even imagine that during gym I'll look at the queue waiting to jump the pommel horse and my classmates will start throwing up one by one – the vomit like porridge around their ankles and fear riveting me to the linoleum – my cheeks as hot as the heating pipes in the ceiling. As soon as I blink, the vision disappears again. To curb my fear, every morning I break a few peppermints into four on the edge of the table and keep them in my trouser pocket. When I feel sick or think I'm going to throw up, I eat one. The mint flavour makes me calm.

The headmaster won't let me leave early. 'There's usually a deeper underlying issue with children who are off school sick for a long time,' he said, looking past me as though he could see Mum and Dad's faces behind me, and the thing that could happen any moment, namely that absent-minded thing called Death who always took the wrong person or, the other way round, let them live.

'As long as you don't start spitting,' I say to the toads, taking two earthworms I got from the vegetable patch this afternoon before Belle came round out of a paper handkerchief. The earthworm is one of the strongest animals because it can be cut in half and still carry on living. They've got nine hearts. The worms wiggle around a bit as I hold them in a pincer grip above the head of the fattest toad; its eyes move back and forth. Their pupils are stripes – a slotted screwdriver, I think to myself. Handy to know if I have to take them apart one day to find out what's wrong with them, the way I did with the toasted sandwich maker that was covered in melted cheese. The toads refuse to open their mouths. I rub my legs together a bit – the knickers from school are itchy. I've been wetting myself a lot recently and hiding the wet knickers under my bed. That's the only good thing about grief: Mum's nose is constantly blocked so she doesn't smell the knickers when she comes to wish me goodnight.

Today there was a mishap at school too. Luckily no one noticed except the teacher. She gave me a pair of knickers from the lost property box – there are things in there that everyone's stopped looking for, so they are properly lost. Red letters on the knickers say COOL. I feel anything but cool.

'Are you cross?' I asked the teacher when she gave me the knickers.

'Of course I'm not cross. These things just happen,' she said.

Anything can happen, I think then, but nothing can be prevented. The plan about death and a rescuer, Mum and Dad who don't lie on top of each other any more, Obbe who is growing out of his clothes faster than Mum can learn the washing labels off by heart, and the way not just his body is growing but also his cruelty; the ticking insects in my belly which make me rock on top of my teddy bear and get out of bed exhausted, or why we don't have crunchy peanut butter any more, why the sweets tin has grown a mouth with Mum's voice in it that says, 'Are you sure you want to do that?' or why Dad's arm has become like a traffic barrier: it descends on you whether you wait your turn or not; or the Jewish people in the basement that no one talks about, just like Matthies. Are they still alive?

One of the toads suddenly moves forward. I hold it back with my hand so that it doesn't tumble off the desk. Do they have silos in their minds? I rest my head back on my hands so that I can look at them close up and say, 'You know what it is, dear toads? You need to use your strengths. If you can't swim as well as a frog and you can't jump as high, you have to be better at other things. You're really good at sitting, for example. A frog can't compete with you on that. So still that you look like lumps of mud. And you're good at digging, I have to give you that. The whole winter we think that you've disappeared but you're just sitting in the earth under our feet. We people are always visible, even when we want to be invisible. Apart from that we can do everything you can do – swim, jump, dig – but we don't find those things as important because we mainly want to do things we can't do, things we have to spend ages learning at school, while I'd rather be able to swim, or dig myself into the mud and let two seasons go by. But maybe the most important difference between you and me is that you don't have any parents any more or you don't see them. How does that go? Did they say one day, "Bye bye, chubby-cheeked kid, you can cope without us now, we're off." Is that how it went? Or did you go paddling one lovely summer's day in July and they floated away from you on a lily-pad, further and further until they were out of sight? Did it hurt? Does it still hurt? It might sound crazy, but I miss my parents even though I see them every day. Maybe it's just like the things we want to learn because we can't do them yet: we miss everything we don't have. Mum and Dad are there, but at the same time they aren't.' I take a deep breath and think about Mum, who is probably downstairs reading the *Reformist* magazine. You can only take it out of its plastic on Thursdays and no sooner. Her knees together and a mug of aniseed milk in her hand. Dad scrolling through teletext for milk prices. If they're good, he goes to make himself a sandwich in the kitchen and Mum gets nervous again about possible crumbs, as though she's from pest control. If the milk prices are disappointing, he goes outside and walks away from us along the dike. Every time I think it's the last time we'll see him. Then I'll hang his overalls on the peg in the hall next to Matthies's coat – Death has its own coat hook here. But the worst thing is the endless silence. As soon as the television's off all you can hear is the ticking of the cuckoo clock on the wall. The thing is, they're not drifting away from us but we're drifting away from them.

'Promise me this will stay between us, dear toads, but sometimes I wish I had different parents. Do you understand that?' I continue. 'Parents like Belle's who are as soft as shortbread just out of the oven and give her lots of cuddles when she's sad, frightened or even very happy. Parents that chase away all the ghosts from under your bed, from inside your head, and run through a summary of the week with you every weekend like Dieuwertje Blok does on TV, so you don't forget everything you achieved that week, all the things you tripped up on before scrabbling to your feet again. Parents that see you when you're talking to them – even though I find it terrifying to look people in the eye, as though other people's eyeballs are two lovely marbles you can continuously win or lose. Belle's parents go on exotic holidays and make tea for her when she comes home from school. They've got hundreds of different sorts including aniseed and fennel, my favourite tea. Sometimes they drink it sitting on the floor because that's more comfortable than sitting in a chair. And they horse around with each other without it turning into fighting. And they say sorry as often as they're nasty to each other.

'What I was wondering, friends, was whether you toads can actually cry or do you go swimming when you feel sad? We've got tears in us but perhaps you seek comfort outside yourselves, so you can sink away in it. But more on your strengths, that's where I started. Of course you have to know what you want to make use of and how you want to do that. I know you're good at catching flies and at mating. I think that last one's a funny business but you do it all the time. And if something you like doing stops then there's something going on. Have you got toad flu? Are you homesick or are you just being difficult? I know I might be asking too much but if you start the mating season, Mum and Dad might get going too. Sometimes someone has to lead by example, the way I always have to set a good example for Hanna, even though the other way round works better. Or are you just mainly kissing now? Belle says there are four bases: kissing, fumbling, more fumbling and mating. I can't talk about it, I haven't even been able to bat yet. Even though I understand you have to start slowly. It's just we don't have much time. Mum didn't even eat her rye bread and cheese yesterday and Dad is constantly threatening to leave. You should know that they never kiss either. Never. Well, just at twelve o'clock on New Year's Eve. Then Mum leans cautiously towards Dad, holds his head briefly like a greasy apple fritter, and presses her lips to his skin without making a kissing sound. Look, I don't know what love is, but I do know it makes you jump high, that it makes you able to swim more lengths, that it makes you visible. The cows are often in love – then they jump on each other's backs, even females on females. So we have to do something about the love here on the farm. But to be honest, dear esteemed toads, I think we've dug ourselves in, even though it's summer.

We're buried deep in the mud and no one is going to get us out. Do you actually have a god? A god who forgives and a god who remembers? I don't know what kind of god we have. Maybe He's on holiday, or He's dug himself in. Whatever it is, He's not exactly on the case. And all these questions, toads. How many fit inside your little heads? I'm no good at maths but I'm guessing about ten. You have to think that if your little heads fit about a hundred times inside mine, how many questions there are in me and how many answers that haven't been ticked off yet. I'm going to put you back in the bucket now. I'm sorry about this but I can't set you free. I'd miss you, because who would watch over me when I sleep? I promise to take you to the lake one day. Then we'll float away together on a lily-pad, and maybe, only maybe, I'll even dare to take off my coat. Even though it will feel uncomfortable for a while, but according to the pastor, discomfort is good. In discomfort we are real.'

14

There's exactly twelve hours between the morning and evening milkings. It's Saturday, which means Dad goes back to bed after the first round – you can hear the floor creaking until it's quiet again upstairs. We're not allowed to take our places around the kitchen table until about eleven, when he feels like breakfast. It's been laid since eight o'clock, and sometimes I walk in hungry circles around it in the hope that Dad will hear my impatience vibrating up through the ceiling. Sometimes I secretly smuggle a slice of gingerbread upstairs and break it in two. One half used to be for Hanna but now it's for my toads. When Dad finally comes to the table – first he has to shave himself so that he's neat and tidy for the Lord's Day – there's still a bit of shaving foam on his neck and collar. It's already past eleven and Dad's bread is still waiting on his plate. I've already walked around the kitchen table four times and Mum has already spread a slice of wholemeal with butter, and put some brawn and a blob of ketchup on top, the way Dad likes it.

The open sandwich reminds me of the run-over hedgehog I saw next to the road yesterday on the way home from school. It was a sorry sight: that flattened body with its innards a bit further up on the verge and its eyes pecked out, must have been by a crow. There were two black holes you could push your fingers through. It lay on a side road through the fields where very few cars or tractors pass. Maybe it was the hedgehog's own choice, maybe he'd been waiting for days for the wrong moment to cross. I squatted down next to the hedgehog sadly and whispered, 'Lord have mercy on us and be near. We are united in this place to say farewell to Hedgehog, who was so mercilessly taken from us. We return this broken life and lay it in Thy hands. Receive Hedgehog and grant him the peace he could not find. Be to all of us a merciful and loving God so that we may live with death. Amen.' After that, I picked a few handfuls of grass and laid them over the hedgehog. I didn't look back as I cycled away.

I place a slice of bread on my plate and cover the entire surface very carefully in chocolate sprinkles. My stomach rumbles.

'Is Dad still in bed?' I ask.

'He didn't even go back to bed,' Mum says. 'I felt the covers – cold.'

She leans over the table and spoons the skin off Dad's cold coffee. She likes skins. I watch the limp brown milk sheet disappear into her mouth and a shiver runs down my spine. Obbe's chair opposite me is empty too. He must be on his computer or with his chickens. Obbe and I each have twenty chickens: white Leghorns, Orpingtons, Wyandottes and a few laying hens. We often pretend to be two successful companies – his is called The Peck About and mine is called The Little Bantam. Once a year we have chicks, little yellow candyflosses on legs. Most of them are raised by the mother who keeps them warm under her wings, but sometimes the mother rejects them, not knowing what her wings are for. The thing is, they can't fly with them – their bodies are too fat and heavy to stay aloft. That's why we put their chicks in an aquarium filled with sawdust in the shed and hang the calves' heat lamps above it. Sometimes I take one upstairs to the attic and let it sleep in my armpit. I wrap a piece of kitchen paper around its bum so I don't get covered in shit. Obbe and I sell our eggs – a box of twelve costs one euro – to the chip man on the square. He makes the most delicious mayonnaise from them or boils the eggs for Russian salad. Obbe used to spend a lot of time with his chickens. He could spend hours sitting on an upturned milk pail watching one of his red hens take a dust bath. Now he spends less and less time there. Sometimes he even forgets to feed them and they fly up against the mesh of their run hungrily. I think he does it deliberately. He has started hating everything, so he probably hates the chip man and his mayonnaise too. That's why I often give them bread and gather the eggs from the laying house and secretly put them in my box. I hope he's finally cleaning out the run. Dad threatened to sell them if he didn't do it very soon. Particularly in this hot weather, there are tons of maggots and chicken lice. You can watch them walking along your bare arms, little brown bodies with six legs, before pinching them dead between your fingers.

Hanna has come to the table too in the meantime. It's taken her just a few seconds to scoff the whole bowl of strawberries. Waiting makes us nervous because we don't know what's coming next – where's Dad? Has he finally plucked up the courage to cycle off for good? Without a skirt guard though, because the cover broke when his bike blew over after church. Or did Dad collapse among the cows only to be trampled? I turn my attention to the strawberries. I'll go fetch some new ones from the vegetable plot: Dad loves them, and he likes to eat them covered in a thick layer of castor-sugar.

'Have you already looked in the cowshed?'

'He knows we have breakfast at this time,' Mum says, putting Dad's mug in the microwave.

'Maybe he's gone to fetch some silage grass from Janssen's?'

'He never does that on a Saturday. Let's just begin without him.'

But none of us makes a move to start eating. It feels strange without Dad. And who's going to thank God 'for need and for abundance'?

'I'll go and have a look,' I say, shunting my chair back and accidently knocking against Matthies's. It wobbles a little and then falls backwards onto the floor. The crash vibrates in my ears. I want to quickly set it upright again but my mother grabs my arm.

'Don't touch it.' She looks at the chair-back as though my brother has fallen again, always falling in our minds, again and again. I leave the chair and stare at it as though it's a dead person. Now she's eaten all the strawberries, Hanna starts on her fingernails. Sometimes there are bloody bits of cuticle between her teeth. A silence follows the crash, no one breathes. And then all bodily functions slowly return:

feeling, smelling, hearing and moving.

'It's just a chair,' I say then.

Mum has let go of me and is clutching a jar of peanut butter.

'You really come from another planet,' she whispers.

I look at the floor. Mum only knows Planet Earth. I know all eight planets, and know that up to now life's only be found on Earth. *My Very Educated Mother Just Served Us Nachos.* Mum never serves us nachos but the sentence is a useful way to remember all the planets. If I'm nervous about something or have to wait too long at the traffic light near school, I repeat the line up to ten times inside my head. The line also makes me insignificant. We are all just nachos in an enormous bowl.

'What on earth is going to become of you?' Mum complains. Her other hand is now clutching the jar of Duo Penotti. Since Matthies's death none of us has eaten it, much too afraid we won't be able to keep the white chocolate bit white, that the colours will get muddled up until it becomes just one black hole.

'We will become Big Friendly People, Mum, and of course this chair isn't just a chair. I'm sorry.'

Mum nods approvingly. 'Where has that man got to?' Again she presses the start button on the microwave. She doesn't put me back in the solar system, but lets me float. Am I really different from the others?

I quickly open the back door and go out into the farmyard, crossing it towards the cowsheds. I take a deep breath and exhale as hard as I can. I repeat this a few times and see that the sky above me is beginning to turn grey. It's a perfect day to escape to the other side. There I'll be in charge of what I do when and I'll be able to eat breakfast whenever I want, but the closer I get to the cowsheds, the slower I begin to walk. I try to skip the half-tiles in the yard. *Otherwise you'll get really ill and you'll get the shits or start vomiting. And everyone will see. Everyone in the village, all your classmates.* I shake my head to get rid of the thoughts and notice that the hatch to the feed silo, which is next to the milking shed, has been left open. There's an enormous pile of feed pellets under it. Dad is always warning us about rats. 'If you spill anything they'll start with the feed and move on to your toes. They'll chew right through the soles of your shoes.' The stream of pellets is getting thinner, and most have already fallen out. I run my hands through the pellets for a moment. They feel cool and pleasant as they slide through my fingers. Then I close the hatch and secure it to the side with a rope.

Suddenly I'm reminded of the rope hanging in the middle of the barn that used to have a blue space hopper attached to it as a diversion for the cows. But one day the space hopper was burst by a new cow that still had horns. The rope was left hanging. Sometimes we nailed the leaves from a walnut tree to it, or one of Obbe's *Hitzone* albums that Dad had confiscated dangled there, its shiny back helping keep away the shit flies, just like the walnut leaves. Now I picture Dad's head hanging there instead of the space hopper. Mum often speaks for Dad. Who knows, maybe that was the case that night when I hid behind the rabbit shed. There are so many ropes in the countryside, but not one of them has a set job.

He's not standing on top of the silo in any case.

Through the door to the cowshed, I see Obbe standing in the feed section. He's forking silage grass in an elegant curve in to the cows, sweat on his face like the morning dew on the shed windows. The cows are restless, whipping their tails from left to right. Some of the tails are matted with dried-up dung. Every now and then we cut it out of the hairs with a hoof knife, more for the way it looks than for the cows themselves. With every elegant toss, Obbe's biceps bulge. He's getting stronger. My eyes dart to the dozens of backs of the cows, to the corners of the shed and the rope in the middle. Then the back door opens and Dad appears. He looks different, as though someone has left the latch open in his head, like a feed silo. The top press studs of his overalls are open, showing his tanned chest. Mum finds that inappropriate – what if a milk customer should see him like that? I think she's worried the milk customer would go off without any milk but with Dad instead. Milk costs one euro a litre. Dad is made up of about fifty litres. That's partly the reason Sunday is Mum's favourite day, because no one can spend or accept money on the Lord's Day. On that day we're only allowed to breathe and partake of the bare essentials, and that's just the love of God's word and Mum's vegetable soup.

Dad is chasing the last cows inside, slapping their haunches with the flat of his hand. He slides the lock on the big stable door. I don't get it. The lock only gets shut in the winter or when nobody's on the farm. It's not winter and we're all home. Dad piles up all the forks in the feed section and wraps them up in the plastic left over from a silage pack. For a moment, Dad looks up to the heavens. He hasn't shaved, I notice. He holds his hands to either side of his face, his jaw tense. I want to tell him that Mum's inside waiting, that she isn't angry, that she hasn't yet asked whether we love her, so she can't be doubting the answer, and that his sandwich is ready on his favourite plate, the one with cowhide patches around the rim, that Hanna and I practised Psalm 100 this morning, the psalm of the week, and that it was as pure as milk.

Dad hasn't noticed me yet. I stand there watching, the china bowl from the strawberries in my hand. Along with Obbe, he fetches the bull from among the young cows; the bull hasn't been there two days yet. We've called him Bello. Dad calls all the bulls Bello. Even when we're allowed to choose and pick another name, they always end up being called Bello. I've already seen his willy. It wasn't for very long because Mum came out of the milking shed right that second and put her hand, which was covered in a rubber glove, in front of my eyes and said, 'They're doing the conga.'

'Why aren't I allowed to see that?' I asked.

Now Dad spots me at last. He makes a shunting gesture with his hand. 'You've got to get out of the shed, now.'

'Yes, now,' Obbe repeats after him, his blue overalls tied around his hips. By the looks of it, he's taking his role as Dad's disciple seriously. I feel a brief stab around the area of my spleen. Here among the cows they suddenly seem to understand each other; they are father and son.

'Why?'

'Just obey!' Dad shouts. 'Close the door.'

The anger in his voice startles me. His eyes are like rock-hard rabbit droppings in his face. Sweat drips down his forehead. At that moment a cow close to me slides over the grating and collapses onto her udders. She makes no effort to get back up again. I give my father and Obbe a questioning look, but they've already turned around and are squatting next to the young cow. I stride out of the shed and slam the door behind me, hearing the wood creak. Let that bloody shed collapse, I think, immediately feeling ashamed of my thoughts. Why aren't I allowed to know what's going on? Why am I kept out of everything?

I crawl under the bird net in the vegetable patch. Lien from next door stretched it out over the rows of strawberries to stop the seagulls and starlings eating them. I fall onto my knees on the damp earth. Because it's Saturday I'm allowed to wear trousers since there's work to be done. I carefully push aside the plants to find the best fruit, the ones that are completely red, and put them in the dish. From time to time I pop one in my mouth – they're deliciously juicy and sweet. I love the texture of strawberries, the little seeds and the hairs on the inside of my mouth. Textures calm me down. Textures create unity, they keep something together that would collapse otherwise. Wok vegetables, cooked chicory and scratchy clothes are the only textures I don't like. Human skin has texture too. Mum's is beginning to look increasingly like the bird net: little compartments drawn in soft skin, as though she's a jigsaw puzzle that's losing more and more of its pieces. Dad's got more of a potato skin – it's smooth and there are a few rough patches, and sometimes a dent from a nail he's walked into.

Once the bowl is full, I crawl back out from under the bird net and wipe the soil from my trousers. Dad's and Obbe's wellies are in the shed, next to the door-mat, one of them still half hanging on the boot-jack. They aren't at the breakfast table but on the sofa in front of the TV, while it's daytime and the screen is supposed to be black during the day. Usually there's just snow to see then. At first I thought we might find Matthies in there, but later I discovered that Dad had simply pulled the cable out. The news was on: 'Farms here have also been struck by foot-and-mouth. God's punishment or bitter coincidence?'

Just like the weather, God can never get it right. If a swan is rescued somewhere in the village, in a different place a parishioner dies. I don't know what foot-and-mouth is and don't get the chance to ask because my mum says I should go and play with Obbe and Hanna, that this isn't going to be a normal day like the rest, and I don't want to interrupt her by saying that the days haven't been normal for a long time, because her face looks just as pale as the creamy crocheted curtains in the windows. I also notice that Mum and Dad are sitting remarkably close to each other. Maybe this is a sign they are going to get naked soon and I should leave them in peace, like the way you shouldn't separate two snails that are on top of each other because it might damage the mother-of-pearl on their shells. I put the bowl of strawberries in front of them on the dresser, next to the open Authorized Version, in case Mum gets hungry after mating and finally wants to eat again. Dad is making strange sounds: he hisses, growls, sighs, shakes his head and says, 'no, no, no'. Different animals make different mating sounds – it must be the same with people. And then I catch a glimpse of a cow's tongue with blisters on the screen. 'What's foot-and-mouth?' I quickly ask all the same. I don't get an answer. Dad leans forward to pick up the remote control and just keeps pressing the volume button.

'Go on!' Mum says without looking at me.

As though the volume stripes on the screen are stairs, I stamp harder and harder as I go up to my room, but no one comes after me. No one tells me what in God's name is about to happen.

15

There's a black note on Obbe's bedroom door that says DO NOT DISTURB in white letters. He doesn't want to be disturbed but if Hanna and I don't go to his room for a while, he does come to ours. We don't have signs on our doors. We want to be disturbed so that we're not so alone.

Around the white letters, he's stuck stickers of pop stars including Robbie Williams and Sugababes from the new *Hitzone 23*. Dad knows Obbe listens to them but he doesn't dare confiscate his Discman – it's the only thing that keeps him quiet, while I'm not allowed to keep saving up for one. 'Buy books with your savings, that's more your thing,' Dad said, and I thought: I've been sidelined by the cool stuff. In any case, Dad thinks all the music on CDs and on the radio is wicked. He'd rather we listened to *The Musical Fruit Basket*, but that's totally boring and for old people, for rotting fruit, Obbe says sometimes. I think that's funny, rotting fruit in a sick-bed: a request for Hymn 11. I'd rather listen to Bert and Ernie from *Sesame Street* because they argue about things normal people would just shrug at; their squabbling calms me down. Then I turn on my CD player and crawl back under the covers and imagine I'm a rare paper clip from Bert's collection.

'Klapaucius,' I whisper, as I gently open the bedroom door

a crack. I see a strip of Obbe's back. He's sitting on the floor wearing his overalls. The door creaks as I open it a bit more. My brother looks up. Just like the note on his door, his eyes are dark. Suddenly I wonder whether butterflies have a shorter life expectancy when they know they can flap themselves to death.

'Password?' Obbe calls.

'Klapaucius,' I say again.

'Wrong,' Obbe says.

'But that was the password, wasn't it?' Dieuwertje's whiskers are still in my coat pocket. They tickle my palm. I'm lucky Mum never empties my pockets, otherwise she'd find out about all the things I want to hang on to, the things I'm collecting to become heavier.

'You'd better come up with something better than that or I won't let you in.' Obbe turns back to his Lego. He is building an enormous spaceship. I think for a moment and then say, 'Heil Hitler.' It's silent for a moment. Then I see his shoulders move up and down slightly as he begins to chuckle, louder and louder. It's good that he's laughing – it seals an alliance. The butcher in the village always winks at me when I come to buy fresh sausages. This means that he agrees that it's a good choice, he's happy that I've come to free him of the sausages he made with so much love and which smell of nutmeg.

'Say it again but with your arm raised.'

Obbe has turned around completely now. Just like Dad, he's left the top press studs of his overalls open. His shiny tanned chest looks like a chicken on a spit. In the background

I can hear the familiar theme tune to *The Sims*. I stick my hand in the air without a moment's hesitation and whisper the greeting again. My brother nods at me as a sign that I can come in, before returning his gaze to his Lego. There are various groups of blocks around him, sorted by colour. He's taken apart the Lego castle he kept the dead Tiesey in for a while until he began to stink.

There's a stale smell in his room, a smell of decay, of an adolescent body that hasn't been washed for a long time. There's a toilet roll on his bedside table with pale yellow wads around it. I play with the wads and carefully sniff the paper. If tears had a scent, no one would cry secretly any more. The wads don't smell of anything. Some of them feel sticky, others are as hard as rock. The tip of a magazine sticks out from under his pillow. I lift it up – there's a naked woman on the cover with breasts like gourds. She looks surprised, as though she doesn't know herself why she's naked, as though various circumstances have combined to make this *her* moment. There are people who are startled by that moment, as though they've been looking forward to it all their life, but once they get there it's still somehow unexpected. I don't know when my moment's coming, only that I'll keep my coat on. The lady must be cold, even though I don't see any goose bumps on her arms.

I quickly drop the pillow again. I haven't seen the magazine before. We don't get anything but the *Reformist Daily*, the *Reformist* magazine, *Dairy Farmer*, some supermarket advertising brochures and Matthies's judo magazine – my parents keep 'forgetting' to cancel the subscription which means that every Friday his death comes crashing onto the door-mat again. Maybe that's why Obbe bangs his head on the edge of his bed – to get the naked women out of it, so that he can zap himself away like the TV channels, and Dad must see it in you if you've had something in your head that isn't pure.

I sit down next to Obbe on the carpet. He's holding a princess captive in the ruins of his Lego castle. She's wearing lipstick and mascara and has long blonde hair to below her shoulders.

'I'm going to inseminate you,' Obbe says, pushing his knight up and down against the princess, the way Bello the bull does with the cows. I can hardly put my own hand in front of my eyes because there's no one to check whether I'm peeking or not. Better to give temptation free rein, I decide. As I watch the scene, he takes from the Lego box a clean tuna tin we've been using to keep our coins and gold medallions in – they smell of oily fish. Obbe holds out his hand.

'Here's your money, whore.' My brother tries to make his voice sound deep. His voice has been breaking since the spring, it shoots from high-pitched to low.

'What's a whore?' I ask.

'A woman farmer.' He looks at the door to check our parents can't hear. I know Mum isn't against women being farmers, even though she considers it more a man's work. I take another knight from one of the broken lookout towers. Obbe pushes his doll against the princess again. They continue to look happy.

I lower my voice. 'What's under your skirt, princess?'

Obbe bursts out laughing. Sometimes it's just as if a young starling has flown down his throat – he chirps. 'Don't you know what's under it?'

'No.' I set the princess upright and study her from all sides. I only know about willies.

'You've got one yourself. A cunt.'

'What does it look like?'

'A custard bun.'

I raise my eyebrows. Dad sometimes brings custard buns home from the baker's. Sometimes there are a few blue spots on the bottom of the bun and the custard has soaked in, but it still tastes quite good. We hear Dad shouting downstairs. He's shouting more often, as though he wants to force his words hard into us. I think it's a proverb from Isaiah: 'Shout it aloud, do not hold back. Raise your voice like a trumpet. Declare to my people their rebellion and to the descendants of Jacob their sins.' What kind of rebellion is he talking about?

'What's foot-and-mouth?' I ask Obbe.

'A disease cows get.'

'What's going to happen?'

'All the cows have to be put down. The entire herd.'

He says it without emotion, but I notice that the hairs around his crown are greasier than at the hairline, like damp silage grass. I don't know how many times he's touched his crown but it's obvious he's worried.

My chest feels increasingly hot, as though I've drunk a mug of hot chocolate too quickly. Someone is stirring it with a spoon, making a whirlpool in my heart – stop stirring, I hear Mum say – and the cows disappear one by one into the whirlpool like chunks of cocoa mixed with milk. I dedicate all my mental energy to thinking about the Lego princess. She's hidden a custard bun under her skirt and Obbe's allowed to lick out the cream, his nose covered in icing sugar.

'But why then?'

'Because they're ill. They're going to die anyway.'

'Is it infectious?'

Obbe scans my face, squinting his eyes into the flat blades we sometimes buy for Lien next door's wood chipper, and says, 'I'd watch out where you breathe and where you don't if I was you.' I clasp my hands around my knees, rocking myself faster and faster. I get a sudden vision of Mum and Dad turning as yellow as Lego figures. They will be stuck to one spot when all the cows have gone if no one picks them up by the backs of their necks and clicks them onto the right place.

After a while Hanna comes to sit with us. She's brought cherry tomatoes, which she peels with her teeth, revealing the soft red fleshy pulp. The care with which she eats the tomatoes, doing everything in layers, touches me. When she eats a sandwich she starts with the filling, then the crusts and only then the soft part of the bread. When she eats a milk biscuit, she scrapes off the milk bit with her front teeth and saves the biscuit till last. Hanna eats in layers and I think in layers. Just when she's about to put a new tomato between her teeth, Obbe's door opens again and the vet folds his face around the edge. It's been a long time since he came round, but he's still wearing the dark green dust-coat with black buttons, the four limp fingers of a rubber glove dangling from his pocket, the thumb folded back. For the second time he's come to bring us bad news: 'They'll come to take samples tomorrow. You can assume they'll all have to go, even the unregistered ones.' Dad has a few unregistered cows to be able to sell a bit of extra milk to the villagers or family members. The money from this 'black-market milk' is kept in a tin on the mantelpiece. For holidays. Nevertheless, I sometimes see Dad open the tin and take a couple of notes out when he thinks no one else is around. My guess is that he's saving up for his 'bottom drawer', for when he moves out. Eva at school's doing that too, even though she's only thirteen. Dad is probably looking for a family where he's allowed to lick his knife after putting it in the apple syrup jar and doesn't have to shout or slam doors, where they don't mind if he leaves his trouser button open after eating and you can see the blond hairs curling up above the waistband of his pants. And maybe he'd even be able to pick out his own clothes there: every morning my mum hangs what he has to wear over the edge of the bed – if Dad doesn't agree with the choice she spends the whole day not speaking to him or gets rids of yet another foodstuff from her diet, which she announces with a sigh as though the item doesn't want her any more.

'If He wants it this way, it must be God's will.' He looks at us one by one with a smile. It's a nice smile, nicer than Boudewijn de Groot's.

'And,' he continues, 'be extra nice to your parents.' We nod obediently; only Obbe stares dourly at the heating pipes in his room. There are a few butterflies drying on them. I hope the vet doesn't see and then tell Mum and Dad.

'I have to get back to the cows,' the vet says, turning around and closing the door behind him.

'Why didn't Dad come and tell us himself?' I ask.

'Because he has to take measures,' Obbe says.

'Like what?'

'Close off the farmyard, install a disinfectant bath, take in the calves, disinfect the tools and the milk tank.'

'Aren't we measures?'

'Of course,' Obbe says, 'but we've been fenced off and tied up since our births. We can't be anything else.'

Then he moves closer to me. He's wearing Dad's aftershave to gain a bit of Dad's natural authority. 'Do you want to know how they're going to murder the cows?'

I nod and think about the teacher who said I'd go far with my empathy and boundless imagination, but in time I'd have to find words for it because otherwise everything and everybody stays inside you. And one day, just like the black stockings which my classmates sometimes tease me about wearing because we're Reformists – even though I never wear black stockings – I will crumple in on myself until I can only see darkness, eternal darkness. Obbe presses his index finger to his temple, makes a shooting sound and then suddenly pulls the cords of my coat together, constricting my throat. I stare him straight in the eye for a moment and see the same hatred as when he shook the hamster around in the water glass. I pull myself away, and shout, 'You're crazy!'

'We're all going crazy – you too,' Obbe says. He takes a packet of mini Aeros from his desk drawer, tears off the wrappers and stuffs them into his mouth, one after the other until they are just a big brown mush. He must have stolen the Aeros from the basement. I hope the Jewish people managed to hide in time behind the wall of apple sauce pots.

16

Dad likes crows' funerals the best. Sometimes when he finds a dead crow in the muck-heap or in the field, he hangs it upside down with a rope from one of the branches of the cherry tree. Soon a whole flock of crows turn up and spend hours circling the tree to pay their last respects to their fellow. No other creature mourns for as long as a crow. Generally there's one that really stands out, a bit bigger than the others and fiercer too, and it crows the loudest of all of them. That must be the flock's pastor. Their black-feathered cloaks contrast beautifully with the pale sky, and Dad says crows are intelligent animals. They can count, remember faces and voices, and hold a grudge against anyone who treats them badly – but after a crow has been hung up, they hang around the farmyard. They stare down from the guttering searchingly as Dad walks between the house and the cowsheds, like cardboard hares at a shooting range, their black eyes boring into his chest like two shot holes. I try not to look at the crows. Maybe they want to tell us something, or they're waiting until the cows are dead. Granny said yesterday that crows in a farmyard are an omen of death. I think that either Mum or I will be next. There must be a reason Dad asked me to lie down in the farmyard this morning so that he could take the measurements for a new bed, which he is making from pallets and oak and the leftover planks from Obbe's chicken coop. I lay down on the cold flagstones with my arms alongside my body and watched Dad unfold a tape measure and lay it from head to toe, and I thought: if you saw off the bed legs and take away the mattress, you could easily turn it into a coffin.

I'd like to be laid facing down in it, with the viewing window at the height of my bum so that everyone could say goodbye and look at my bum hole, since that was where the entire problem was located. Dad folded his tape measure back up. He had insisted I stop sleeping in Matthies's bed as 'little Johnny can't bear it any more'. And over the past weeks I've looked so pale that Lien from next door has started bringing around a crate of mandarins every Friday evening. Some of them are wrapped like me in jackets, made of paper. I keep holding my breath all the time not to inhale any germs, or to get closer to Matthies. It's not long before I collapse to the floor and everything around me fades into a snowy landscape. Once I'm on the floor, I regain consciousness quite quickly and see Hanna's worried face. She holds her clammy hand to my forehead like a flannel. I don't tell her that fainting is nice, that in that snowy landscape there's more chance I'll meet Matthies than there is of meeting Death here on the farm. The crows circled above me when I was lying out in the yard and Dad was noting down the centimetres in his accounts book.

Mum has put a clean fitted sheet over the new mattress and shaken up my pillow. She presses her fist twice into the middle of the case, where my head will come to lie. I look at my new bed from my desk chair. I miss the old one already, even though my toes touched the end and it seemed like I was lying in a thumb-screw that turned me tighter and tighter. It was a safe feeling at least, as though something was setting boundaries so I didn't grow any more. Now I've got so much room to wiggle around and I can lie diagonally. I'll have to dig a hollow to be able to lie in it now Matthies's shape has gone. His measurements are nowhere to be found any more.

Mum kneels on the edge of my bed, her elbows resting on the duvet that smells of liquid manure because the wind was blowing the wrong way, which it is doing more and more often. It won't be long before the smell of cows doesn't get into anything, before it disappears from even the inside of our heads and all we can smell is longing and each other's absence. My mum pats the duvet gently. I get up submissively and crawl under the sheets, lying down on my side so that I can still see Mum's face. From here my blue striped duvet cover makes her seem miles away from me. She's somewhere on the other side of the lake, her body as skinny as a moorhen frozen in an ice hole. I shift my feet to the right so that they end up beneath Mum's folded hands. She moves them immediately as though I'm electric. There are dark rings under her eyes. I try to gauge how the news of the foot-and-mouth has affected her and whether the crows have come for me or for her.

'Do not allow yourselves to be beaten by evil, but beat evil with good,' Reverend Renkema preached in the morning service. I was sitting with Hanna and some other children from the village, next to the organ on the balustrade. From up there I suddenly saw Dad rising from a sea of black hats which, from above, looked like the yolks of rotten eggs that were speckled with black because no one had collected them from the nest. Some of the children around me had been in the nest too long as well, and sat there with sleepy faces staring into space.

Dad glanced around him, ignoring Mum's little tugs at the seam of his black overcoat, and cried out, 'The pastors are the cause of it.' There was deathly silence in the church. Everyone looked at my father and everyone on the balustrade looked at Hanna and me. I let my chin sink further into the collar of my coat and felt the cold zip against my skin.

To my relief I saw the organ player feel for the white keys and start on Psalm 51, causing the congregation to rise to their feet, and Dad's protest fell away among the villagers like a lump of butter among egg yolks, and in between that the soft hissing of the gossips. Not long after that, we saw Mum flee the pew with a wet nose, the hymn-book clamped under her arm. Belle had poked me in the side: 'Your dad's not right in the head.' I didn't reply but thought about the foolish man in the children's song who built his house on sand – the rain streamed down and the floods came and the house collapsed with a plop. Dad was building his words on sinking sand. How could he blame the pastor? Maybe it was our own fault? Maybe it was one of the plagues – and a plague here is never a natural phenomenon but a warning.

Mum began quietly to sing, 'Higher than the blue skies and

the stars of gold, abides our Father in the Heavens; Matthies, Obbe, Jas and Hanna he beholds.' I don't sing along but turn my thoughts to the bucket under my desk. Mum thinks toads are dirty, unpleasant creatures. She sometimes sweeps them up with a dustpan and brush from behind the boot-jack and carries them to the muck-heap like a pile of potato peelings. The toads aren't doing too well either. They look a bit peaky, their skin is getting drier, and they spend a lot of time sitting with their eyes closed – maybe they're praying and they don't know how to round it off, the way I don't with conversations. I just start shuffling my feet and staring ahead until someone says, 'OK, bye then.' I hope the moment won't come that I have to say 'bye' to the toads, but if they don't eat soon, that's going to happen.

After she's stopped singing, Mum puts her hand into the pocket of her pink dressing gown and takes out a little parcel wrapped in silver foil. 'I'm sorry,' she says.

'What for?'

'For the stars, for this evening. It's because of the cows, the shock of it.'

'It doesn't matter.'

I take the parcel. It's a crumpet topped with cumin cheese. The cheese is warm from her pocket. Mum watches me take a bite.

'You're just so odd, you and that funny coat of yours.'

I know she's only saying this because Lien from next door mentioned it again when she came round to find out how the cows were doing, and therefore us too. Even the vet brought up the subject of my coat with Mum. When she came in a bit later after feeding the calves, she got up in the middle of the kitchen, on the stepladder she normally only unfolded to get down the spider's webs. To every web with a spider in it, she'd say, 'Be off with you, old spinster.' It's the only joke Mum tells, but we still cherish it like an insect caught in a jam-jar. This time she didn't climb the stepladder to get rid of a spider but to get me out of the web she'd spun herself.

'If you don't take off your coat immediately, I'll jump.'

She stood there high above me in her long black skirt, her arms folded in front of her chest, her lips a bit red from the cherries – one of the few things she still eats – like the body of a spider squashed on pristine white wallpaper. I gauged the fall. Was it enough for Death? According to the pastor, the devil was afraid of the village because we were mightier than evil. But was that true? Were we stronger than evil?

I pushed my fist into my belly to calm the excruciating stabbing feeling that had arisen, and clenched my buttocks in a reflex, as though I was trying to keep in a fart. It wasn't a fart but a storm, a storm that raced through me. Just like the hurricanes on the news, mine also had a name. I called it the Holy Ghost. The Holy Ghost raced through me and my armpits stuck to the fabric of my coat. I would get ill without my protective layer. Frozen to the spot, I continued to look at Mum, at her polished mule slippers, at the steps on the ladder that had splatters of paint on them.

'I'll count to ten: one, two, three, four . . .'

Her voice slowly faded away, the kitchen grew hazy, and

whatever way I tried to bring my hand to the zip, I couldn't manage it. Then I heard a dull thud, bones hitting the kitchen floor, a crash and a cry. All of a sudden the kitchen was filled with people, with lots of different coats. I felt the vet's hands resting on my shoulders as though they were the heads of two calves, his voice calm and guiding. Slowly my vision became sharper and zoomed in on Mum, who was lying in the wheelbarrow Dad had used to take the beans to the muckheap. Obbe pushed her across the farmyard to the doctor in the village. I only saw some crows fly up – they looked like streaks of mascara through my tears. Dad refused to take her in the Volkswagen. 'You don't take rotten mandarins back to the greengrocer's,' he said. Meaning it was her own fault. It wouldn't be much longer, I thought, before we'd wheel her away for good. And Dad didn't say a single word for the rest of the evening. He just sat there flat out in his overalls watching TV, a glass of genever in his hand, smoking a cigarette. He was getting more and more holes in his overalls from the burning cigarette ends he laid on the edge of his knee for want of an ashtray, as though being here was suffocating him and he needed more air holes.

The vet, who has been here constantly since the news, had taken me and Hanna for a drive around the village. Sitting in the car is the nicest way to sit still: everything around you moves and changes and you can see it without having to move yourself. We drove to the rapeseed fields and sat on the bonnet and watched the combine mowing the plants out of the ground. The black seeds ended up in a big container.

The vet told us that they would make lamp oil, cattle feed, biofuel and margarine from them. A flock of geese flew over. They were headed to the other side. For a moment I expected them to fall from the sky like manna from heaven and land at our feet, their necks broken, but they flew on, further and further, until I could no longer see them. I looked at Hanna but she was deep in conversation with the vet about school. She'd taken off her shoes and was sitting on the bonnet in her stripy socks. I wished I could take off my green wellies too, but I didn't dare. An illness could get in on every side, just like burglars, even though Mum and Dad underestimated their cunning – they only locked the front door when they left, assuming only people they knew would come in through the back.

We didn't even mention once what had happened at home. There weren't any words to take the edge off fear, the way the blades of the combine decapitated the rapeseed plants to keep only the bit you can use. We silently watched the sun go down and on the way back got a bag of chips from the chip man which we ate in the car, making the windows steam up, and my eyes too because for the first time I briefly didn't feel alone: chips unite people more than any other type of food.

An hour later, we lie in bed with greasy fingers, smelling of mayonnaise, after an evening that was filled with hope despite the odds. But because of the chips, I don't feel like eating the crumpet. Only I don't want to disappoint Mum so I take a bite anyway. I keep seeing her lying in the wheelbarrow, her injured foot dangling over the edge. Obbe, who suddenly looked so fragile that I wanted to comfort him. In Romans 12, it says, 'If your gift is serving, then serve; if it is teaching, then teach; if it is to encourage, then give encouragement; if it is giving, then give generously; if it is to lead, do it diligently; if it is to show mercy, do it cheerfully.' I don't know what my gift is – maybe my gift is to shut up and listen. And that's what I did. I just asked him how his Sims were doing, whether they were already kissing. 'Not now,' he said, shutting himself away in his bedroom. The new *Hitzone* came out of his speakers so loudly that I could sing along to the lyrics under my breath. No one said anything about it.

Mum is growing limper, just like the frozen beans. Sometimes she just lets things fall from her hands and blames us. I said the Lord's Prayer five times today. The last two times I kept my eyes open to keep watch on everything around me. I hope Jesus understands – cows sleep with one eye open so that they can't suddenly be attacked. I can't help being more and more afraid of everything that could take me by surprise in the night: from a mosquito to God.

Mum stares with hollow eyes at my fluorescent duvet cover. I don't manage to swallow the bite of crumpet. I don't want her to be unhappy because of me. I don't want her to get out the kitchen stepladder again, because that way it would be easier to reach the rope or climb up the feed silo. She'd only have to kick the ladder away with her foot. Obbe says it doesn't take long – it only takes time for the person hanging themself because they get a rush of things to contemplate. The contemplations in church last at least two peppermints. And if her fear of heights didn't stop her this time, it wouldn't stop her on the silo either.

My mouth full, I say, 'It's so dark here.'

Mum's eyes look at me hopefully. I think about Belle's friendship book. Mum had crossed out the answer to the question 'What do you want to be?' and replaced it with 'A good Christian.' It meant no one noticed I'd had a growth spurt at the question 'What's your height in centimetres?' I wonder whether I am a good Christian. Maybe if I give something to my mum to cheer her up again.

'Dark? Where then?' she asks.

'You know, everywhere,' I say, swallowing my mouthful.

Mum turns on the globe on my bedside table and pretends to creep out of the room carefully, with her sore foot bandaged up and the belt of her dressing gown tied tight. It's a game we used to play when Matthies was still alive. I couldn't get enough of it.

'Big Bear, Big Bear! I can't sleep, I'm frightened.'

I peek through my fingers as she walks to the window, opens the curtains and says, 'Look, I've fetched the moon for you. The moon and all the twinkling stars. What more can a bear want?'

Love, I think to myself, like the warmth in the cowshed of all those breathing cattle with a common goal – survival. A warm flank to rest my head against, like during the milking. All the love they can give consists of poking out their tongues now and again when you offer them a chunk of mangel.

'Nothing, I'm a happy bear.'

I wait there until the stairs stop creaking and then I close the curtains, try to think of my rescuer so that the oppressive feeling around my stomach disappears, making way for a longing, a longing that birds can best express. I notice that my bed creaks with every movement and that this means my parents must know what I get up to in the night. I stand up on my mattress to put the rope hanging from the beam in the attic around my neck. It's too loose. I can't move the knot – it's been tied for too long – but for a moment I wrap it around my neck like a scarf, feeling the rough fibres against my skin. I imagine what it would be like to slowly suffocate, to be a swing and to know which movements are expected of you, to feel the life glide out of me, the way I feel a little bit when I'm lying on the sofa butt-naked being a soap dish.

17

'This is an initiation,' I say to Hanna, who is sitting cross-legged on my new mattress. There's a Barbie's head on the front of her pyjamas. It's got long blonde hair and pink lips. Half of the face has worn off, just like the Barbie dolls on the edge of the bath. We scrubbed off their smiles with a scourer and a bit of soap. We didn't want to give Mum the impression there was anything to smile about here, especially not now the cows are sick.

'What's that? An "initiation"?' Hanna asks. Her hair is in a bun. I don't like buns – they are much too tight and people call us 'black stockings' even more then, because the buns of the women in the church look just like balled-up socks.

'A ritual to welcome someone or something. My bed is new and this is its first night here.'

'All right,' Hanna says, 'what do I have to do then?'

'Let's start by welcoming it.'

I sweep my hair behind my ear and say loudly and clearly, 'Welcome, bed.' I lay my hand on the bottom sheet. 'And now for the ritual.'

I lie down on my belly on the mattress with my head sideways under my pillow, so that I can still look at Hanna and tell her that she's Dad and I'm Mum.

'Sure,' Hanna says.

She lies on her front next to me. I pull the pillow further over my head, pressing my nose into the mattress. It smells of the furniture shop where Mum and Dad bought it, of a new life. Hanna copies me. We lie there for a moment like shot-down crows; neither of us speaks, until I take away my pillow and look at Hanna. Her pillow is moving softly up and down. The mattress is a ship, our ship. 'For we know that if the earthly tent we live in is destroyed, we have a building from God, an eternal house in heaven, not built by human hands.' For a moment I'm reminded of the lines from Corinthians. I turn my attention back to Hanna and whisper, 'From now on this will be our operating base, the place where we are safe. Repeat after me: Dear bed, we, Jas and Hanna – Mum and Dad – are pleased to initiate you into the dark world of The Plan. Everything said here and longed for here stays here. From now on, you're one of us.' Hanna repeats the words, even though it's more like muttering because she's lying with her face in the mattress. I can hear from her voice she's finding it boring, that it won't be long before she's had enough and wants to play a different game. Even though this isn't a game, it's deadly serious.

To give her an idea of the seriousness of all of this, I rest my hand on the pillow covering the back of her head, then take both ends of it and press down hard. Hanna immediately begins to twist the lower part of her body, which means I have to use more force. Her hands thrash around, clawing into my coat. I'm stronger than her; she can't get out from under me.

'This is an initiation,' I repeat. 'Anyone coming to live here has to feel what it's like to almost suffocate, just like Matthies, to almost die. Only then can we become friends.'

When I remove the pillow, Hanna begins to sob. Her face is as red as a tomato. She greedily tries to take air. 'Idiot,' she says, 'I almost suffocated.'

'That's part of it,' I say. 'Now you know how I feel every night, and now the bed knows what can happen.'

I snuggle up to the sobbing Hanna and kiss her cheeks dry, the salty fear.

'Don't cry, little man.'

'You're frightening me, little woman,' Hanna whispers.

I slowly begin to move against my sister, as I often do with my teddy bear, and whisper, 'Our days may be longer if we show daring.'

My body gets hotter and hotter from my movements; my coat sticks to my skin. I only stop when I feel that Hanna is about to fall asleep. We don't have time for sleep now. I sit up in bed again.

'I choose the vet,' I say suddenly, trying to make my voice sound decisive. There's a moment's silence. 'He's kind and he lives on the other side and he has listened to lots of hearts, thousands,' I continue.

Hanna nods and the Barbie's head does too. 'Boudewijn de Groot is much too ambitious for girls like us,' she says.

I don't know what she means by this – girls like us. What actually makes us who we are? How can people tell by looking at us that we're all Mulders? I think that lots of girls like us exist, it's just we haven't run into them yet. Fathers and mothers meet each other one day too. And since everyone has a parent inside them, they can finally get married.

It's still a mystery how our parents found each other. The thing is, Dad's hopeless at looking. When he's lost something it's usually in his pocket, and when he goes to do the shopping he always comes back with something different than what was on the list: Mum's the wrong kind of yoghurt, but one he was happy enough with and vice versa. They've never told us about how they met – Mum never thinks it a good time. There are rarely any good times here, and if we have them we only realize afterwards. My suspicion is that it was exactly like with the cows, that one day Granny and Grandpa opened my mum's bedroom door and put Dad in with her like a bull. After that they shut the door and hey presto: there we were. From that day on, Dad called her 'wife' and Mum called him 'husband'. On good days 'little man' and 'little woman', which I found strange, as though they were worried they'd forget each other's sex, or that they belonged to each other.

I fibbed to Belle about how they met. I told her they bumped into each other in the Russian salad section of the supermarket and they'd both picked the beef version, their hands touching briefly as they reached for the tubs. According to our teacher, eye contact isn't necessary for love, touch is more than enough. I wondered then what you should call it when both of them are lacking: eye contact and touch.

Even though I think there are girls like us, I nod at Hanna. Maybe they don't smell of cows all the time, or of Dad's anger and cigarette smoke, but there's probably something you can do about that.

I briefly press my own hand to my throat. I can still feel the impression of the rope in my skin, and I think about earlier, the wobbly kitchen stepladder and the crash, and then the rope seems to be a bit tighter, a double knot under the larynx. Everything seems to stop just below the throat, just like the strip of light from Dad's tractor headlights on my duvet. We can hear him outside, spreading cow manure across the fields. He has to do it secretly because no one's allowed to muck-spread any more, to reduce the chances of contamination. We don't know what we're supposed to do with it otherwise. The planks on the muck-heap you roll the wheelbarrow along have sunk away into the muck – there isn't room for any more. Dad said that not a soul would notice if he spread it across the fields at night. There was even someone from the fallen stock company who came in a white suit, and brought dozens of rat boxes filled with blue poison to spread around the farm so that the rats couldn't pass on the foot-and-mouth. Hanna and I have to stay awake. Dad mustn't suddenly slip away from us. The strip of light moves from the foot end to beneath my chin and begins again from the bottom after a while.

'Tractor accident or a fall into the slurry pit?'

Hanna squashes up close to me beneath the duvet. Her dark hair smells of silage grass. I breathe in the smell deeply for a moment and think about how often I have cursed the cows, but now they're about to be killed, I'd like nothing more than for them to stay with us – that it will never become so quiet on the farm that we can only remember the sound of them, that only the crows in the guttering are left to keep an eye on us.

'You're as cold as frozen bread,' Hanna says. She lays her head in my armpit. She isn't joining in with the game. Maybe she's worried that if she says something it will actually happen. That like in *Lingo*, we'll be able to predict beforehand who is going to take the lucky green balls for the jackpot, and that we'll be able to predict death too.

'Better a frozen loaf than a defrosted bag of beans,' I say, and we laugh with the duvet pulled over our heads so that we won't wake up Mum. Then I move my hand from my throat to Hanna's neck. It feels warm. I feel her vertebrae through the skin.

'You're closer to the perfect thickness than me, little woman.'

'What for, my little man?' Hanna plays along.

'For a rescue.'

Hanna pushes my hand away. For a rescue you don't need the perfect thickness – it's actually the absence of perfection that means we're fragile and need to be rescued.

'Are we fragile?'

'As fragile as a blade of straw,' Hanna says.

Suddenly I realize what's going on. Everything from the recent past falls into place, all the times we were fragile, and I say, 'This is another of the plagues from Exodus, it must be. Only they're coming to us in the wrong order. Do you understand?'

'What do you mean?'

'Well, you had a nosebleed which meant water changed into blood. We've had the toad migration, head lice at school, the death of the firstborn, horseflies around the muck-heap, a grasshopper squashed by Obbe's boot, ulcers on my tongue from the fried egg, and hailstorms.'

'And you think that's why there's a cattle plague now?' Hanna asks with a shocked expression. She's laid her hand on her heart, exactly above the Barbie's ears, as though she's not allowed to hear what we're discussing. I nod slowly. After this, there's one more to come, I think to myself, and that's the worst one: darkness, total darkness, daytime eternally clad in Dad's Sunday overcoat. I don't say it out loud but we both know that there are two people in this house who long constantly for the other side, who want to cross the lake and make sacrifices there, whether Fireball gobstoppers or dead animals.

Then we hear the tractor cut out. I switch on the globe on my bedside table to combat the darkness now that the tractor lights are no longer illuminating my bedroom. Dad has finished the muck-spreading. I picture him in his overalls standing looking at the farm from a distance. The only light shining is at the front of the farm, the oval-shaped window that is lit up as though the moon has tumbled a few feet downwards half-drunk. When he looks at the farm he sees three generations of farmers. It belonged to Grandpa Mulder and he took it over from his father. After Grandpa's death, many of his cows lived on. Dad used to often tell the story of one of Grandpa's cows that also had foot-and-mouth and wouldn't drink. 'He bought a keg of herrings and forced it into the mouth of the sick animal. It didn't just get some protein but also it made it very thirsty, so that it got over the pain of the blisters and started drinking again.' I still think it's a nice story. You can't treat tongue blisters with herring any more; Grandpa's cows will be put down too. Dad's entire living will be taken from him in one go. That's how it must feel to him – Tiesey but then times the number of cows, times one hundred and eighty. He knows every cow and every calf.

Hanna disentangles herself from me – her sticky skin slowly pulls free from mine. I sometimes feel as though she's one of the celestial bodies on my ceiling that fall down from time to time, meaning that I've run out of wishes to make; although I've learned that the heavens aren't a wishing-well but a mass grave. Every star is a dead child, and the most beautiful star is Matthies – Mum taught us that. That was why I was afraid on some days that he would fall and end up in someone else's garden, and that we wouldn't notice.

'We have to get ourselves to the safe zone,' Hanna says.

'Exactly.'

'But when then, when are we going to the other side?'

My sister sounds impatient. She doesn't know much about waiting and always wants to do everything right away. I'm more cautious; that's why so many things pass me by, because things can be impatient sometimes too.

'You're good at talking but not much comes of it.'

I promise Hanna I'll try harder and say, 'When the mice are away, love will play.'

'Is that another plague? Mice?'

'No, it's protection for when the cat comes back.'

'What's love?'

I think for a moment and then say, 'Like the eggnog Granny on the less religious side used to make that was thick and golden yellow: to get it to taste nice, it was important to add all the ingredients in the right order and the right proportions.'

'Eggnog's gross,' Hanna says.

'Because you have to learn to like it. You don't like love at first either but it starts to taste better, and sweeter, with time.'

Hanna clamps on to me briefly – she holds me the way she holds her dolls, under my armpits. Mum and Dad never cuddle; that must be because otherwise some of your secrets end up sticking to the other person, like Vaseline. That's why I never spontaneously give hugs myself – I'm not sure which secrets I want to give away.

18

Dad's clogs are next to the door-mat, with blue plastic covers around their hard noses to prevent any further contamination. I wish I could stick a plastic cover over my face so I could only breathe my own breath. I wear his clogs to empty the basket of peelings onto the muck-heap, tipping them out onto cow pats white with dew, and suddenly it occurs to me that this might be the last pile of cow shit that I'll see for a while. Just like the sound of the early morning mooing, the feed concentrate mixers, the milk tank's cooling system turning on, the coo-ing of the wood pigeons attracted by the corn feed that build nests in the rafters of the barn, everything will ultimately fade into something we only recall on birthdays or when we can't get to sleep at night, and everything will be empty: the cows' stalls, the cheese shed, the feed silos, our hearts.

A trail of milk runs from the milk tank to the drain in the middle of the farmyard – Dad has opened the tap. The milk can't be sold any more, but he continues to milk the cows as though nothing's about to happen. He secures the cows between the bars, attaches the cups to their udders, then uses one of my old underpants covered in salve to clean them after-wards. I often used to feel embarrassed when Dad rubbed one of my worn-out pairs of knickers on the udders, or cleaned the milking cups with them without any kind of bashfulness – but sometimes at night I've thought about the crotch that has passed through so many other people's hands, from Obbe's to Farmer Janssen's, and that they touch me that way, with calluses and blisters on their palms. Sometimes a pair of knickers gets lost among the cows before finally getting kicked between the gratings. Dad calls them udder cloths; he doesn't see them as underpants any more. On Saturdays Mum washes the udder cloths and hangs them to dry on the washing line.

I pick a leftover apple core from the bottom of the peelings basket with my fingernail, and see out of the corner of my eye the vet squatting next to a white tent. He sinks a syringe into a jar of antibiotics and presses the needle into a calf's neck. The calf's got diarrhoea – mustard yellow has splattered against her sides, legs trembling like fence poles in the wind. Even on a Sunday the vet is here, but if we were to lie on the bathroom rug with thermometers up our bare bums, things would be put off until Monday. Mum would sing the Dutch nursery rhyme about Kortjakje – 'often is Kortjakje sick, never on Sundays but always in the week'. And I thought, Kortjakje's a coward: she can't go to school but she can go to church – that's a bit wet. It wasn't until I started secondary school that I understood. Kortjakje was frightened of everything unfamiliar. Was she bullied? Did she get tummy ache as soon as she caught sight of the school playground like I do? When school trips were announced and all the germs would go along too? Did she break peppermints on the edge of the table to stop feeling sick? Actually, you had to feel sorry for Kortjakje.

The plastic covers crunch with every step. Dad once said, 'Death always comes wearing clogs.' I hadn't understood. Why not ice skates or trainers? Now I get it: Death announces itself in most cases, but we're often the ones who don't want to see or hear it. We knew that the ice was too weak in some places, and we knew the foot-and-mouth wouldn't skip our village.

I escape to the rabbit shed where I'm safe from all the illnesses, and I press the limp carrot tops through the wire mesh. I briefly think about a rabbit's neck vertebrae. Would they crack if you twisted the head? It's a scary thought that we hold other beings' death in our hands, however small mine are – like bricklaying trowels, you can use them to build, but also to chop things to the right size with the sharp edge. I slide away the manger, let my hand descend onto the fur, and stroke Dieuwertje's ears flat to his body. The edges of his ears are hard from the cartilage in them. For a moment I close my eyes and think of the lady with the curls from children's TV. The concern in her eyes when she explains that Saint Nicholas's helpers have all got lost, and everyone's going to wake up to empty shoes next to the fireplace and the carrots next to them for his horse, gone floppy from the heat, their orange skins all wrinkly. I also think about the meringues on her table, the gingerbread men, and the way I sometimes fantasize that I'm a gingerbread man allowed to get very close to her, closer than to anyone before. She'd say, 'Jas, things grow and shrink, but people always stay the same size.' The way she'd reassure me because I can no longer reassure myself.

When I open my eyes again, I take my rabbit's right ear

between my fingers. Then I feel the place between Dieuwertje's back legs. It just happens, like with the little porcelain angels in the past. At that moment the vet comes in. I quickly withdraw my hand, bending my head to put the manger back in front of the hatch. If your head turns red it's heavier, because embarrassment has a larger mass.

'They've all got a fever, some of them even forty-two degrees,' he says. The vet washes his hands in the water barrel with a bar of green soap. There's algae on the inside of the barrel. I urgently have to clean it with a brush. I peer over the edge. The froth from the soap makes me feel sick, and when I place my hand on my lower belly I can feel my swollen intestines. They feel just like the fennel sausages from the butcher's that are impossible to digest.

The vet puts the bar of green soap between the stone feeding troughs on a wooden table. They are from earlier rabbits, most of which died of old age. Dad buried them with a spade in the furthest field where we're never allowed to play. Sometimes I worry about the rabbits there, whether their teeth might carry on growing a long time after death and stick out of the ground where a cow could get caught on them, or worse, my dad. That's why I give Dieuwertje a lot of tops, and I pick buckets of grass for him so that his teeth don't grow too long and he's got enough to chew on.

'Why can't they get better? Children get better again when they have a fever, don't they?'

The vet dries his hands on an old tea-towel and hangs it back on a hook on the wall of the shed. 'It's too infectious, and you can't sell any of the meat or the milk. You'd only make a loss then.'

I nod, even though I don't get it. Isn't it a greater loss this way? All those steaming bodies we love so much will soon be killed. It's like with the Jewish people, only they were hated, and then you die sooner than when you go to your grave out of love and powerlessness.

The vet turns a feed bucket upside down and sits on it. His black curls hang like party streamers around his face. I feel like I'm all legs now I tower over him. It's difficult anyway to know what to do with the extra centimetres only noted in friendship books. We used to mark them on the door-post. Dad would fetch his tape measure and a pencil, and score a line in the wood at the place your head reached. When Matthies didn't come home, he painted the door-post olive green; the same green as the shutters at the front of the house that have been kept shut all the time recently – no one is allowed to see us growing up.

'It's a sorry business.' He sighs as he turns the palms of his hands upwards. You can see the blisters on the inside. They're just like the air cushions in the envelopes Dad sent off vials of bull sperm in, which sometimes stood, lukewarm, among the breakfast things on the table. In the winter I'd hold them to my cheek when I'd just got up and the cold of the floor had reached my cheeks via my toes – hearing Mum in the background spitting on the little windows in the wood-stove before polishing them with a piece of kitchen roll. She always did that before Dad was allowed to put in the kindling, which he lit with some old newspaper. She said you could feel more heat if you could see the flames fighting for a piece of wood.

Mum didn't like me holding the vials to my cheeks – she said it was unsavoury. She said calves were forged from it, like Granny made new candles from the candlewax that everyone in the village saved for her. But the stuff in the vials was whitish, sometimes watery, sometimes very thick. One time I secretly took some up to my bedroom. Hanna insisted we open the vial once it had cooled down and we could no longer warm ourselves up with it. When the vial got as cold as our bodies, we each dipped our little fingers in it, and, counting to three, stuck it in our mouths. It tasted insipid and salty. In the evening hours we fantasized that calves would come out of us, until the plan to find a rescuer blossomed in our minds and we felt bigger than ever: we'd turn into liquid in the rescuer's hands, just as fluid as the semen in the test tubes.

'Is your coat comfortable?'

It's a while before I can answer. My thoughts are still taken up with the blisters on his palms.

'Yes, very.'

'Not too hot?'

'Not too hot.'

'Do you get teased about it?'

I shrug. I'm good at thinking of answers but less good at saying them. Every answer gives rise to an observation. I don't like observations. They're as persistent as when a butter brush covered in cheese wax falls onto your clothes – almost impossible to wash out.

The vet smiles. I only notice now that he has the widest nostrils I've ever seen, which must mean he spends a lot of time picking his nose. It creates a bond I mustn't forget. There's a stethoscope around his neck. For a moment I imagine the cold metal on my chest and him listening to everything moving inside me and changing. The vet drawing a worried frown across his forehead and pushing his thumb and index finger between my jaws to feed me, just like the calf. He'd keep me warm under his green dust-coat.

'Do you miss your brother?' he asks suddenly. He lays his hand around my lower leg and gently squeezes. Maybe he's feeling whether I'm sick: you can tell from the fleshiness of calves' legs how healthy they are. He rubs his hand softly back and forth, which makes the skin under the denim grow hot, and the warmth spreads through my whole body like the thought of homecoming and hot chocolate on a cold winter's day, a thought that is quite a lot less warm by the time you get home. I stare at his neatly trimmed fingernails. You can see the impression of a ring around his ring finger – the skin is lighter there. Loved ones always remain visible in your heart or under your skin, the way my chest seems like it will split when my mum sits on the edge of my bed and asks in a porcelain voice whether I love her and I reply, 'From hell to heaven.' Sometimes I hear my ribcage crack and I'm afraid I'll split for good.

'Yes, I miss him,' I whisper.

It's the first time anyone's asked me whether I miss Matthies. Not a pat on the head or a pinch of the cheek but a question.

Not: how are your parents doing? How are the cows doing? But: how are you doing? I stare at my shoes.

When I look at the vet, he suddenly appears cast down, the way Mum often looks, as though she's been carrying a glass of water on top of her head to the other side all day without spilling a drop. That's why I say, 'But I'm doing so well I may even speak of happiness, praise the Lord until the knees of my jeans are replaced by patches featuring comic-book characters.'

The vet laughs. 'You know you're the prettiest girl I've ever seen?'

I feel my cheeks fill with colour like the circles after multiple-choice questions. I don't know how many girls he's seen in his life but I still feel flattered. Someone finds me pretty. Even with my faded coat that's beginning to fray at the seams. I don't know how to respond. Multiple-choice questions often have traps, according to my teacher, because they all contain part of the reality and at the same time are lies. The vet hides his stethoscope under his shirt. Before he goes out, he winks at me. 'To make peace,' Mum sometimes says when Dad does that to her. She says it angrily because peace died out long ago. Still, something sears inside my ribcage, something different than inside my heart, which often blazes like a bramble bush.

19

We are growing up with the Word, but words are lacking more and more frequently at the farm. Now it's long past coffee time and yet we're still sitting silently in the kitchen, nodding our heads at unasked questions. The vet is sitting in Dad's place at the head of the table. He takes his coffee black, I take my squash dark. Like every afternoon before feeding time, Dad has set off on his bike for the lake to see whether he's missed anything, a blue clothes peg on his left trouser leg so that it doesn't flap into the spokes. There's a lot Dad misses. He looks at the ground or up at the sky more than at the things at eye height. At my current size I'm right between those things, and I'll either have to make myself bigger or smaller to be seen by him. Some days I watch him through the kitchen window until he's just a speck on top of the dike, a bird fallen from its flock. In the first weeks after my brother's death, I kept expecting him to be brought back on the carrier of Dad's bike, albeit frozen to the bone. Then everything would be all right again. Now I know Dad always returns with an empty carrier and that Matthies will never come back, just like Jesus will never descend on a cloud.

There's silence around the table. There's less talk in general and that's why most of the conversations only take place inside my head. I'll have long chats with the Jewish people in the basement and ask them how they'd describe my mother's state of mind, whether they happen to have seen her eat anything recently, whether they think that she'll just drop down dead one day, like my toads that keep refusing to mate. I fantasize there's a laid table in the middle of the basement between the shelves of flour packets and pots of gherkins, with Mum's favourite nuts in those greasy packets – although she only likes whole nuts, not the half ones, which she gives to Dad. And she has put on her favourite dress, the sea blue one with daisies on it. I ask the Jewish people whether they'll say the Song of Songs for her because she finds that one so lovely, and whether they'll take care of her, in happiness or in adversity.

The conversations about my dad are different. They're often about his bottom drawer. I hope his new family will talk back to him more if he leaves us, that someone will dare to challenge him and doubt him, the way we sometimes doubt God. Sometimes I even hope that someone will get angry with him and say, 'Your ears are full of mangels, you can only hear yourself, and that traffic-barrier arm that's so loose, we'll have to repair it, there shouldn't be any hinges.' That would be nice.

Obbe sticks his tongue out at me. Every time I look at him he sticks out his tongue, which is brown from the chocolate meringue biscuits they gave us with our squash. I took mine apart so I could scrape off the white cream with my teeth. I don't realize that my eyes are filled with tears until the vet winks at me. I think about the science lesson we had at school about Neil Armstrong, the first man on the moon, about the way the moon must have felt when someone took the trouble to come closer by for the first time in its existence. Maybe the vet's an astronaut too and someone will finally take the trouble to see how much life is left in me. I'm hoping it will be a good conversation. Only I'm not sure what a good conversation would consist of. It will have to contain the word 'good', that seems clear to me. And I mustn't forget to look the other person in the eye for a long time, because people who look away too often have secrets to hide, and secrets are always hidden in the deep-freeze compartment of your head, like containers of minced meat in the freezer. As soon as you take them out and leave them unattended, they go off.

'All the animals have got the runs. It can't get much worse,' the vet says in an attempt to break the silence. Mum has balled her hands into fists. They lie on the table like rolled-up hedgehogs. I'd told Hanna they were hibernating but that soon she was sure to feel along the veins of our jaws, the way she sometimes did with her index finger before scraping the dried milk from the corners of our mouths.

Then the hall door opens and Dad comes into the kitchen. He unzips his skipper's jersey and throws a bag of frozen bread onto the work counter. He stands next to the table and eats his meringue biscuits with large bites.

'They're coming tomorrow around coffee time,' the vet says.

Dad thumps the table. Mum's biscuit bounces up slightly, and she lays her hand protectively over it – if only I was a meringue biscuit, I'd fit perfectly inside the bowl of her hand.

'What have we done to deserve this?' Mum asks. She shunts her chair back and goes to the counter. Dad pinches his septum, his fingers like a bread clip so that he won't dry out by starting to cry.

'Upstairs, all of you,' is all he says. 'Now.'

Obbe gestures at the loft. We follow him up to his room – his curtains are still completely closed. This afternoon, the teacher said at the end of the science lesson that if you breathe through your nose, everything gets filtered by the little hairs in it. If you breathe through your mouth everything gets right inside you, you can't stop illnesses getting in. Belle had started breathing loudly through her mouth, which made everyone laugh. I'd only looked at her anxiously: if Belle got sick, it would mean the end of our friendship. Now I only breathe through my nose; I keep my lips firmly sealed. I only open them to say something, even though that's less often now.

'You have to drop your trousers, Hanna.'

'Why?' I ask.

'Because it's a matter of life or death.'

'Does Dad need more pants for the cows?'

I think about my own. Maybe Mum found the knickers under my bed and she saw that they were yellow and hard from the dried-up piss. Obbe raises his eyebrows as though I'm the one asking funny questions. Then he shakes his head.

'I know something fun to do.'

'Not about death again?' Hanna asks.

'No. Not about death. It's a game.'

Hanna nods eagerly. She loves games. She often plays

Monopoly on her own on the carpet in the sitting room.

'Then you have to take off your knickers and go and lie on the bed.'

Before I can ask what his plan is, Hanna's taken off her trousers and her pants are around her ankles. I look at the slit between her legs. It doesn't look like the custard bun Obbe was talking about. More like the slug Obbe once cut open behind the boot-jack with his penknife, that slime came out of.

He sits on the bed next to Hanna. 'Now close your eyes and spread your legs.'

'You're peeking,' I say.

'Am not,' Hanna says.

'I saw your eyelashes quiver.'

'That's the draught,' Hanna says.

Just to be sure, I lay my hand over her eyes and feel her eyelashes tickling my skin. I watch Obbe take a can of Coke and begin to shake it around wildly. Then he holds the can to her slit and forces her legs as wide open as possible, affording me a view of the pinkish flesh. He shakes the can a few more times then holds it as close as possible to the opening. Suddenly he opens the ring pull and the Coke squirts in a straight line into her flesh. Hanna's hips jerk, she cries out. But what I see in her eyes when I take away my hand in shock is not something I know. Not pain but more like peace. She giggles. Obbe shakes a second can and repeats the procedure. Hanna's eyes grow bigger, her lips press damply against my palm, she moans quietly.

'Does it hurt?'

'No, it feels nice.'

Then Obbe breaks the ring pull off one of the cans and lays it on the little pink ball sticking out from the slit. He gives it a quick jerk as though he wants to open her like a can of Coke. Hanna moans louder now and writhes across the duvet.

'Stop, Obbe. You're hurting her!' I say. My sister lies on the pillow, sweating and wet from the fizzy drink. Obbe is sweating too. He picks up the half-empty Coke cans from the floor and gives me one. I drink it greedily and see over the top of it that Hanna's about to put her knickers back on.

'Wait a minute,' Obbe says, 'you have to keep something safe for us.' He gets the bin out from beneath his desk, empties it onto the floor and fishes out dozens of Coke ring pulls from among the failed test papers. Then he pushes them into Hanna one by one.

'Otherwise Mum and Dad will notice that you two have been stealing cans,' he says. Hanna doesn't complain. She seems like someone else all of a sudden. She almost looks relieved, even though we'd promised each other we'd feel eternally burdened to take the weight off our parents. I look at her angrily. 'Mum and Dad don't love you.' It's out before I realize it. She sticks out her tongue. But I see the relief slowly fading from her eyes, her pupils becoming smaller. I quickly rest my hand on her shoulder and say that it was a joke. We all want Mum and Dad's love.

'We'll have to make more sacrifices,' Obbe says. He sits down at his computer which springs buzzing to life. I don't know what kind of sacrifice we've just made but I daren't ask any more questions, afraid he'll come up with a new mission. Hanna sits down next to him on a folding chair. They both act as though nothing happened, and maybe that's the case and I'm worrying unnecessarily, the way I worry about night falling every time. It's just part of the process. However afraid I am of the dark, in the end it always gets light again – like now, even though the light's artificial, the light of the screen, but still the darkness of just then has largely disappeared. I pick up a forgotten ring pull and put it in my coat pocket with the whiskers and the shards of my piggy bank. We have to be careful with Hanna – she could betray us with every step – you can probably hear the tinkle of ring pulls inside her body, the way they sometimes break off when you're drinking and fall into the can and can be heard with every sip. I look at my brother and sister's backs. It suddenly dawns on me that I can no longer hear the fluttering of butterfly wings against the lids of the cottage cheese tubs. A line from Matthew springs to mind: 'If your brother sins against you, go and tell him his fault between you and him alone. If he hears you, you have gained your brother.' Obbe and I really need to talk. And even though it's never just the two of us but three, I have to make sure that Hanna's ears are closed, just for a moment.

After dinner, I quickly slip outside, step over the red ribbon around the cowshed, and hold my hand in front of my mouth like a paper face mask as I go in. Since no doors or stable windows are allowed to be open, there's a strong whiff of ammonia, mixed with the smell of silage. I run the manure shovel across the gratings behind the cows and pile up the runny shit in the middle. The slurry falls between the gratings – I hear it ending up in the sub-basement. You have to keep the shovel at a good angle from your body otherwise it keeps getting stuck between the gaps. From time to time, I push against a cow's hoofs to tell it to move. Sometimes you have to do it more roughly or they just ignore you. I walk along behind the gutter to the dry cows, which stand there chewing amiably as though unmoved by the fact that this is their last meal. I let Beatrix lick my hand. She's a black cow with a white head and brown patches around her eyes – all cows have blue eyes because they have an extra layer that reflects the light. In the winter I do that with the calves – I let them suck on my frozen fingers until they're totally vacuum-packed, like the sadness inside my chest. Every time I hear that sucking sound it makes me think of that story of Obbe's. He said that Janssen's son didn't put his fingers in there but something else, but those were just stories that went around the village like the stink of muck-spreading once a month, and it was better to turn your nose up at them.

I let the cow lick my hand again. First you have to gain their trust and only then do you strike without mercy, that's what Obbe taught me. That was how he'd caught the butterflies for his collection. I let my hand glide from her head along the backbone to the place between her hip bone and tail. Along with their ears, it's the place cows like being touched the most. Every evening I search for a similar place on my own body with a torch, but I don't find anything worth stroking, anything that calms me down or makes me breathe faster. As if of its own accord, my hand glides further from her hip bone towards her tail. I can see her bum hole opening and closing like the mouth of a hungry baby. Without thinking about it, I push my finger into the cow's bum hole. It's warm and spacious. Underneath it I can see something hanging that does indeed look like the custard bun Obbe was talking about, but then pinker, with a tuft of hair at the end of it. Between the two, I feel another hole, this one narrow and soft. It has to be the cow's cunt, I think. Immediately she clenches her hips and holds her tail close to her, shifting her leg back restlessly. Hanna flashes through my mind and I move my finger in and out, quicker and quicker until it begins to get boring. I put my other hand in my coat pocket and all of a sudden I feel the cheese scoop between the shards of piggy bank, the Coke ring pulls and Dieuwertje's whiskers. I'd forgotten about taking it from the cheese shed. I get it out of my coat pocket and turn it a few times in the air to examine it from all angles. An idea pops into my head. A rescuer needs to be tested, the way divers need to get a diving licence. This is going to be a test for the vet, because if he can save a cow from a roving cheese scoop, he can save a girl's roving heart too. I squeeze my eyes into slits in anticipation of the pain Beatrix must feel, and then carefully insert the cheese scoop into her bum hole. I press harder and harder so that her bum hole becomes wider and shapes itself around the scoop, until I can go no deeper. My hand and wrist completely inside the cow, I let go and pull my arm back. It's covered in shit. I pat her warm flank, the way my dad patted my lower leg when he was finished with the soap.

'There's something wrong with Beatrix,' I say to the vet after I've cleaned my arm with the stuff my mum uses to clean the milking pails, rinsed the soles of my wellies with the hose and turned off the tap.

'I'll go take a look,' he says, walking to the cowshed. When he returns a few moments later, I can't make out anything in his gaze. No worried frown between the eyes, no grim set to his mouth.

'Well?' I ask.

'She's royalty, you know. They always make a song and a dance when they have a bit of pain. Nothing wrong there, that animal is as healthy as can be, and just to think that the poor creature is going to be put down tomorrow. This foot-and-mouth is an abomination in God's eyes.'

I smile at him, the way the TV lady from *Lingo* smiles when someone has failed to grab the green ball.

20

'The first cow is going down now,' Mum says. She's standing next to the cowshed door with a thermos flask in each hand – one of them has got TEA written on it in waterproof marker, the other COFFEE. As though she can keep her balance this way. A packet of pink-glazed cakes is clamped under her arm. Her voice sounds hoarse. I follow her into the cowshed, and at that very moment the first cows fall down dead on the gratings, and their unwieldy bodies are pulled along the ground by their back legs to the grab loader, which picks them up like cuddly toys at the fair and drops them into the truck. Two bovines stand under the rotating cattle brush chewing idly, their noses covered in thick scabs. They stare feverishly at their fellows whose legs are giving way, or who are slipping and smacking down onto the floor blocks in the stalls. Some of the calves are still alive as they go into the carcass-disposal truck, others get a stud shot into their foreheads with a bolt stunner. The moaning and the sound of banging against the side of the truck causes small cracks under my skin, and my body begins to feel feverish. It's no longer enough to pull my collar up to my nose and chew on my coat cords. Even Maxima, Jewel and Blaze are killed without remorse. They collapse and are gone, folded up like empty milk cartons and thrown into the container.

Suddenly I hear Dad shouting. He's standing with Obbe in the feed section among the men in blue-green overalls wearing bathing caps and face masks. At the top of his voice he quotes Psalm 35, verse 1, until it becomes a scream, spittle gathering at the corners of his mouth. 'Contend Lord, with those who contend with me; fight against those who fight against me. Take up shield and armour; arise and come to my aid. Brandish spear and javelin against those who pursue me.' Saliva drips slowly down his chin onto the floor in the feed section. I concentrate on the drops, on the sadness trickling out of him, like the runny manure and the blood from the dead cows that flow between the ridges of the tiles and end up in the drain, mixing with the milk from the cooling tank.

The calves were the first to go, so that they didn't have to see their mothers being brutally murdered. In protest, Obbe has hung the youngest calf in the yard upside down by its leg from the branch of a tree, tongue dangling from its mouth. Each farmer in the village has hung up one of his dead cows or pigs next to their drive. Some of them have also sawn down a tree and laid the trunk across the farm track so that the disposal service can't get through. After that the man in the white suit, the one who had put the rat poison boxes around the farm previously, took the corpses away and carefully put them in the disposal service's van. The same care was missing now; he just tossed the poison pellets into the black container.

'Thou shalt not kill,' Dad cries. He's standing next to a cow that used to belong to Grandpa and is now lying on the floor with its legs in the air. There are broken-off tails on the gratings. Horns. Chunks of hoof.

'Murderers! Hitler!' Obbe shouts afterwards. I think about the Jewish people who met their fate like hunted-down cattle, about Hitler who was so terrified of illnesses that he started to see people as bacteria, as something you can easily stamp out. The teacher told us during the history lesson that Hitler had fallen through ice when he was four and had been saved by a priest, that some people can fall through ice and it's better if they're not rescued. I wondered then why a bad person like Hitler could be saved and not my brother. Why the cows had to die while they hadn't done anything wrong.

And I see the hate in Obbe's eyes as he begins to hit one of the men in masks. Farmer Evertsen and Farmer Janssen pull him back by his overalls and try to calm him down, but he tears himself away and runs out of the cowshed, past Mum, who is still riveted to the door opening holding the two thermos flasks. If I take one from her hand, she'll probably collapse to the ground just as hard as the dry cows whose turn it is now. The stench of death sticks in my throat, like a chunk of congealed protein powder. I try to gulp it down and blink away the calves in the corners of my eyes like thunderbugs, until they begin to smart and I can only get rid of them with tears. Every loss contains all previous attempts to hang on to something you didn't want to lose but had to let go of anyway, from a marble bag filled with the most beautiful marbles and rare shooters, to my brother. We find ourselves in loss and we are who we are – vulnerable beings, like stripped starling chicks that fall naked from their nests and hope they'll be picked up again. I cry for the cows, I cry for the three kings – out of pity, and then for my ridiculous self, wrapped in a coat of anxiety, wiping the tears away quickly again. I have to go and tell Hanna we can't go to the other side for the time being. We can't leave Mum and Dad behind like this. What's going to become of them when the cows have gone?

I hold my hand in front of my mouth to combat the smell and keep whispering, 'My Very Educated Mother Just Served Us Nachos, My Very Educated Mother Just Served Us Nachos, My Very Educated Mother Just Served Us Nachos.' It doesn't help, I don't calm down. I look at my dad; he's holding a pitchfork that he points angrily at the men every now and again. If only they were bales of hay or silage grass, I think to myself, then we'd be able to lift them up together and move them, or wrap them in green plastic and put them out in the fields for the view, and then let them dry out. One of the men, the tallest of the group, is standing next to the cowshed door with Mum, eating a pink iced cake; his face mask dangles under his chin like a sick bag. He scrapes the icing off with his front teeth and only after he's done that does he eat the cake, while around him cows are flying into walls and bullets are being fired into heads. When he whisks a second cake out of the packet and carefully strips it of its icing, the cracks in my skin seem to grow bigger – this is how a caterpillar must feel when it's about to become a butterfly, but it has something that keeps holding it back, even though it can see the cracks forming around it, the light of freedom falling through them

– and my heart begins to beat so wildly behind my ribs that I'm afraid for a moment that the entire village can hear it, the way I'm sometimes afraid they'll hear in the night when I'm lying on my bear, moving past the darkness. I wish I could scream and kick the men in their stomachs or tie two face masks in front of their eyes so they can't see the cows any more, only the darkness of their deeds, that are black and sticky and will cling to them with every step they take. I'd drag their stupid heads through the stained stalls and then grab them by their legs with the grab loader and drop them above the container.

Dad drops the fork and raises his head to the rafters of the shed, where doves are flying up with every bang. Their feathers are dirty – peace always comes in white, but this is war. And I briefly hope that Dad will come to me and pull me tightly to him, so that the press studs of his overalls press into my cheek, so that I can lose myself in the longing to cling on to him tightly, but the only thing I can lose myself in now is loss itself.

When I go outside, I see Obbe taking off his disposable overalls. He throws them into the protest fire built from dried reeds that is burning in the field next to the muck-heap, with a handful of lost farmers standing around it. If only we could take off our bodies in the same way, freed of the dirt upon us.

PART III

I

All of a sudden, Obbe presses his mouth to my ear and whispers slowly and emphatically: 'God-damm-it.' A strip of light falls through the chink in the curtains onto his forehead. The red gash from the banging has become a scar, like the seam of my sock. I squeeze my eyes shut and feel his warm toothpaste breath containing the forbidden word, which he repeats, disappear into the vortex of my eardrum. Lucky they're my ears and not my parents', because that is the worst word we can say and think and no one on the farm has ever said it before. I feel myself getting sad, more for God than for myself. He can't help the way things are going here and yet His name is being taken in vain. The more he says the word, the more I shrink under my covers.

'You used the *Sims* password.' Obbe hovers over me in his striped pyjamas. His hands rest on either side of my pillow.

'Just the once,' I say quietly.

'Not true – your avatars never have to work again because they're filthy rich. You've been cheating. You should have asked my permission first, Goddammit!'

I smell Dad's aftershave: a mixture of cinnamon and walnut. I'll have to satisfy Obbe in the same way as Dad, I decide, before instinctively rolling onto my belly, and pulling down my pyjamas and knickers to bare my bum. Obbe takes his mouth away from next to my ear and says, 'What are you doing?'

'You have to put your finger in my bum hole.'

'But that's dirty!'

'Dad does it, though, so that I can poo every day. You make a tunnel ready, you know, like we made tunnels for the ants we put in the aquarium filled with sand? It'll only take a moment.'

Obbe rolls up his shirt-sleeves, carefully parts my buttocks as though they're an animal encyclopaedia he's taking good care of and that only he is allowed to touch, and pushes in his index finger as though pointing out a rare creature, a cockatoo for example.

'Doesn't it hurt?'

'No,' I say, trying to hold back the tears by clenching my jaws. I don't tell him he's supposed to push in some Sunlight green soap, which isn't green at all but a kind of yellowish brown. I don't want my lips to start frothing, like some of the cows that had foot-and-mouth. Dad is forgetting to do it more and more often. Someone has to take over the job so that I don't have to go to the doctor or be exterminated.

Obbe pushes in his finger as far as he can.

'Don't you dare do a fart,' he says.

When I look back, I see that his pyjama bottoms are tight around his crotch. I think about the last time his willy performed a trick, and wonder how many fingers' worth of thickness he'd be, whether we could put that in to make the tunnel even bigger. But I don't mention it, not now: asking questions creates expectations and I don't know if I can live up to them. When the teacher asks me a question, my thoughts sometimes seem to have been Tippexed away. And I mustn't make Obbe even angrier. Imagine if his swearing woke up Mum and Dad. Suddenly Obbe begins to move his finger backwards and forwards, faster and faster as though he wants to give the rare creature in his collection a poke so that it will come to life. My hips slowly begin to move up and down: I want to run away and stay at the same time. I want to sink and I want to stay afloat. A snowy landscape appears around me.

'Do you know how long eels live?'

'No,' I whisper. There's no reason to be whispering but my voice becomes quieter and hoarser on its own. My mouth fills with saliva. I briefly think about my toads. They're sitting on top of each other and call each other 'little man' and 'little woman'. Their long tongues swing around each other, as though they're fighting for the same imaginary bluebottle. Does a toad have a willy? And can it pull it back into its sheath like a bull can, the way Obbe's wooden revolver can go back into its holster?

'They can live to be eighty-eight and they've got three enemies: cormorants, maw-worms and fishermen.'

Obbe abruptly withdraws his finger from my bum hole. The snowy landscape begins to melt. Alongside relief I also feel disappointment inside my chest, as though he's pushed me back into my pitch-black mind – a torch that is shone onto you to give you a stage but then switched off again. I'm spending more and more time escaping the farm by lying on my belly moving my crotch against my teddy bear, making my bed slats squeak, harder and harder until I can no longer hear it, until I've got rid of all of the day's tension and all I can hear is the whooshing in my ears, the sea so much closer than during the day.

'Mum and Dad are forty-five and they don't have any enemies.'

'That doesn't mean anything,' I reply, as I pull my knickers and pyjama bottoms back up. I hope Dad won't be angry I've taken his job away from him, even though he failed to do it himself and has stopped touching me completely. I don't want to be even more of a burden to him.

'No, it doesn't mean anything,' Obbe says.

He swallows audibly a couple of times, pretending not to be bothered by it, or that he's not scared we're going to lose them even sooner than ourselves. He makes a face as he looks at his index finger. He has a quick sniff.

'That's what a secret smells like,' he says.

'You're gross.'

'Don't say anything to Mum and Dad, otherwise I'll murder Dieuwertje and pull that stupid coat off you, Goddammit.' Obbe pushes me away from him and strides out of my bedroom. I hear him go downstairs where he opens kitchen cupboards, then slams them shut again. Now the cows have gone we no longer have breakfast at a fixed time. Sometimes there isn't any breakfast to be had, just some dry crackers and instant porridge. Dad forgets to fetch bread on Wednesdays from the baker in the village. Or he's suddenly become afraid of the mould. We have to stand in front of him in the afternoons. He'll be sitting in his smoking chair next to the window with his right leg crossed over his left, which doesn't suit him – legs wide apart is better – in his hand the blue fountain pen from his accounts book. We're the new stock and we have to be checked for potential illnesses; we have to show our bare backs like the undersides of our egg cakes. Dad inspects us for blue and white spots.

'Promise me you won't die,' he says, and we nod and don't mention the hunger in our bellies or the fact you can die of that too. In the evenings we get tinned soup with meatballs and extra vermicelli that Mum breaks above the pan. That way it seems as though she's still cooked for us. Some of the vermicelli strands float like lifebuoys in the soup bowls decorated with hens.

I move my legs a bit under the dinosaur duvet cover until they no longer feel heavy but their normal weight, even though I don't know exactly how legs are supposed to feel, probably weightless. Everything that's part of you is weightless and the things that are alien feel heavy. Obbe's toothpaste breath mixed with the swear-word hangs around me like a demanding milk customer: they're not satisfied with anything and stride into other people's farmyards as though they own them, heads held high. I push off the duvet and cross the landing to Hanna's room. She sleeps at the end of the corridor, her bedroom door always open a chink. She insists the landing light stays on the whole time. Hanna thinks that burglars are attracted to lamps like moths and that Dad could chase them outside again in the morning.

I gently push open her door. My sister is already awake and is lying reading a picture book. We read a lot – we like heroes and carry them with us inside our heads, continuing their story there, but now with a leading role for ourselves. One day I'll be Mum's hero so that Hanna and I can go to the other side with peace of mind. Then I'll free the toads and the Jewish people, and buy my dad a cowshed full of brand-new blazed cows, and get rid of all the ropes as well as the feed silo. No heights any more, no temptations.

'Obbe swore. He said G-d-it,' I whisper as I sit down on the foot of the bed. Hanna's eyes widen. She puts her picture book down.

'If Dad hears that . . .' she says. There's sleep in the corners of her eyes. I could wipe it away with my little finger, the way Obbe and I once got a snail out of its shell with a filling knife and smeared the slimy creature onto the tiles.

'I know. We have to do something . . . Maybe we should tell Mum that Obbe's being mean? Remember when Evertsen wanted to get rid of his dog? He said it was a nasty animal and a week later it was put down,' I say.

'Obbe's not a dog, you idiot.'

'But he is mean and nasty.'

'Yes, but we have to give him something. Something more like a bone than an injection – to keep him quiet,' Hanna says.

'What then?'

'An animal.'

'Dead or alive?'

'Dead. That's what he wants.'

'That's not nice for the poor creature. I'll have a talk with him first,' I say.

'Don't say anything stupid, you'll just make him angry. And we have to talk about The Plan. I don't want to stay here much longer.'

I think about the vet – he didn't manage to find the cheese scoop so it's impossible he'll be able to save my heart. I don't mention it – there are more important things going on.

Hanna takes a bag of Fireballs from her bedside table. There's a cartoon character with flames coming out of its mouth on the front. She tears open the plastic and gives me a red ball. I put it in my mouth and suck. As soon as it gets too hot, I take it out of my mouth again. It keeps changing colour – from red to orange to yellow.

'Once we're on the other side and have been saved, we might set up a Fireball factory. We can swim laps through the red balls every day,' Hanna continues. She moves her gobstopper from cheek to cheek. We buy them in the little sweet-shop at the back of the village on the Karnemelkseweg. The lady who sells the sweets always wears the same cute white apron and has black uncombed hair that sticks out all over the place. Everyone calls her 'the Witch'. Some horrible stories about her are doing the rounds. According to Belle, she turns stray cats into cat-shaped liquorice sweets and children who try to steal sweets into toffee. All the children in the village still buy their sweets from her, though.

Dad doesn't actually allow us to buy them. 'She's a heathen

disguised as a God-fearing Christian. I sometimes see her trimming her hedge on a Sunday.' One time I'd crept round the back with Belle and we'd peeked into her garden over the hedge. It was so overgrown the plants could touch the stars. I scared her by saying that the Witch secretly visited anyone in the night who peeked into her garden, and she could turn you into a plant she'd later re-pot outside her back door.

As well as sweets, the shop also sells stationery and magazines with tractors on the cover or naked women. A bell tinkles when the door opens which is unnecessary because her husband, who wears a dust-coat as white as his face, his body as slender as a whippet's, is always standing behind the counter watching everyone who comes in. His eyes stick to you like magnets. Next to him there's a parrot in a cage. Mr and Mrs van Luik talk all the time to that brightly coloured bird, though it's more like complaining about the new ballpoint pens that haven't arrived, the liquorice laces that have dried out which you could break a window with, the weather that is too hot or too cold or too stuffy.

'You have to go now otherwise Mum and Dad will wake up,' Hanna says. I nod and bite the Fireball into chewing gum. The sweet cinnamon taste fills my mouth. Hanna picks up her picture book and pretends to read on, but I can see she's no longer able to concentrate on the words. The words are dancing the way they often dance inside my head, finding it harder and harder to form an orderly queue and come out of my mouth.

2

Two forks lie with their teeth through each other in the farmyard, like hands praying. Obbe is nowhere to be seen. I look for him in the empty stalls which smell of dried blood and where the odd broken-off tail is stuck to the ground. No one has been here since the cows were taken. I carry on to the vegetable patch and see my brother collapsed on the ground next to his beetroot plants. His shoulders are shaking. I watch from a distance as he cradles a dead beetroot in his arms and angrily pushes his finger into the soil to plant new seeds, the way he just did between my buttocks. This time he pushes more roughly. Obbe's other hand strokes the leaves of the beetroot plant – on good days he will also stroke a chicken's plumage. He has had no influence on what has happened here: Death has come. I wrap my arms around my coat. It's only November but it froze last night already.

Obbe suddenly pushes himself up, looks back and sees me standing here. I'm reminded of a line from Exodus: 'If you see the donkey of someone who hates you fallen down under its load, do not leave it there; be sure you help them with it.' I smile at Obbe to show I have come in peace, that I always come in peace, even though I sometimes long to come with war in mind, the same way I sometimes take a broken toy to the vegetable patch and bury it among the red onions, next to the one-winged angel. I know, though, that we'd have to come from a better family to be able to bury our childhood – we'd have to lie under a layer of earth ourselves, but the time isn't ripe for that yet. We still have our missions which have been keeping us on our feet until now, even though Obbe's half lying on the damp earth, looking back at me, unmoved. I shuffle my welly awkwardly back and forth over the ground and become aware of the goose bumps on my arms. The elastic of my pyjama bottoms is baggy around my waist. Obbe jumps to his feet; there's still a trace of tears on his face. He pats the mud from his striped pyjamas. The things that move us will finally cause us to fall apart like a chunk of crumbly cheese.

Obbe stands before me. His bushy eyebrows are like strips of barbed wire above his eyes, a warning not to come any closer. He rubs his cheeks dry with the back of his hand, holding in his other a couple of wilted plants. The beetroots at their tips are wrinkled and display traces of mould. The leaves are brown.

'What you just saw never happened,' he whispers.

I nod briefly and look at the coffee grounds around the cauliflowers to keep away pests. Are Mum and Dad the pests that keep eating away at us? Obbe turns around. There's wet soil on his pyjama top. For the first time I imagine digging a hole in the vegetable garden, laying Obbe in it and closing it, raking it over and letting the frost come over it like you do with kale, hoping it makes things better. I'd get a better version I could call a brother and whom I'd give my milk biscuits to when the drawer gets too full to fit any more. A brother I don't have to be ashamed of any more in the school playground when he gets into a scrap again or when he shows off in the bike sheds, putting out his Lucky Strike cigarettes on a garden spider.

'Do not curse if God does not curse; do not swear when the Lord does not swear.'

Obbe stops at the wheelbarrow that Mum had lain in and which now has rainwater in the bottom. I angrily kick at the wheelbarrow with my foot so that it tips over, and the water streams out onto the earth and around the ankles of Obbe's wellies. Matthies's rusty go-kart lies next to the wheelbarrow. The red side seat has faded and there's a big tear in its back. No one has driven it since his death. Obbe smiles.

'You're always so good, aren't you?'

'I just don't want you to swear – do you want Mum and Dad to die or something?'

'They're already dead.' Obbe makes a cutting motion across his throat with his finger. 'And you're going to die soon too.'

'You're making things up,' I say.

'Unless you make a sacrifice.'

'Why a sacrifice?'

'When the time's right, I'll show you.'

'But when will the time be right?'

'When it's the colour of a good beef tomato. If you leave them on the vine too long, they split and burst open and the mould gets in. It's about finding the right moment,' Obbe says, walking away from me with the beetroot plants clamped under his arm. They leave mud patches on his pyjamas.

3

One by one, Dad puts the silver cows into a binbag and pulls the yellow loops at the sides towards each other – the opening looks like a cow's bum, with its sphincter clenching. He pauses for a moment, holding the binbag. I look at him over the top of my nature book, at his washed hair which he has combed neatly into a side parting, making lines with the teeth of the comb like a ploughed field, at his lip which has a dent in it like an ashtray – there's a cigarette stuck in it now. The side parting makes him look a bit like Hitler, but I don't say so. Dad might get the idea that I hate him too, and then he'd walk even more crookedly, closer to the soil, closer to Matthies's double grave where there's still room for one more family member – 'first come first served,' Mum once said. I hope they don't make a competition of it.

On both the day of his death and his birthday we go to the graveyard next to the Reformed church where death smells of conifers. When we reach the grave, Mum cleans the photo on his gravestone with a bit of spit and a hanky, as though she's wiping away the imaginary milk residue from around Matthies's mouth. Dad lights a lantern and waters the plants and flowers around the grave. The gravel beneath our feet crunches as we change positions. I always stay as still as possible so as not to knock against Mum by accident. We don't speak. I always look at the graves next to and behind Matthies's. There's a girl who fell off a boat in the summer and ended up in the propeller; a woman with an enormous butterfly sculpture on her grave because she wanted to fly but didn't have wings; a man who was only found when he began to smell. But one day, this is what it says in the Bible, all the graves will break open, one day the dead will return. I'd always found that a scary thought: I pictured all the bodies coming out of the earth and marching through the village like a procession of biology models, with chattering teeth and hollow eyes. They'd bang on the doors claiming to know you, saying they were relatives. I remember the lines from Corinthians that Granny once read to me when I was worried we'd no longer recognize Matthies: 'How foolish! What you sow does not come to life unless it dies. When you sow, you do not plant the body that will be, but just a seed, perhaps of wheat or of something else. But God gives it a body as he has determined, and to each kind of seed he gives its own body. So will it be with the resurrection of the dead. The body that is sown is perishable, it is raised imperishable; it is sown in dishonour, it is raised in glory; it is sown in weakness, it is raised in power; it is sown a natural body, it is raised a spiritual body.' I didn't understand why we'd had to plant Matthies in the ground like a seed if above the earth he'd have been able to blossom into something wonderful. We never know it's time to leave until Dad turns around. I usually run my hand along the conifers as I walk past them, as though I'm offering Death my sincere condolences, out of respect, out of fear.

Dad has fixed his side parting with hair wax. I don't want the Jewish people to see him through the gaps in the floorboard like that – he'd frighten them unnecessarily. Though sometimes I doubt they're still living in the basement. It's so quiet and now winter's coming it's starting to get freezing cold down there, so cold that their bodies will freeze over time, like the bottles of blackcurrant cordial. I'd put them up in the hay barn where it's warmer.

I carry on reading my nature book about ants and their carrying capacity: I hope for Mum's sake that the Jewish people are still there because if you take away a queen ant's subjects, I read, it's not long before she dies of loneliness; and vice versa, as the subjects also die if the mother lays downs her wings and ceases to be. Without her, Dad, who is now tying a tight knot in the binbag, wouldn't survive for long. He once won two silver medals for the cows called Boude and Wijn who had produced a hundred thousand litres of milk. They were his favourite Blaarkoppen and they'd been featured in the *Reformist Daily*, complete with pictures. That Sunday we received weak handshakes after the church service and a free slice of vanilla sponge in the Hoeksteen, where people discuss the sermon afterwards. For a short while it had seemed as though Dad was emitting light among the members of the congregation, like my glow-in-the-dark stars. He spoke with sweeping hand gestures and grinned from cheek to cheek – the same smile as when he'd sold a calf to a cattle dealer. I looked at him and thought: this isn't Dad, this is a stranger we'll be going home with shortly, who will lose his light when the rest around him light up again. That's why we had to stay dark, as it formed a nice contrast for Dad. I was impressed by him and the way he told people about Boude and Wijn's success. Sometimes you have to sell yourself – it's something we'll have to learn one day. Dad is good at that. One day he'll close a deal on me and Hanna – even though we're impatient to take matters into our own hands. As I was listening to Dad talk that Sunday, I picked off the greasy darker edges of the slice of cake in my hand and put them in my coat pocket. I resolved to stand on the edge of the sofa back home and offer the strips to Mum, like worms dangled above the beaks of young starlings. I wondered about putting them on Matthies's grave – he liked cake, especially with whipped cream and chocolate sprinkles and when the centre was still a bit moist, but then I thought it might attract worms and beetles.

Out of the window I see Dad putting the binbag into the black container. When he returns he sits down in the smoking chair next to the window. The smoke of his cigarette causes half of his face to become foggy. Without looking at me, he says, 'We shouldn't have hung a calf in the tree as a protest, but a farmer. It would have made a bigger impression on those filthy heathens, those spineless shortbreads.' Dad often uses 'short-breads' as a swear-word. I immediately picture Dad hanging upside down from a branch with his tongue hanging out of his mouth. Now he's probably going to threaten to leave for good. Now he asks me whether I still remember the story of the man who got on his bike one day and rode to the edge of the world. As he was cycling he discovered that his brakes didn't work, which was a relief to him because now he couldn't stop for anything or anyone. The good man cycles off the edge of the world and tumbles and tumbles, the way he's been tumbling all his life, but now there's no end to it. That's what death will feel like – like an endless fall without getting back up again, without plasters. I hold my breath. The story has frightened me a bit. Once Hanna and I had folded bottle tops around the spokes of Dad's bike so that he couldn't secretly go after the man. I didn't realize until later that Dad was the man. Dad was the one tumbling.

'Have you already pooed?' he asks all of a sudden.

I feel my body stiffen at once. I hope for a moment he'll be covered entirely in fog and disappear for a while. The only thing that came out of me was watery like chocolate milk and not really worth giving a name. Dad's talking about a real poo, the kind you really have to try hard to get out.

'And what rubbish are you reading there? You'd be better off reading the Authorized Version,' he continues.

I close my nature book in shock. Ants can carry up to five thousand times their own weight. People are puny in comparison – they can barely lift their own body weight once, let alone the weight of their sorrow. I pull my knees up to protect myself. Dad taps his cigarette ash into his coffee cup. He knows Mum hates him doing that – she says it makes the coffee taste of wet cigarettes, of the number one cause of death.

'If you don't start pooing, they'll have to make a hole in your tummy and your shit will run into a bag. Do you want that?'

Dad pushes himself up from the smoking chair to stoke the fire. He stacks his worries like the sticks of kindling next to it: they blaze up in our feverish minds. We all want Dad's worries, even though they only burn briefly and don't give off much heat.

I shake my head. I want to tell him about Obbe and his finger, that it will all be fine. At the same time, I don't want to disappoint him because you mustn't just make people superfluous – he could go rusty.

'You're holding it in deliberately, aren't you?'

I shake my head again.

Dad comes and stands in front of me. He's holding a piece of kindling in his hand. His eyes are dark – the blue seems to have been swallowed up by the pupil.

'Even dogs shit,' he says. 'Show me your stomach.'

I carefully put my legs back down on the ground. He takes hold of the seam of my coat. But the drawing pin, I think then. If Dad sees it, he'll pull it out roughly, like an ear tag from a dead animal. Mum and Dad will definitely never go on holiday then because the only place I want to go to is myself.

'Friends,' we suddenly hear behind us. Dad lets go of my coat. His expression changes at once: the sky often clears unexpectedly inland, as Dieuwertje Blok says on her pre-Christmas show. She's been back on TV for a week now. Sometimes she winks at me and then I know what we're doing is right – that once Hanna and I have gone, she'll keep an eye on things. This reassures me a bit. Dad opens the stove door and throws the stick in.

'The animal's healthy from the front but sick at the back end.'

The vet looks from Dad to me. It's an expression he used for the cows but that is now intended for me. The vet nods and opens the press studs of his green jacket one by one. Dad begins to sigh now. 'She's got a problem with her arsehole.' I think about all the bars of soap I've hidden in my bedside table. There are eight of them. I could make the entire ocean froth with them. All the fish, walruses, sharks and sea-horses would be washed clean. I'd make a washing line for them and hang them up with Mum's clothes pegs.

'Olive oil and a varied diet,' the vet says. His nose is running. He sniffs and wipes it on his sleeve.

I clutch my nature book even tighter. I forgot to fold over the corner of the page I was at. If only there was somebody to do that for me so that I'd know my place, where to live my story from again, and whether that place is here or on the other side: the Promised Land.

Dad turns around abruptly and walks to the kitchen. I hear him rummaging around in the herb cupboard. He comes back with an old bottle of olive oil; there are yellow crusts around the edge of the lid. We never use olive oil in the food. Dad is the only one who sometimes uses it, to grease the door hinges to stop them from creaking.

'Mouth open,' he says.

I look at the vet. He doesn't look back but stares at a wedding photo of Mum and Dad on the wall. It's the only picture in which they're really looking at each other, where you can see that they were in love, even though Mum has a dubious smile on her lips and Dad is leaning awkwardly on one knee on the grass, his deformed leg handily out of shot. Their bodies are still supple, as though they'd been coated in olive oil for the shot. Dad is wearing a brown suit and Mum a milk white dress. The longer I look at the photograph, the more doubting their smiles become, as though they already know what the future has in store for them, the cows around them in the field like bridesmaids.

Before I can do anything, Dad squeezes my nose shut, holds the bottle's spout to my lips and pours the oil into me. I begin to splutter. Dad lets go.

'There we are. That should be enough.'

I try to swallow the nasty oil and cough a few times. I wipe my mouth on my knee – it's like a greased baking tin – and wrap my arms around my belly. Don't throw up, don't throw up or you'll die. Dad points outside – the vet follows his finger. I don't hear what they are saying. All I can hope is that one day God will pick up the farm like the grab loader picked up the dead cows. I clench my hand tighter around my belly. I want to let go of my poo and I don't want to let go of it. Maybe Obbe should stick in something bigger? If it came out I'd carefully fold up a few pieces of toilet paper – the rule is eight for poo, four for pee – and run my hand between my buttocks like a manure shovel. Should I take a sip of Mum's rennet that makes holes pop up in the cheese? Then I'll get holes in me too and everything will be able to get out at last.

4

I mash the florets of broccoli on my plate. They're just like mini Christmas trees. They remind me of the evening that Matthies didn't come home, the hours I spent sitting on the windowsill with Dad's binoculars around my neck. They were actually supposed to be for looking for the greater spotted woodpecker. I didn't see a greater spotter woodpecker and I didn't see my brother. The cord of the binoculars left a red stripe behind at the back of my neck. If only I could bring closer what was becoming increasingly far from us by just reversing my gaze, by looking through the big end of the binoculars. I'd searched the sky often enough with them – looking for the angels from the tree that Obbe and I had secretly got out of the box in the attic a week after our brother's death. We'd rubbed them forcefully against each other ('my juicy little angel', Obbe had groaned affectedly, to which I'd replied 'my sweet little piece of china') before letting them fall out of his skylight into the gutter. The weather has turned them green. Some of them lie buried under leaves from the oak tree. Every time we go to check whether they're still there, we're disappointed. If the angels here lose the ability to fly after the most minor set-back, how can they be with Matthies in heaven? How can they protect him and us?

Eventually I twisted the lens caps back onto the binoculars and returned them to their case. I never got them out again, not even when the greater spotted woodpecker did return – their view will stay black forever.

I take a big mouthful of broccoli. We always have a hot meal at lunchtime. Everything here is cold in the evening: the farmyard, the silence between Mum and Dad, our hearts, the bread spread with Russian salad. I don't know how to sit on my chair. I shuffle around a bit to try to feel my burning bum hole, reminding me of Obbe's finger, as little as possible. I mustn't give anything away, otherwise my brother will make my rabbit as cold as the evenings. And I must have wanted it myself, right? You keep bulls calm by showing them your buttocks if you're a cow.

I can't keep my eyes off the stethoscope lying next to the vet's plate on the table. It's the second time I've seen one in real life. I saw one once on Nederland 1, but you didn't see the body because that would be too much nudity. I fantasize for a moment that the stethoscope is on my bare chest, that the vet lays his ear to the metal and says to Mum: 'I think her heart is torn. Does it run in the family or is this the first time it's happened? Perhaps she should go to the seaside where the air is clear. All that liquid manure gets into your clean clothes and the heart can get infected more quickly.' I picture him taking a Stanley knife out of his trouser pocket, like the one Dad uses to cut the ropes of the silage grass packing – whoosh whoosh until it falls free of its shape. Then he'd draw lines on my chest with a felt-tip pen. I think about the Big Bad Wolf that ate the seven little goats and was cut open so they could be taken out alive – maybe a big girl would come out from inside me, freed of her fears, or someone who would be seen in any case, the girl who'd been hidden for too long beneath layers of skin and coat. When the stethoscope leaves my skin, he'll have to lay his ear to my chest, and then just by breathing in and out, I can make his head go up and down so that he understands me. I'd say that it hurts everywhere and point to places where no one has ever been – from my toes to the crown of my head and everything in between. We could draw guiding lines between the freckles to give ourselves boundaries or to cut a figure out of me, just like those dot-to-dot pictures. But if he doesn't hear my cry for help I'll have to remove the metal from my chest, open my mouth as wide as possible and poke the round tip as far down my throat as I can. Then he'll have to listen. Choking is never a good sign.

Obbe elbows me in the ribs.

'Hello, Earth to Jas, pass the gravy will you.'

Mum hands me the jug. Its handle has broken off. There are globules of fat floating in the gravy. I quickly pass it to Obbe before he puts a downer on things by asking me what I was thinking about. He'd start listing all the boys at school, while the boy I do actually think about a lot has a memorial plaque at the place he always parked his bike. Things aren't very cheerful anyway now the cows have gone and the vet is talking about the impact of foot-and-mouth on all the farmers in the village. Most of them don't want to talk about it and those are the most dangerous ones, he says, most likely to be weighed down and end up doing something silly.

'Hard to understand that,' Dad says without looking at anyone, 'you've always got your kids still.'

I glance at Obbe whose head is almost touching his plate, as though he's studying the structure of broccoli and seeing whether the florets can be used as umbrellas to hide ourselves under. I can see from his balled fists that he's angry about what Dad said, or what Dad hasn't said. We all know that Mum and Dad can be lead weights too, like the ones we use to keep the curtains hanging down in their place. I keep on watching the vet. From time to time he runs his tongue along the silver metal of his knife. It's a handsome tongue – dark red. I think about the plants in Dad's greenhouse, and how he uses a knife to cut across a vein before planting the cuttings with the leaves pointing upwards in the potting soil, then fastening them with a fence staple. I imagine the vet's tongue touching my tongue. Will I finally uncurl then? When Hanna poked her tongue into my mouth a while back, I tasted that she'd eaten the last honey drop. I ask myself whether the vet's tongue tastes of honey, whether that will calm the tickling insects in my belly.

Dad sits at the table with his head in his hands. He's no longer listening to the vet, who suddenly leans forward in a secretive manner and whispers, 'I think your coat looks lovely on you.' I don't know why he's whispering because everybody can hear, but I've seen people do that at other times, as though they want everyone to lean in a little, to prick up their ears, to be drawn towards them like a magnet and then to put everyone back in their place. It's got something to do with power. I think it's a shame that Hanna's staying at a friend's house. Otherwise she'd be able to hear that it won't be much longer before we're rescued. Maybe I should forget the incident with the cheese scoop. It did make me lose a bit of my belief in him, just like the time – I was in the fourth year of primary school – when Dad called me to the table. It was the first and last time we'd have a conversation at the table that wasn't focused on the cows.

'I need to tell you something,' Dad had said. My fingers felt for my knife and fork, to have something to hold on to, but it was long before dinner and the table hadn't been laid yet.

'Saint Nicholas doesn't exist.'

Dad didn't look at me as he said it but stared at the coffee grounds in his cup, holding it aslant. Dad cleared his throat again. 'The saint at school is our Tjerre, the regular milk customer, the bald one.' I thought about Tjerre who sometimes rapped his head with his knuckles as a joke, making hollow sounds with his mouth. We loved it, every single time. I couldn't imagine him with a beard and a red mitre. I tried to say something but my throat was as full as the rain metre in the garden. At last it overflowed and I began to sob. I thought about everything that was a lie: sitting in front of the open fire, singing Christmas songs in the hope he'd hear us, though at best only a coal tit had heard us; the mandarins we received in our left-out shoes that made our socks smell acidic. Maybe Dieuwertje Blok was fake too. The fact we had to behave, otherwise we'd be put in the saint's empty sack and taken to Spain.

'And Dieuwertje Blok then?'

'She's real, but the Saint Nicholas on television is an actor.'

I looked at the pepernoten that Mum had put in a coffee filter for me. Everything we were given was carefully weighed, even these miniature spiced cookies. I left them untouched on the table, the tears kept on coming. Then Dad got up from the table, fetched a tea-towel and dried my tears roughly with it. He kept on scrubbing even though I'd stopped crying, as though my face was covered in boot polish – the polish that fed the illusion, the soot smears worn by the saint's helpers. I wanted to pound on his chest the way he'd pounded on the door for years, and then run away into the night and not come back for the present. They'd been lying all this time. Yet over the years that followed I tried to believe in the holy man just as determinedly as I believed in God – as long as I could picture them or see them on TV, and as long as I had something to wish or pray for, they existed.

The vet puts the last broccoli floret on his plate into his mouth, leans forward again, and lays his knife and fork in a cross on his plate as a sign he's finished eating.

'How old are you?' he asks.

'Twelve.'

'Then you're almost complete.'

'Completely nuts, you mean,' Obbe says.

The vet ignores him. The idea that I'm almost complete and ready for someone makes me feel proud, even though it's actually like I'm falling more and more apart – but I do know that complete is always a good sign. My collection of milk caps is almost complete; there are only three empty plastic cases, so at a certain point I'll get the same feeling as when I leaf through my file and think about all the games I've won and lost. Though it must be harder to leaf through yourself, but perhaps you have to be a grown-up to do that, to stay at the same stripe on the door-post, no longer able to rub out your old height. And Rapunzel was twelve when she was locked up in a tower and rescued by a prince. Not many people know that her name is the German word for lamb's lettuce.

The vet looks at me for a long time. 'I don't know why you don't have a boyfriend yet. When I was your age I would have known what to do.' My cheeks get as hot as the sides of the gravy jug. I don't know what the difference is, why he would have known what to do as a twelve-year-old but as an older man my father's age he no longer does. Aren't adults supposed to know everything?

'Chance of rain tomorrow,' Dad says out of the blue. He hasn't listened to any of the conversation. Mum keeps on walking between the counter and the table so that no one will notice that she's barely eaten a thing. I read in my nature book that ants have two stomachs: one for themselves and the other to feed other ants. I find this touching. I want two as well – then I could use one stomach to keep my mother at a reasonable weight.

The vet winks at me. I decide to tell Belle about him tomorrow. Finally I've got someone to whisper about. I won't tell her he's got a lot of wrinkles, more than an unironed tablecloth, that he coughs like a calf with swine fever, that he's maybe even older than my father and has got wide nostrils you could fit at least three chips in. I'll tell her he's even more handsome than Boudewijn de Groot. And that means something. After school, Belle and I often listen to his music in my attic bedroom. When we feel very sad – Belle can sometimes get very down when Tom doesn't text her a big X at the end of a message but just a small one, even though when you type a full stop, the big one comes automatically and so he's gone to the trouble to replace the capital letter with a small one – we say to each other, 'There's a drowned butterfly inside me.' Then we simply nod, knowing exactly how the other feels.

5

Carrying the shovel that still has a bit of white paper from Obbe's lantern sticking to it, and wearing my pyjamas, I go into the field behind the breeding stable we privately call the sperm barn. I dig a hole just next to the place where Tiesey is buried and where Obbe patted down the overturned earth with the back of the spade, and this time didn't poke in a stick because it isn't something we want to remember, that we want to look at. As I dig, the stabbing feelings in my belly get more and more intense. It makes me short of breath and I clench my buttocks tightly, whispering softly, 'Wait just a little while, Jas, you can almost go.' Once the hole is deep enough, I glance around quickly. Dad and Obbe are still asleep and Hanna is playing with her Barbies behind the sofa. I don't know where Mum's got to. She might even have popped next door to see Lien and Kees, who has just bought a new milk tank for when the new stock arrive – a twenty thousand litre one.

I quickly untie the cords of my striped pyjama bottoms and drop them and my knickers to my ankles, feeling the ice-cold wind on my bottom, and then I squat and hover over the hole. In a last attempt to solve my poo problem by looking it up in the Bible yesterday evening, Dad came across a reference in Deuteronomy: 'Designate a place outside the camp where you can go to relieve yourself. As part of your equipment have something to dig with, and when you relieve yourself, dig a hole and cover up your excrement.' He'd leafed on and closed the Bible with a sigh, meaning there was nothing useful for this problem there, but the lines had stuck in my head. It had kept me awake in the night. I tossed and turned in the dark and kept thinking of those three words, 'outside the camp'. God must have meant outside the farmyard. Was that the only place I'd be able to poo? I didn't say anything to my parents about my plan because not being able to poo is the only thing we still talk about, the only thing that makes them look up when I stand in front of them in the kitchen and lift my T-shirt, my swollen belly like an egg with a double yolk, feeling the same pride as when one of my silky fowl lays a massive white egg.

I look back between my legs and feel the pressure in my bum. Whether it's due to the olive oil or the Bible verses, it works. Only instead of a steaming brown trail descending into the earth like an enormous worm, a few droppings come out of my bum. I keep on pressing as the tears run along my clenched jaw and I feel myself grow dizzy. I have to go on and get everything out otherwise I'll burst one day, and then I'll be even further from home and from myself. The droppings look a bit like the ones my rabbit Dieuwertje does, but then one size bigger. Mini pasties. Granny once said that poo is healthiest when it looks like the greasy veal sausages she sometimes makes. My poo looks like anything but that.

More and more steam comes out of the hole. I pinch my

nose to keep out the smell, which is much worse than a stable full of crapping cows. When nothing else comes, I look around in search of leaves and suddenly notice that everything is bare or buried under a thin layer of frost. I don't want to freeze shut like the plug in the bath-tub in the field which the cows drink water from in the summer. And so I pull my knickers and pyjama bottoms back up without wiping my bum, trying not to let the fabric touch the skin, otherwise everything will get dirty. As I turn around, I bend over the hole for a moment like an eagle hovering over its chicks. I look at the droppings lying there in a heap and begin to close the hole to cover the excrement. I flatten the earth with the shovel, stamp on it a few times with my wellies, and poke a stick in it so I'll remember where I lost a piece of myself. I leave the field, put the shovel back among the other shovels and pitchforks, and think briefly about the boys next door who actually find in the toilet bowl all the things they've lost: a blue button, a Lego brick, plastic bullets from a gun at the fair, a bolt. For a moment I feel big.

6

Belle says, 'Sadness doesn't grow, only the space it takes up.' It's easy for her to talk. The space she's talking about is only the size of a fish tank and came about when her two guppies died. Now she's twelve and it has become an aquarium. That's as far as it goes, while in my case it grows and grows and can no longer be stopped: at first it was six foot tall and now it's as big as the giant Goliath from the Bible. I nod at Belle anyway. I don't want the glass of the aquarium to break and for her tears to escape. I can't handle people crying – I want to wrap them up in silver foil like my milk biscuits and put them in a dark drawer until they've dried out. I don't want to feel any sadness, I want action; something to pierce my days, like bursting a blister with a pin so that the pressure is eased. But my thoughts keep straying to this afternoon when Mum had a shindy after the vet left. That's what Dad calls everything we're not to take too seriously: a shindy. Out of the blue, Mum suddenly said, 'I want to die.' She had simply continued clearing the table, filled up the dishwasher, and brushed the potato shoots that were on the chopping board into the peelings basket to give to the chickens.

'I want to die,' she repeated, 'I've had enough. If a car ran over me tomorrow and left me as flat as a squashed hedgehog,

I'd be happy.' For the first time I saw desperation in her eyes.

Obbe had got up from the table. He pressed his fists into his crown. It didn't calm him down. 'Drop dead then, if you want.'

'Obbe!' I whispered. 'She's about to break.'

'Can you see anyone breaking here? The only thing breaking is us.' He'd thrown his mobile at the wall above the stove tiled in Delft blue, shouting, 'Goddammit.' His Nokia fell apart. I thought about the *Snake* game on there – the snake was probably dead now. Usually it only got tangled up in itself when it ate too many mice and started bulging out of the screen. Now it was broken.

There was a deadly silence in which I only heard the tap dripping. Then Dad stormed in from the sitting room, his gammy leg bumbling behind him. He pushed Obbe roughly to the kitchen floor and held his arms behind his back.

'Do it then – kill yourself – otherwise I'll murder you all!' my brother screamed.

'Thou shalt not take the name of the Lord thy God in vain; for the Lord will not hold him guiltless that taketh his name in vain,' Dad cried. Mum squirted some washing-up liquid on a scouring sponge and scrubbed the oven dish.

'You see,' she whispered, 'I'm a bad mother. You'd be better off without me.' I'd clamped my hands over my ears until the screaming stopped and Dad let go of Obbe, until Mum opened the oven and pressed her wrist a few seconds to the still-hot baking tray to warm herself up inside.

'You're the best mother,' I said, hearing in my voice that I was lying – it was as empty and hollow as the cowsheds. There was no life left in it. But Mum seemed to have forgotten what had just happened already.

Dad raised his arms in the air. 'You're driving us mad, bonkers!' he said, setting off for the wood store. Granny on the more religious side always said you had to nip arguments in the bud immediately. Were we the bud? And I thought, no, parents live on in their children, not the other way round – the madness lives on in us.

'Do you really want to die?' I asked Mum.

'Yes,' she said, 'but pay no attention, I'm a lousy mother.' She turned on her heels and carried the peelings basket to the shed.

I was frozen to the spot for a moment and held my hand out to Obbe. His nose was bleeding. Obbe batted my hand away. 'Shit-pants,' he said.

Belle and I are sitting in the sperm barn on the dusty stone floor. In the middle of the barn there's a dummy cow consisting of a metal frame with a piece of hide on top that's supposed to drive the bulls crazy. Beneath the hide are metal rails with a black chair on them. The chair is made of leather. You move it forward and back to be able to catch the sperm. The hide is torn in places. It's called Dirk IV and is named after a famous bull that sired hundreds of calves. They made a bronze statue of him and put it on a pedestal in the middle of the village square. I interrupt Belle in her argument that sadness always begins on a small scale and then expands. She knows life the way tourists know a village: they don't know how to find the dark alleyways, the path forbidden to trespassers. I say, 'Lie down on Dirk.' Without asking why, Belle climbs up onto the dummy cow. I sit on the black leather chair beneath her. The hide is hollow on the inside where it's reinforced with a tube. Belle's feet dangle down over the sides – the toes of her All Stars are covered in mud, her shoelaces grey.

'And now move your hips like you're riding a horse.'

Belle begins to move. I lean to the side to have a look. She's taken hold of the top of the hide for a better grip.

'Faster.'

She goes faster. Dirk IV begins to squeak. After a few minutes she stops. Panting, she says, 'This is boring and I'm tired.'

I adjust the chair so that I am sitting exactly beneath her hips. I can go four holes further.

'I know something exciting we could do,' I say.

'That's what you always say, but this is totally dumb.'

'Give it a chance.'

'Pretend the cow's Tom. You can do that.'

'And then?'

'Move again.'

'What's supposed to happen?'

'In the end you'll see wonderful colours, like a Fireball that keeps changing, and you'll get to the other side of the bridge where there's no sadness, where your guppies are still alive and where you'll be in charge.'

Belle closes her eyes. She begins to move back and forth.

Her cheeks grow redder, her lips moister with saliva. I let myself sink back in the chair. Maybe I should put together a presentation for Mum and Dad, I think. I'd give it on toads and I'd explain how they're supposed to mate. It's important that Mum lies on top of Dad – her back is as fragile as a gingersnap. And that's the only way Mum is going to start eating again, so that Dad will have something to hold on to. We should organize a toad migration through the farm. We'd put Dad at one side of the room and Mum on the other side and have them cross. We could also fill the bath so that they could swim together, just like the day when we got the new mint green bath-tub – it was two days before that day in December, and Mum and Dad had gone in it together. 'Now they're totally naked,' Matthies had said and we'd giggled so much, picturing two apple fritters plunging into the frying fat. They'd come out golden brown, towels wrapped around their waists like paper napkins.

The dummy cow's hinges squeak even louder. Dad was proud of Dirk IV. He always patted the creature on its fake flank after using it. I suddenly feel my throat burning, my eyes stinging. The first snow of the year falls early, descending into my heart. It feels heavy.

'I can't see any colours.'

I scramble up from the chair and stand next to Belle whose eyes are still closed. I quickly put on Dad's pale green raincoat that was hanging over a chair next to the work counter in the shed. Then suddenly the door opens and Obbe pokes his head around it. His gaze goes from me to Belle and then back.

He comes in and closes the door behind him.

'What are you playing?' he asks.

'A stupid game,' Belle says.

'Get lost,' I say. Obbe can't join the game otherwise he's sure to do something mean. He's as unreliable as the weather here in the village. He's still got blood on his nose from when he was pushed onto the kitchen floor.

Some part of me feels sorry for him. Even though I'm not feeling it as much now he's started swearing – and what's more, he often steals food, or money from the holiday tin on the mantelpiece, reducing the chances of us going camping to nil, and ruining Dad's savings for his bottom drawer. Now the most he'll be able to buy is a toaster and a drying rack. One day he'll steal Mum and Dad's hearts too. He'll dig a hole for them in the field, like one of the stray cats holding a cormorant it has caught in its mouth.

'I know something fun,' he says.

'You're not allowed to play.'

'I don't mind if you do. Jas only thinks of boring things.'

'See, Belle says I can,' Obbe says, taking some silver-coloured AI guns from the cupboard above the work counter and a box of Alpha sheaths. These are long sticks with coloured tips. They're used to inseminate the cows that have failed to get pregnant. Obbe hands me a pair of blue gloves. When I don't want to look at him I focus on the stubble on his chin. They feel like the cumin seeds that Mum sometimes has me stir into the curd. He started shaving a few days ago. I follow all his movements tensely.

'You can be my assistant,' he says.

Again the cupboard bangs open. This time he takes out a little bottle containing some kind of gel. He smears some on the gun. 'Lubricant' it says on the label.

'Now you have to take off your trousers and lie on your front on top of the cow.' Belle follows his instructions without complaining. I suddenly realize she hasn't been talking about Tom much recently, more about my brother. She wants to know what his hobbies are, his favourite food, whether he prefers blondes or brunettes and so on. I don't want Obbe to touch her. What if the aquarium broke? What would we do then? Once Belle is lying on Dirk IV, I have to hold her buttocks apart, exposing her bum hole like the fountain pen holder at school.

'It won't hurt, will it?' Belle asks.

'Don't be afraid,' I say with a smile on my face, 'you are worth more than many sparrows.' It's from Luke, and Granny had once said those words when I was staying the night and got scared I'd die in the night.

Obbe stands on an upturned feed bucket so that he can see better, aims the gun between Belle's buttocks and pushes the cold metal into her without warning. She screams like a wounded animal. I let go of her buttocks in shock.

'Stay where you are,' Obbe says, 'otherwise it will hurt even more.' Tears pour down her cheeks, her body shakes. I think feverishly about my leaky fountain pen. The teacher said I should leave it standing in cold water for a night, and then rinse it and blow it dry the next day. Should I lay Belle in cold water too? When I look at Obbe worriedly, he nods at the container in the corner where the straws of bull sperm are kept in nitrogen. Dad forgot to lock up the container. I'm guessing Obbe has had the same idea – rinse. I unscrew it, take out a straw and pass it to Obbe. The gun is still sticking out between Belle's buttocks.

'You're the best assistant in the world.'

The ice is beginning to melt a little. What we're doing is good. Sometimes you have to make sacrifices that aren't that nice, like when God asked Abraham to sacrifice Isaac and he finally gave him an animal. We also have to try different things before God is satisfied with our attempts to meet Death and leave us in peace.

Now Obbe pushes the straw into the gun. There are so many alternatives and still we do it, without knowing that the nitrogen will burn her skin. I feel cowardice making my legs heavier when I run out of the sperm barn with Obbe hot on my heels. We both fly to the other side of the farmyard. 'And lead us not into temptation but save us from evil,' I whisper to myself, as I see Hanna lean her bike against the side of the farmhouse. Her pillow is clamped under her luggage binders. She's carrying her overnight bag in her hand. When she hasn't been to Granny's for a long time, it gets full of silverfish. We crush them between our thumbs and forefingers, rubbing them to dust, then blow them from our fingers.

'Come with us,' I say, running ahead of her to the stack of hay-bales behind the rabbit shed. We crawl between a few bales of hay so that we're out of sight of Dad, the crows and God.

'Will you hold me?' I ask.

I try not to cry about Belle's screams that are still ringing in my ears, her eyes opened wide, burst like half-full fishbowls.

'Why? What's happened?' Hanna gives me a worried look. 'You're shaking all over.'

'Because . . . because otherwise I'll burst,' I say, 'just like that hen of Dad's when the egg was too big and was sticking half out of its bum. If Dad hadn't killed it, it would have burst into pieces and its innards would have flown everywhere. I'm about to burst like that.'

'Oh, yes,' Hanna says, 'that poor creature.'

'I'm a poor creature too. Won't you hold me now?'

'I'll hold you.'

'You know,' I say, as I press my nose into her hair which smells of baby shampoo, 'I do want to be bigger, but not for my arms to grow too. Right now you fit in them perfectly.'

Hanna is silent for a moment, then she says, 'When they get too big, I'll just wrap them around me twice, like my winter scarf.'

7

That night I dream about Belle. We're in the woods at the edge of the village, just by the ferry, and we're playing the Fox Hunt game. I don't know why, but Belle's wearing my mum's Sunday overcoat and her Sunday hat with the kind of gauze over it and a black ribbon on the side. The seam of the coat drags along the ground, picking up sticks and mud; it rustles as she walks. Only then do I notice that Belle and the fox have fused into something part human, part animal. We walk further into the woods and end up lost between the tall, thin trees that resemble upright boot-jacks in the dark. Wherever I walk, Belle appears with her rusty red fox's body.

'Are you the fox?' she asks.

'Yes,' I say, 'get lost before I eat you up like a fresh chicken.' She raises her chin disdainfully and tosses back her hair.

'Moron,' she says, 'I'm the fox. Now I have to ask you a question and if you can't answer it, you'll throw up or get the runs and you'll die a premature death.' Her nose and ears have suddenly become pointed. Everything sharp has extra value: teeth to bite through food, hearing to listen to sounds. The fox's body suits her. Each time she takes a step forwards, I take one back. I'm expecting her to let out an eerie scream at any moment like in the barn, that her eyes will open as wide as those of a pike caught on a hook. Helpless.

'Is your brother really dead or is Death your brother?' she asks at last. I shake my head and study the toes of my shoes.

'Death has no family, that is why he keeps looking for new bodies so that he won't be lonely. Until that person is under the ground, then he looks for a new one.'

Belle reaches out her hand. In the dream I suddenly hear what the pastor once said: 'The only way to combat your enemy is to make him your friend.'

I look back to take in a breath of fresh air, one without any germs in it, and ask, 'What would happen if I gave you my hand?'

Belle moves closer. She smells of burning flesh. Suddenly her bum is covered in sticking plasters. 'I'd eat you up in a flash.'

'And if I didn't give you my hand?'

'I'd eat you up slowly, that would hurt more.'

I try to run away from her but my legs turn to jelly beneath my body, my wellies are suddenly too big for my feet.

'Do you know how many voles in the belly of a fox would mean he no longer had to fathom his own emptiness?' When I finally run away from her, she calls after me with an inbuilt echo effect, a voice for playing hide-and-seek. 'Dear vole, vole, vole.'

8

Dad squints to figure out how high the silver-plated skates should hang. He has three screws clamped between his lips in case one falls, and he's holding an electric drill. Mum stands, damp-eyed, watching from a distance, the vacuum cleaner hose held aloft. I look at her white vest which is visible because the belt of her dressing gown has come loose, and I can see her saggy breasts through the thin fabric. They look just like two egg meringues, the kind Obbe sometimes makes and sells in the playground in freezer bags, four at a time. If the egg is too old the white gets thinner and this makes the meringue soggy. Dad climbs down the kitchen steps and Mum turns off the vacuum cleaner, making the silence seem silver too.

'They're crooked,' Mum says then.

'They aren't,' Dad says.

'Yes, they are. Look, from here you can see they're crooked.'

'Then you shouldn't stand there. Crooked doesn't exist, they hang differently from every angle.'

Mum pulls her dressing gown belt tight, hurries out of the living room, pulling the vacuum cleaner along with her by its hose – it follows her around the house all day like an obedient dog. Sometimes I'm jealous of that ugly blue beast – she seems to have more of a relationship with it than with her own children. At the end of every week I see her cleaning its tummy with great love and putting a new hoover bag in it, while mine is about to burst.

I look at the ice skates again. The insides are lined with red velvet. They're not hanging straight. I don't say anything about it. Dad has gone to sit on the sofa and is staring ahead glassily. There's a bit of dust on his shoulders. He's still holding the drill in his hand.

'You look like a scarecrow, Dad,' Obbe, who has just come in, says in a challenging tone. I hadn't heard my brother come back until about five in the morning. I lay waiting, my heart pounding, analysing every sound: the slaloming of his footsteps, the way he felt along the wall, forgot to skip the creaking steps – the sixth and the twelfth. I heard him hiccuping and not long after that he threw up into the toilet in the bathroom. This has been the pattern for a few nights in a row. My pyjamas are constantly soaked in sweat. According to Dad, vomiting is an old leftover sin the body needs to get rid of. I knew Obbe erred by killing animals, but what he did wrong by going to barn parties, I didn't understand. What I did know was that he kept putting his tongue in different girls' mouths. I could see that through my bedroom window – he stood there in the light of the stable lamp as though he was Jesus, surrounded by a heavenly glow, and then each time I'd press my mouth to my forearm and use my tongue to run circles on my sweaty skin. It tasted salty. This morning I didn't say much to Obbe, so as not to inhale any bacteria that would make me throw up too. It reminded me of the first and last time I'd been sick, when Matthies had still been alive.

It was a Wednesday – I was about eight – and I'd gone with Dad to fetch bread from the bakery in the village. On the way back, he gave me a currant bun, an extra-large one. It was still deliciously fresh, without blue and white spots. When we arrived at Granny's – we always dropped her off a feed-bag full of bread – I started to feel nauseous. We walked around the back because the front door was more for decoration, and I'd thrown up onto the soil of her vegetable patch, the currants swimming in the brownish puddle like swollen beetles. It was the spot where Granny planted her carrots. Dad had quickly kicked a layer of soil over it with his boot. When the carrots were pulled up, I expected Granny to get sick at any moment and die because of me. At the time I wasn't yet afraid I would die myself, because that only came when Matthies didn't come home, when the incident in the garden became multiple versions of itself. In the worst version, I'd escaped death by the skin of my teeth. I sometimes wondered whether the girls pushed their tongues so far down Obbe's throat that this was why he threw up, like when you stick a toothbrush too far into your mouth and it makes you gag. Mum and Dad didn't ask where he'd been or why he kept stinking of beer and cigarettes.

'Shall we go for a bike ride?' I whisper to Hanna, who is sitting behind the sofa, drawing. None of her figures has a body, only a head, reflecting the way we're only focused on other people's moods. They look sad or angry. She has her overnight case clenched under her right arm. Since she came back from her sleepover, she's been carrying her case around all over the place, as though she wants to hang on to the possibility of escape. We're not allowed to touch it or even comment on it.

'Where to?'

'To the lake.'

'What do you want to do there?'

'The Plan,' is all I say.

She nods. It's time to set our plans in action – we can't stay here any longer.

In the hall Hanna puts on her anorak that hangs on the blue coat peg. Obbe's is yellow, mine is green. Next to mine there's a red peg. The coat isn't missing but the body that should be wearing it is. Only Mum and Dad's hang on wooden hangers, which are warped from the damp of rain showers in their collars. They were once the only reliable shoulders in the house but are now sagging more and more.

I suddenly think of the time that Dad took hold of me by my hood. Matthies had only been dead a couple of weeks. I'd asked Dad why we weren't allowed to talk about him, and whether he knew if there was a library in heaven where you could borrow books without getting a fine if you were late taking them back. Matthies didn't have any money with him. We forgot to return our books so often – particularly the Roald Dahls and the Angry Witch series, which we read in secret because our parents said they were godless books. We didn't want to entrust them back to the librarian. She was never nice to us. Matthies said she was afraid of children with greasy fingers and children who folded over the corners of the pages. Only children who didn't have a real home, a place they could always return to, made dog-ears – this was why they had to keep a record, the way I would later myself even though mine were more like a mouse's ears. When I asked Dad that question, he'd picked me up by my hood and hung me from the red peg. I dangled around a bit with my feet swinging but I couldn't get myself free. The ground had disappeared from beneath my feet.

'Who asks the questions around here?' he said.

'You do,' I said.

'Wrong. God does.'

I had a good think. Had God ever asked me a question? I couldn't remember one, though I thought of lots of answers to questions people could potentially ask me. Maybe that was why I didn't hear God.

'You can hang there until Matthies comes back.'

'When's he coming back then?'

'When your feet are back on the ground.'

I looked down. From my earlier experiences of growing, I knew this could take quite a long time. Dad pretended to leave but came back after a few seconds. My coat zip was digging into my throat painfully, breathing was difficult. I was set back down on the floor and never asked another question about my brother. I deliberately built up a big fine at the library and sometimes read the stories out loud under my duvet in the hope that Matthies could hear them in heaven, ending with a hashtag the way I did when using my Nokia to leave a message for Belle about an important test.

*

I cycle along the dike behind Hanna; her case is on her cargo rack. We pass our neighbour Lien halfway. I try not to look at her son who is sitting on the back of her bike, even though I know I'm not a paedophile. There's something angelic about him with his blond hair and I love angels, whether they're older or younger than me. But Granny says you should never leave the fox to watch the geese. Granny doesn't have a fox or any geese, but I can imagine it not going well if you left the two together. Lien greets us from a distance. She looks worried. Now we have to smile back cheerfully so she doesn't ask any questions, not to us or our parents.

'Pretend to be happy,' I say quietly to Hanna.

'I've forgotten how to.'

'As though it's for the school photo.'

'Oh, right.'

Hanna and I smile our broadest grins, and the corners of my mouth pull. We pass Lien without any difficult questions. I glance back for a moment at her son, suddenly picturing him dangling from the rope in the attic – angels always have to be hung up so that they can spin on their own axis and offer everyone around them the same support. I blink a few times to get rid of the horrible image and think about what Reverend Renkema said last Sunday during the service. It was from Luke: 'Evil does not enter us from the outside but from the inside. Therein lies our ailment. The tax collector beat his breast and prayed. He beat his breast as though to say: here is the source of all evil.'

I press my fist to my chest for a moment, so hard that all of my body tenses and I begin to lurch on my bike, whispering to myself, 'Forgive me, God.' Then I put my hands back on the handlebars to be a good example to Hanna. She's not allowed to cycle no-handed. When she does, I tell her off, just like how every time a vehicle wants to pass us, I cry 'Car!' or 'Tractor!'

There's a gap between Hanna's front teeth like a planting machine. I feel more air enter my tense chest momentarily. Sometimes it's like there's a giant sitting on me, and when I hold my breath at night to get closer to Matthies, he sometimes watches from my desk chair, with big eyes like a newborn calf. He encourages me, saying, 'You have to hold on for longer, much longer.' Sometimes I think that the Big Friendly Giant has escaped from my book because I once left it open on my bedside table and fell asleep. But this giant isn't friendly, more angry and domineering. He doesn't have gills and yet he can hold his breath for ages, sometimes all night.

When we reach the bridge we throw our bikes onto the verge. There's a wooden sign at the start of the railings that has the following painted on it: 'Be sober, be vigilant; because your adversary the devil, as a roaring lion, walketh about, seeking whom he may devour.' It's from Peter. There's an empty chewing gum packet in the grass. Someone wanted to get to the other side with fresh breath. The lake is calm, like a pious face in which no lies can be found. There's already a thin layer of ice here and there at the water's edge. I throw a pebble at it. It lands on top of the ice. Hanna steps onto one of the boulders. She puts her case down next to her and stares at the other side, her hand sheltering her eyes.

'I've heard they hide themselves away in pubs.'

'Who?' I ask.

'Men. And you know what they like?'

I don't reply. Seen from behind, my sister isn't my sister but someone who could pass for anybody – her dark hair is getting longer. I think she's deliberately let it grow so long so that Mum has to plait it every day, meaning Mum has to touch her every day. My hair is always fine as it is.

'Chewing gum that doesn't lose its taste.'

'That's impossible,' I say.

'You always have to be sweet and stay sweet.'

'Or they should chew less.'

'In any case you mustn't be too sticky.'

'Mine always loses its taste really quickly.'

'But you do chew like a cow.'

I think about Mum. Her jaws chew so much each day, there must be increased tension, and increased tension is a reason to jump off a feed silo, or to break the thermometer Mum uses to measure the temperature of the cheese and swallow the mercury – Dad has been warning us about mercury since we were very small: it would be a fast death, he said. It taught me that you die fast or slowly and that both things have their advantages and disadvantages.

I stand behind Hanna and lay my head against her anorak. She is breathing calmly.

'When do we leave?' Hanna asks.

The cold wind blows right through my coat. I shiver.

'Tomorrow after the coffee break.'

Hanna doesn't reply.

'The vet said I was complete,' I say then.

'What does he know of those things? He only sees complete animals – the incomplete ones get put down.' Hanna's voice suddenly sounds bitter. Is she jealous?

I put my hands on either side of her hips. One push and she'd just topple into the water. I'd be able to see then how Matthies got underwater, how it ever could have happened.

And then I do it. I push her from the boulder into the water and watch her as she gets a ducking before coming back up again spluttering, her eyes wide with fear like two black fishing floats. I shout her name, 'Hanna, Hanna, Hanna.' But the wind beats my words onto the boulders. I kneel at the water's edge to pull her out by her arm. After that nothing is the same any more. I lie on top of my wet sister with my entire weight, repeating, 'Don't die, don't die.' We don't get up until the church bell tolls five times. Water drips from my sister from every side. I take her hand and hold it tightly, squeezing it as though it's a wet dish-cloth. We're as empty as the Queen Beatrix biscuit tin on the breakfast table we once won on the Postcode Lottery: no one can fill us up. Hanna picks up her overnight case. Her body is shivering as much as the red and white wind sock blowing next to the bridge. I've almost forgotten how to cycle, how we're ever going to get home. I no longer know where we're going. The Promised Land on the other side has suddenly become a drab postcard.

'I slipped,' Hanna says.

I shake my head, hold my fists to my temples and force my knuckles into the skin.

'Yes, I did,' Hanna says, 'that's the story.'

9

That night my dreams are feverish again, but this time they're about my sister. She is skating over the lake with her hands behind her back, puffing out clouds. Reverend Renkema has parked his Volkswagen on the side of the ditch with its headlights pointing across the ice. The strip of light indicates how big Hanna's laps should be. Renkema is sitting on the bonnet in his black vestment, the Bible on his lap. Everything around him is white from snow and ice.

Then the headlights slowly start to move towards me. I'm not a person but a folding chair that has been abandoned next to the jetty. No one needs me any more to hold on to as they skate. My legs are cold to the touch, my back misses hands. Every time Hanna comes past and I hear her skates scraping the ice, I want to shout to her. But chairs can't shout. I want to warn her about the treacherous wind holes in the ice but chairs can't warn people. I want to hold her, press her to my back, take her in my lap. My sister glances at me each time she comes round. Her nose is red and she's wearing Dad's ear muffs that we sometimes put on when we're longing for his hands to be wrapped around our cold heads. I want to tell her how much I love her, so much that my back, the chair-back, begins to glow for a moment – the wood becomes warm like after a day of having borne a visitor. But chairs can't say how much they love someone. And nobody knows it's me: Jas disguised as a piece of furniture. A little way off, some coots slide past. I'm reassured they don't sink through the ice, though my sister must weigh about thirty-five coots. When I search the ice again, I see that Hanna has moved outside the strip of light and is disappearing from sight. Renkema begins to toot his horn and flash his headlights. My sister's yellow knitted hat slowly sinks like the setting sun. I don't want her to go under. I want to be an ice-pick and bore myself into her, pinning myself to her. I want to save her. But chairs can't save people. They can only be silent and wait until someone comes to have a rest on them.

10

'Where you see sticks in the ground, that's where the mole traps are,' Dad says, handing me a spade. I take hold of it by its middle. I feel sorry for the moles, falling into traps in the darkness. I'm just like them: during the day it seems to get blacker and blacker, and in the evening I can't see my hand in front of my eyes. I dig a little around my feet, turning up everything we've pushed under the turf. This morning I turned on the globe on my bedside table and there was a brief flash of light before it went pitch black. I pressed the switch again but nothing happened. For a moment the ocean seemed to flow out of the globe – my pyjamas were soaking wet and smelled of piss. I held my breath and thought about Matthies. Forty seconds. Then I let some fresh air in and unscrewed the globe. The bulb still looked perfect. I thought briefly: this is the darkness, the last plague, then we'll have had them all. I quickly dismissed the idea.

The teacher had been right when she told my mum and dad at parents' evening that I had an overactive imagination, that I built a Lego world around myself. It was easy to click it together and apart – I determined who was an enemy and who was a friend. She also told them I'd given a Nazi salute at the door to the classroom – I had indeed raised my arm in the air and said 'Heil Hitler' as Obbe had told me to. He said it would make the teacher laugh. The teacher didn't laugh but made me write up lines after school: 'I shall not mock history, just as I shall not mock God.' And I thought – you don't know that I belong to the right side, that Mum is hiding Jewish people in the basement who are allowed to eat sweets, including mini biscuits, and drink an infinite amount of fizzy drinks. I tell her the mini biscuits have two sides: one is chocolate and the other is gingerbread. I've got two sides too – I'm both Hitler and a Jew, good and evil. I'd taken off my wet pyjamas in the bathroom and spread them over the floor, which was heated. Wearing clean knickers and my coat, I was leaning against the bath, waiting for them to dry, when the door opened and Obbe came in. He looked at my pyjamas as though a corpse was lying there.

'Have you pissed your pants?'

I shook my head firmly. I clutched the bulb from the globe tightly in my hand. It was a flat little bulb.

'No, the water came out of my globe light.'

'Liar, it didn't have any water in it.'

'It did too,' I said. 'There are five oceans.'

'Why does it smell of piss here then?'

'That's just what the sea smells like. Fish pee too.'

'Whatever,' Obbe said. 'It's time for the sacrifice.'

'Tomorrow,' I promised him.

'Good,' he said, 'tomorrow's the day.' He glanced at my pyjamas again and then said, 'Otherwise I'll tell everyone at school that you're a little piss monster.' He'd closed the door behind him.

I'd lain flat on my belly on the bathroom floor and practised butterfly stroke, which turned into just moving my crotch against the fluffy mat as though it was my bear, as though I was swimming in the ocean among the fish.

I follow Dad into the field. The frost has turned the grass rock hard under my wellies. Since the cows no longer go into it, he's been checking the traps every day; he's holding a couple of new ones in his right hand to exchange with the old ones that have clapped shut. When I'm doing my homework, I can see him through my bedroom window often taking the same path across the fields. Some days Mum and Obbe go with him. From above, the land looks just like a ludo board and I feel the same relief when they're safely back in the farm, in the stables, like pawns. Even though it's getting more difficult for all of us to be in the same place. Each room in the farm can only tolerate one pawn, and as soon as more come along there's an argument. Dad will lay his mole traps inside then, too. He hasn't got anything else to do and sits in his smoking chair all day like a stuffed heron, not saying anything until he can turn us into his prey. Herons love moles. If he does say anything it's often an interrogation about the Authorized Version. Who lost his hair and there-fore all his powers? Who turned into a pillar of salt? Who was swallowed by a whale? Who killed his brother? How many books are there in the New Testament? We avoid the smoking chair as though it's the plague but sometimes you have to go past it, just before a meal for example, and then

Dad keeps on asking questions until the soup's gone cold and the breadsticks soggy. One wrong answer and you're sent to your bedroom to reflect on things. Dad doesn't realize there are already so many things to reflect on, that more keep on turning up, that our bodies are growing and that these contemplations can no longer be switched off with a peppermint, like in the church pew.

'In the olden days, you used to get a guilder per skin. I'd nail them to a plank to let them dry,' Dad says. He squats down next to one of the sticks. Now he feeds the moles he catches to the herons behind the cowshed. They dip them in the water first – they can't swallow them dry – and gulp them down without chewing, as though they're Dad and God's word, which slips down in the same way.

'Yes, kiddo, you have to keep your head doing this – if it claps shut you'll be as dead as a doornail,' Dad whispers as he pokes the stick deeper into the ground. Nothing in it. We go to the next trap: again nothing. Moles like to live alone. They go into the darkness alone, like everyone has to fight their dark side in the long run. It's pitch black more and more often inside my head. Hanna digs herself up from time to time, but I don't know how to get out of that damned tunnel system where I can block Mum and Dad at every corner, arms like weak springs next to their bodies, trapping them like the rusty mole traps in the shed.

'Much too cold for those animals,' Dad says. A drip hangs from his nose. He hasn't shaved for a few days. There's a red scratch on his nose where he scraped himself on a branch.

'Yes, much too cold,' I agree, pulling up my shoulders like a wind-break.

Dad stares at the sticks in the distance and then suddenly says, 'People are gossiping about you in the village. About your coat.'

'What's wrong with my coat?'

'Are there molehills growing under it? Is that it?' Dad grins. I turn red. Belle's have slowly started to grow now. She showed me in the changing rooms during gym; her nipples were pink and swollen like two marshmallows.

'Now you,' she'd said.

I shook my head. 'Mine grow in the dark, just like cress. You mustn't disturb them otherwise they'll get drowsy and go limp.' She understood, but it wouldn't be long before she became impatient. Even though Obbe and I had shut her up for a while. She hadn't told her parents what had happened, because there'd been no angry phone call. Only at school now there was a history book between our tables, like the Berlin Wall. She hadn't wanted to speak to me since the incident and had lost all interest in my collection of milk biscuits.

'Every healthy girl has molehills,' Dad says.

He gets to his feet and stands before me. His lips are chapped from the cold. I quickly point at a stick a little way away,

'I think there's a mole in that one.'

Dad turns for a moment and peers at the place I pointed out to him. His blond hair has got long, just like mine. It stops just above our shoulders. Normally Mum would have sent us

260

to the hairdresser's on the square a long time ago. Now she's forgotten. Or maybe she wants us to be overgrown, for us to slowly disappear like the ivy covering the whole of the front of the house. Then no one will be able to see how little we amount to.

'Do you think you'll ever be able to marry before God like that?'

Dad stamps his spade into the earth – one-nil to him. There isn't a single boy in my class who looks at me. They only point me out when I'm the butt of one of their jokes. Yesterday Pelle had put his hand down his trousers and stuck his finger through the fly.

'Feel this,' he said. 'I've got a stiffy.'

Without thinking about it, I'd taken hold of his finger and pinched it. I felt the bones through the thin skin that was yellowish from smoking. The whole class began to whoop. A little bewildered, I'd gone back to my chair next to the window, while the laughing became louder and the Berlin Wall shook in its foundations.

'I'm never going to get married. I'm going to the other side,' I say, with my thoughts still in the classroom. It just slips out before I realize. The colour drains from Dad's face, as though I've said the word 'naked', which is worse than suggesting we're talking about developing tits.

'Anyone who gets it in their head one day to brave the bridge will never return,' he says in a loud voice. Ever since that first day when Matthies didn't come home, he's been warning us and making the city out as a slurry pit that would suck you down if you went into it, and intoxicate you.

'Sorry, Dad,' I say in a whisper, 'I wasn't thinking about what I said.'

'You know how things ended for your brother. Do you want that too?' He pulls his spade out of the ground and walks away from me, giving the wind the chance to come between us. Dad squats next to the last trap.

'Tomorrow you'll take your coat off. I'll burn it and we won't mention the matter again,' he cries.

Suddenly I picture Dad's body between the blades of a mole trap, us sticking a branch in next to his head so that we know where the pawn died. Rinsing the trap with the garden hose in the barrel in the rabbit shed, I shake my head to get rid of the nasty image. I'm not afraid of molehills but I am afraid of the darkness they grow in.

We return to the farm without any loot. On the way back, he whacks some of the molehills with the spade to flatten then.

'Sometimes it's good to frighten them a bit,' Dad says, following this with, 'Do you want to be as flat as your mother?'

I think about Mum's breasts, which are as slack as two collection bags in the church. 'That's because she doesn't eat,' I say.

'She's full of worries, there's no space left for anything else.'

'Why has she got worries?'

Dad doesn't reply. I know it's got something to do with us, that we can never act normally – even when we try to be normal we disappoint, as though we're the wrong variety, like this year's potatoes. Mum thought they were too crumbly and then too waxy. I don't dare say anything about the toads under my desk and that they're about to mate. I know it's going to happen and then they'll start eating again and everything will be all right.

'If you take your coat off, she'll fill out again.' Dad gives me a sideways glance. He attempts to smile but the corners of his mouth seem frozen. I feel big for a moment. Big people smile at each other, they understand each other, even when they don't understand themselves. I lay my hand on my coat's zip. When Dad looks away, I pick some snot from my nose with my other hand and put it in my mouth.

'I can't take my coat off without getting sick.'

'Do you want to make us look like twits? You'll be the death of us with that funny behaviour of yours. Tomorrow it's coming off.'

I slow my pace until I'm walking behind him and look at Dad's back. He's wearing a red jacket and has a trapper's pouch on his back. No moles in it or anything else. The grass crackles under his feet.

'I don't want you to die,' I scream into the wind. Dad doesn't hear. The mole traps he's carrying in his hand gently knock against each other in the wind.

II

The toads' heads rest on the surface like floating sprouts. I cautiously use my index finger to push the plumper of the two down in the milk pan I've secretly taken from the kitchen, until it plops up again. They're too weak to swim, but floating is going well.

'Just one more day and then we'll leave for good,' I tell them, getting them out of the water. I dab their bobbly skin dry with a stripy red sock. I can hear Mum shouting downstairs. She and Dad are arguing because one of their old milk customers has complained to the congregation. This time not about the milk that was too pale or too watery, but about us, the three kings. I look pale in particular and my eyes are a bit watery. Mum said that it was Dad's fault, that he didn't give us any attention, and Dad said that it was Mum's fault because she didn't give us any attention. After that they both started threatening to leave but that turned out to be impossible: only one person could pack their bags at a time, one only person could be mourned at a time, and only one person could come back later and act like nothing had happened. Now they're arguing about who's going to leave. Secretly I hope it's Dad because he usually comes back around coffee time. He gets a headache if he doesn't drink coffee. I'm not so sure about Mum: we can't tempt her back with sweets. We have to beg her and make ourselves vulnerable. It seems they're moving further and further apart. Like when they cycle over the dike to the Reformed church on Sundays, and Mum goes faster and faster and Dad keeps having to close the gap. It goes the same way with arguments – Dad has to solve them.

'They're going to take my coat off me tomorrow,' I whisper.

The toads blink, as though they're shocked by this announcement.

'I think I'm just like Samson, though my strength isn't in my hair but in my coat. Without my coat I'll be Death's slave, do you get that?'

I get up and hide the wet sock under my bed with the wet knickers. I put the toads in my coat pocket and go to Hanna's room. The door is open a chink. She's lying with her back to it. I go inside and lay my hand under her nightdress on her bare back. Her skin has goose bumps – it feels like a Lego sheet. I could click myself onto it and never let go again. Hanna turns over sleepily. I tell her about the moles and Dad saying I have to take off my coat, about the argument, them threatening to leave, always threatening to leave.

'We'll be orphans,' I say.

Hanna is only half listening. I see in her eyes that her thoughts are somewhere else. It makes me nervous. Usually we roam around the farmyard when we're together. We think of escape routes, we fantasize about better lives and pretend the world is like *The Sims*.

'Has a mole trap gone off or is the mercury out of the thermometer?'

Hanna doesn't reply. She lights up my face with the torch; I hold my arm in front of my eyes. Can't she see we're not doing very well? We're slowly floating away from Mum and Dad on a lily-pad instead of the other way around. Death hasn't only entered Mum and Dad but is also inside us – it will always look for a body or an animal and it won't rest until it's got hold of something. We could just as easily pick a different ending, different from what we know from books.

'I heard yesterday that you can fantasize yourself dead, that more and more holes will appear in you because it will nag away at you until you break. It's better to break by just trying it – that's less painful.' My sister brings her face close to mine. 'There are people waiting on the other side who can only lie on top of you in the dark, like the way night presses day to the ground, only nicer. And then they move their hips. You know, the way rabbits do. After that, you're a woman of the world and you can grow your hair as long as Rapunzel in her tower. And you can become anything you like. Anything.' Hanna begins to breathe faster. My cheeks grow warm. I watch as she lays the torch on the pillow and lifts up her nightdress with one hand. She pushes against her colourful spotted underpants with the other. She closes her eyes, her mouth open slightly. Her fingers move against her knickers. I don't dare move when Hanna starts to moan and her little body curls like a wounded animal. She pushes it backwards and forwards a bit, the way I do with my teddy bear, only this is different. I don't know what she's thinking about, only that she's not longing for a Discman or thinking about mating toads. What is she thinking about then? I pick up the torch from the pillow and shine it on her. There are a few droplets of sweat on her forehead, like condensation from a body that has got too warm in a space that is naturally cold. I don't know whether I should rush to her assistance, whether she's in pain or whether I should fetch Dad from downstairs because Hanna's feverish, maybe even hitting forty degrees.

'What are you thinking about?' I whisper.

Her eyes are glassy. I see she's somewhere that I'm not, just like that time with the can of Coke. It makes me nervous. We're always together.

'Naked man,' she says.

'Where did you see him then?'

'In Van Luik's shop, the magazines.'

'We're not allowed there. Did you buy Fireballs? The hot ones?'

Hanna doesn't answer and I begin to worry. She raises her chin, squeezes her eyes shut, sinks her teeth into her bottom lip, groans again and then lets herself fall back onto the bed, next to me. She's covered in sweat – a lock of hair is sticking to the side of her face. It looks like she's in pain but also isn't. I try to think of explanations for her behaviour. Is this because I pushed her into the water? Will she break out of her skin like a butterfly coming out of its cocoon and then batter herself to death against the window, against the insides of Obbe's hands? I want to tell her I'm sorry, I hadn't meant it that way when I pushed her into the lake. I wanted to see how Matthies sunk under the water, but Hanna's body wasn't my brother's. How could I ever have got them confused? I want to tell her about the nightmare and ask her to promise never to skate on the lake, now that winter is coming to the village on a sled. But Hanna looks happy, and just as I'm about to turn away from her angrily, I hear the familiar crackle. She takes two red Fireballs from the pocket of her nightdress. We lie next to each other, contentedly sucking and blowing and laughing at each other when our Fireballs get too hot. Hanna presses against me. I hear the sitting room door slam next to us, Mum's crying. Apart from that it's quiet. I used to sometimes hear Dad's hand patting her back like a carpet beater to get out everything she'd inhaled during the day: all that greyness, the dust of days, layers of sadness. But the carpet beater has been missing for a long time.

Hanna blows a big bubble. It pops.

'What were you doing just now?' I ask.

'No idea,' she says. 'It's just been coming over me recently. Don't tell Mum and Dad, will you?'

'No,' I say softly, 'of course not. I'll pray for you.'

'Thank you. You're the sweetest sister.'

When I wake up my plans always seem bigger, just like how humans are bigger in the morning because of the moisture in your intervertebral discs which makes you a couple of centimetres taller. We're going to the other side today. I don't know if that's why I'm feeling strange and everything around me seems darker. Obbe and I stand behind the cowshed as the first snow falls on us, fat flakes sticking to our cheeks, as though God is sprinkling icing sugar the way Mum did over the first doughnuts of the season this morning. The grease drips from the corners of your mouth when you sink your teeth into them. Mum was early this year – she'd fried them herself and built up in three layers in a milk pail: doughnuts, kitchen roll paper, apple fritters. She took two full buckets to the basement, to the Jewish people, because they deserved a new year too. Her fingers were totally bent after peeling the apples for the fritters.

Obbe's hair is white with snow. He promised that if I make a sacrifice he won't tell anyone that I still wet the bed, so the Day of Judgement can be delayed. He's taken one of the cockerels from the coop. Dad is so proud of the creature, sometimes he says, 'As proud as a cow with seven udders.' This is because of its bright red saddle feathers and green hackle feathers, its large earlobes and shiny comb. The cock is the only being that has remained unaffected by everything and now parades around the farmyard, its chest thrust out. It's calmly watching us now with leaden eyes. I feel the toads moving in my coat pocket. I hope they don't catch a chill. I should have put them inside a glove.

'You can stop once it's crowed three times,' Obbe says.

He hands me the hammer. I clench its handle for the second time. I think about Mum and Dad, about Dieuwertje, my brother Matthies, my body filled with green soap, God and his absence, the stone in Mum's belly, the star we can't find, my coat that has to come off, the cheese scoop in the dead cow. It crows once before the claw hammer sticks into its flesh and the cockerel lies dead on the flagstones. My mum made me smash my piggy bank with that hammer. Now it's blood not money that comes out. It's the first time I've killed an animal with my own hands – before this I was just an accessory. When I once stood on a spider in Granny's sheltered housing that didn't have a shelter, Granny said, 'Death is a process that disintegrates into actions and actions into phases. Death never just happens to you, there is always something that causes it. This time it was you. You can kill too.' Granny was right. My tears begin to melt the snowflakes on my cheeks. My shoulders jerk irregularly. I try to hold still but don't manage it.

Obbe casually pulls the hammer out of the cockerel's flesh and rinses it under the tap next to the cowshed, saying, 'You're really sick. You did it too.' Then he turns around, picks up the cockerel by its legs, and walks toward the fields with its head dangling softer back and forth in the wind. I look at my shaking hands. I've made myself small in shock and when I stand up again, it's as though there are split pins in my joints that keep everything connected but also moving independently. And all of a sudden a magpie moth flutters around me, black patches like spilled ink on its wings. I guess it has escaped from Obbe's collection. It's the only possibility; you don't see butterflies or moths in December – they hibernate. I catch it in my palms and hold it to my ear. You're not allowed to touch anything of Obbe's, not his hair or his toys, otherwise he gets furious and begins to swear. You're not even allowed to touch the crown of his head, while he presses on it the whole time himself. I hear the moth fluttering in panic against the inside of my hands and clench them into a fist, as though holding a scrap piece of paper with irreverent words on it. Silence.

Only the violence inside me makes noise. It grows and grows, just like sadness. Only sadness needs more space, like Belle said, and violence just takes it. I let the dead moth fall out of my hands and into the snow. I slide a fresh layer over it with my welly: it's an icy grave. Angrily I punch the shed wall, skinning my knuckles. I clench my jaw and look at the stalls. It won't be long before they're filled again – my parents are waiting for the new stock. Dad has even given the feed silo a new lick of paint. I'm worried it will stand out too much and attract Mum, a glimmer in her death wish. The problem is it's going to seem as though everything has gone back to normal, as though everyone is just continuing with their lives after Matthies and the foot-and-mouth. Except for me. Maybe a longing for death is infectious, or it jumps to the next head – mine – just like the lice in Hanna's class. I let myself fall back into the snow, spread my arms and move them up and down. I'd give a lot to be able to rise up now, to be made of porcelain and for someone to drop me by accident so that I'd break into countless pieces and someone would see that I was broken, that I can no longer be of any use, like those damned angels wrapped in silver paper. The clouds coming from my mouth lessen. I can still feel the hammer's handle in the flesh of my palms, hear the cock crowing. 'Thou shalt not kill nor avenge thyself.' I took revenge and that can only mean one more plague.

I suddenly feel two hands under my armpits and I'm lifted to my feet. When I turn around Dad is standing before me – his black beret isn't black but white. He slowly raises his hand to my cheek. For a moment I think we're going to start slapping our hands like at the cattle market, that we'll assess my meat as healthy or sick, but his fingers curl and stroke my cheek so fleetingly that I wonder afterwards whether it actually happened and whether I haven't invented a hand made of our misty breath from the cold, that it was only the wind. Trembling, I stare at the blood patch in the yard, but Dad doesn't see it, and the snow slowly hides the death.

'Go inside. I'll come and take off your coat in a moment,' Dad says, as he walks to the side of the shed to work the beet crusher. He turns the handle firmly – the rusty wheel squeaks as it turns, bits of sugar beet fly around him, most of them landing in the metal basket. They're for the rabbits – they love them. As I walk away, I leave a trail behind in the snow. My hope that someone will find me is growing steadily. Someone to help me find myself and to say: cold, cold, lukewarm, warm, getting warmer, hot.

When Obbe comes back from the fields, there's nothing noticeable about him. His back to Dad, he stops in front of me, puts his hand on my coat zip and roughly jerks it upwards, catching the skin of my chin. I scream and step backward. I carefully pull the zip down again and touch the painful patch of skin, abraded by the metal hooks of the zip.

'That's what betrayal feels like, and this is just the beginning. You'll be in for it if you tell Dad that it was my idea,' Obbe whispers. He makes a cutting gesture across his throat with his finger before turning around and holding up a hand to greet Dad. He is allowed into the cowshed with him. For the first time in ages, Dad is going back into the place where all his cows were exterminated. He doesn't ask whether I'd like to join them and leaves me behind in the cold, bits of skin stuck in the zip and one cheek burning from his touch. I should have showed my other cheek, like Jesus, to see whether he meant it. I walk back towards the farm and see Hanna rolling a ball of snow.

'There's a giant sitting on my chest,' I say once I reach her. She pauses and looks up, her nose red from the freezing cold. She's wearing Matthies's blue mittens the vet had brought with him from the lake, and which lay defrosting on a plate behind the stove like pieces of meat for the evening meal. My brother had thought it childish that Mum had tied a string to them because she was worried he'd lose them, and frozen fingers were the worst thing, she said, not thinking about a heart that stayed cold for too long and how bad that was.

'What's the giant doing there?' Hanna asks.

'Just sitting there, being heavy.'

'How long's he been there?'

'Quite a long time, but this time he's refusing to get off again. He arrived when Obbe went into the cowshed with Dad.'

'Oh,' Hanna says, 'you're jealous.'

'Not true!'

'You are. The Lord hates lying lips.'

'I'm not lying.'

I make my chest swell and then cave in again, as though a claw hammer has been stuck into me too. I keep on feeling it, the same way I still feel the impression of Obbe's body after he's lain on top of me, long after taking a shower. I'm not jealous because Obbe's with Dad, but because he has the death of Dad's favourite cockerel on his conscience just as much as I do and it hasn't made him fall backwards into the snow. Why does he never catch a chill from the ice-cold plans he drags us into? I want to tell Hanna about the cockerel, tell her the sacrifice I had to make to keep Mum and Dad alive, but I don't say anything. I don't want to worry her unnecessarily. And maybe she'll never cuddle up to me again in bed, leaning against the chest that contains so much that is hidden and that is capable of more than she thinks. This is one of those afternoons, I think, that I stick to the next page with Pritt stick in my diary, only to carefully peel apart again later. First to get rid of it and later to see whether it really happened.

'You can shrink giants by making yourself bigger,' Hanna says, stacking two snowballs on top of each other – the head and the middle section. It reminds me of the time I built a snowman with Hanna and Obbe – on Christmas Day – and called it Harry.

'Do you still remember Harry?' I ask Hanna. The corners of my sister's mouth curl upwards until her cheeks bulge like two mozzarella balls on a white plate.

'When we put the carrot in the wrong place? Mum was in a total state, and fed the entire supply of winter carrots to the rabbits.'

'It was your fault,' I say, grinning.

'It was because of that magazine in the shop,' Hanna corrects me.

'The next morning Harry was gone and Dad was in the front room, dripping with snow.'

'This is a serious announcement – Harry is dead,' Hanna says in a fake deep voice.

'Then we never ate peas with carrots, just the peas – they were much too afraid we'd have dirty thoughts if we ever saw another carrot.'

Hanna arches her back laughing. Before I've realized it, I've spread my arms. Hanna wipes the snow from her knees and stands up. She takes hold of me. It's strange to cuddle in broad daylight, as though our arms are stiffer during the day and seem coated with udder ointment in the evenings, like

275

our faces. She takes a broken cigarette from her coat pocket. She found it in the farmyard. It must have fallen from behind Obbe's ear – he keeps one there because all the boys in the village keep their cigarettes behind their ears. Hanna clamps it between her lips for a moment, then presses it into the snowman under the carrot.

I look at my hand. The knuckles are red, two of them are skinned – the flesh is pinker there with red bloody edges like ruptured prawns' heads. I go to the shed and put one foot on the heel of the other to take off my boot without touching it. I don't want to use the boot-jack, which has been standing there in solitude now that no one asks for help any more. Since the cows went, Mum and Dad have only been wearing their black clogs. A long time ago we had a cast-iron boot-jack but it got bent because of Dad's deformed leg. I kick my boots off and go through the dividing door into the kitchen. It's spotless and even the chairs are at an equal distance from the table, coffee cups upside down on a tea-towel on the counter, teaspoons lined up neatly next to them. On the counter there's a memo pad upon which is written, 'Slept badly.' And above it the date, one day before the cows were put down. Mum has been keeping a diary in short sentences ever since the outbreak of foot-and-mouth. On the day the cows were killed, it says, 'Circus has begun.' Nothing more and nothing less. Next to the memo pad, there's a note: 'Guests in the front room, be quiet.'

I tiptoe into the sitting room in my socks and lay my ear to the door of the front room. I can hear the elders talking in solemn voices. Once a week they come to see whether 'the preaching has borne fruit', whether 'crops have grown after the Word was sown'. Are we faithful believers and do we listen to God and to Renkema's sermons? After this, they always start to talk about forgiveness, as they stir vortices into their coffee, like the ones their piercing glances cause in my belly. Usually Mum and Dad take the house visits and we, the three kings, only have to join them once a month. We're mainly asked which part of the Bible we know well, how we cope with or think we're going to cope with the internet and alcohol, with the exuberance of growing up, our appearance. After that comes the standard warning: 'Sanctification follows justification. They cannot be separated. Beware the leaven of the Pharisees.'

Now the new stock of cattle is coming, Dad is busy with the preparations, so Mum has to take the house visit alone. On the other side of the door, I hear one of the elders ask, 'How pure is your way of life now?' I press my ear harder to the wood but can't hear the answer. When Mum whispers that usually says enough; she doesn't want God to hear while we all know that the ears of the consistory also belong to Him – He shaped them, after all.

'Would you like a shortbread biscuit?' I suddenly hear Mum ask loudly. The biscuit tin with Queen Beatrix's head on it is opened. I can smell the fragile sweet smell of shortbread from here. You should never dip shortbread in your coffee – it collapses immediately so that you have to scrape the crumbs from the bottom with your teaspoon. Yet the elders still dunk their biscuits in their mugs every time, as carefully as the pastor who dunks the fragile children being baptized into the water, as he quietly recites the baptismal formula from the Book of Matthew.

I look at the clock and see that the house visit has only just begun, so they'll be here for at least another hour. This is perfect; no one will disturb me. I knock gently on the basement door and whisper, 'Friend.' No reaction. After killing Dad's cockerel, I can no longer be counted among the 'friends', but when I say 'foe' I don't hear anything – no nervous shuffling, no one quickly hiding behind the apple sauce, even though it's almost all been eaten.

I push open the door and feel along the wall for the light cord. The light flickers slightly as though it's wondering whether to illuminate or not, and then comes on. There's a greasy cooking smell in the basement that issues from the milk pails filled with doughnuts and apple fritters. I can't see the Jewish people anywhere, nowhere the light of the glow-in-the-dark stars on their coats. The bottles of blackcurrant cordial stand untouched on the shelf next to dozens of tins of frankfurter sausages and jars of egg liqueur. Maybe they've fled? Did Mum warn them and hide them somewhere else? I close the door behind me and walk deeper into the basement, my head bent to avoid the spider's webs, a grey gossamer of silence now there's no longer anyone hiding here. I feel the toads in my pocket. They're finally sitting on top of one another and stick to the fabric of my coat like ice cubes. 'I'll free you in a minute,' I reassure them, thinking of the words from Exodus: 'Do not oppress a foreigner; you yourselves know how it feels to be foreigners, because you were foreigners in Egypt.'

It's time I let them go, because their skins feel as cold as the chocolate frogs and mice filled with fondant that Mum bought at the HEMA and whose silver jackets I always smooth out with my nail and keep. On TV yesterday, Dieuwertje Blok bit the head off a purple frog. She showed the white filling: on the inside they were made of ice cream. She winked and said that everything was going to be all right, that the saint's helpers had got lost but a sharp-eyed farmer had found them and they were on their way again. Every child would still get their presents in time, as long as the chimney was well swept, clean like all children's hearts.

After that, Mum had watched *Lingo* from behind the ironing board. Hanna suggested that Mum should go on TV sometime, that we should put her name down. I'd nervously shaken my head: once Mum was behind the glass of the TV set, we'd never get her back, or maybe only in pixels when the screen was snowy, and what would become of Dad then? And who would guess the jumbled-up word? Mum was good at that – yesterday it began with the letter D. For the first time she didn't guess but I knew at once: d-a-r-k-n-e-s-s. It seemed like a sign I couldn't ignore.

I stop in front of the freezer next to the wall. I move the cloth hanging over it with fruit weights on its corners – which are unnecessary because there's never any wind in the basement – and open the lid. I see only frozen Christmas Stollen: Mum and Dad get them every year from the butcher, the skating association and the trade union. We can't eat them all and the chickens have had enough of them too, and leave them untouched in the run where they slowly rot away.

The freezer's lid is incredibly heavy – you have to pull hard before it comes free from the rubber seal. Mum always warned us about that, saying that 'if you topple in, we won't see you again until around Christmas'. I always pictured Hanna's body as frozen food and Mum scooping her out.

Once I've got the lid open, I quickly push the pole standing next to the freezer into the rim so that it stays open, and squeeze myself through the opening, through the hole in the ice. I think about Matthies. Is this how he felt? Was his breath so abruptly cut off? Suddenly I remember what the vet said when he fished my brother out of the water with Evertsen: 'When people have hypothermia, you have to handle them like porcelain. The smallest touch could be deadly.' All this time we've been so careful with Matthies that we don't even talk about him, so that he can't break into pieces inside our heads.

I lie down among the Christmas Stollen and fold my hands over my stomach, which is bloated again and overfull. I feel the drawing pin pricking through my coat, the ice on the sides of the freezer, hear the clap of ice skates. Then I take the toads out of my coat pocket and put them beside me in the freezer. Their skins look bluish, their eyes are closed. I read some-where that when toads climb on top of each other, the male gets black horny lumps in its thumbs so that it can hold the female more tightly. They are sitting so quietly and close to one another I feel touched. I take the smoothed-out, coloured silver foil papers from the chocolate frogs out of my other coat pocket and fold them carefully around the toads' bodies so that they'll stay warm. Without giving it any further thought, I kick the pole out from under the lid and whisper, 'I'm coming, dear Matthies.' A loud bang follows, the freezer light flips off. Everything is pitch dark and silent now. Icily silent.